PENGUIN BOOKS

The World in Winter

Sam Youd was a British author who wrote under a number of pseudonyms, including Stanley Winchester, Hilary Ford and Peter Graaf, as well as under his own name. In total he published fifty-six novels and numerous short stories, spanning general fiction, gothic romance, detective thrillers, social comedy and other subjects. He is best known as John Christopher, pioneer of the young adult dystopian fiction genre and author of the Tripods trilogy, among many other science fiction classics, including *The Death of Grass*. Sam Youd was born in Lancashire in 1922 and died in 2012.

Hari Kunzru is the author of the novels *The Impressionist*, *Transmission*, *My Revolutions* and *Gods Without Men*, as well as a novella and a story collection. His writing has appeared in the *New York Times*, *Guardian* and *New Yorker*, among many other publications. He has won literary prizes including the Somerset Maugham Award and the Betty Trask Prize and was previously named one of *Granta*'s Twenty Best Young British Novelists. Hari Kunzru lives in New York and his next novel, *White Tears*, will be published by Hamish Hamilton in 2017.

The World in Winter

JOHN CHRISTOPHER

With an introduction by
Hari Kunzru

PENGUIN BOOKS

PENGUIN BOOKS

UK | USA | Canada | Ireland | Australia
India | New Zealand | South Africa

Penguin Books is part of the Penguin Random House group of companies
whose addresses can be found at global.penguinrandomhouse.com.

Penguin
Random House
UK

First published in Great Britain by Eyre & Spottiswoode Ltd 1962
Published in Sphere Books 1978
Reissued with a new introduction by Penguin Books 2016

002

Copyright © International Authors N.V., 1962

Introduction copyright © Hari Kunzru, 2016

The moral right of the copyright holders has been asserted

Set in 11/13 pt Bembo Book MT Std
Typeset by Jouve (UK), Milton Keynes
Printed in Great Britain by Clays Ltd, St Ives plc

A CIP catalogue record for this book is available from the British Library

ISBN: 978-0-241-97554-1

www.greenpenguin.co.uk

MIX
Paper from
responsible sources
FSC® C018179

Penguin Random House is committed to a
sustainable future for our business, our readers
and our planet. This book is made from Forest
Stewardship Council® certified paper.

Introduction

by Hari Kunzru

The light of the sun is getting weaker. An Arctic winter descends on Britain, rendering it all but uninhabitable. London is fenced off from the rest of the country, which is left to descend into starvation and anarchy. Good speculative fiction knows how to find appropriate metaphors for the reader's anxieties and desires, and in 1962, when John Christopher's *The World in Winter* was published, the fear of decline was pervasive. The Suez debacle had exposed Britain's inability to project power without the support of the Americans. Decolonization was stripping the mother country of her once-mighty empire, as immigration from those former colonial possessions was changing the lily-white complexion of her streets. It seems unlikely that Enoch Powell was a science fiction fan, but if he ever put down his copy of the *Aeneid* and picked up this novel, he would have found something to make his rivers of blood run cold. Here is the very thing that the old demagogue most feared, the story of what happens when 'the black man has the whip hand over the white man'.

In Christopher's tale of national and racial *Untergang*, the sun has set, there's no more pink on the map, and the centre of civilization and commerce has moved southwards to Africa. White British refugees find themselves grubbing for a living in the slums of Lagos, servants and supplicants to black masters. *The World in Winter* is both a reactionary jeremiad (fear the loss of your status!) and a progressive thought experiment. The reader is invited to lament the terrible fate of a middle-class white hero, who finds himself a beggar in a far-off land where the colour of his skin counts against him. Imagine, for a moment, Mr Powell, that the Oxford brogue is on the other foot. Wouldn't you perhaps hope for a kinder reception than 'no blacks, no dogs, no Irish'?

Christopher is no white supremacist, indeed his anger at crude prejudice is there on the page, but *The World In Winter* is also a book of its time, which is to say that it's animated by a sense that racial difference is a kind of abyss, and between black and white there can be no complete understanding or identification. The plot hinges on ideas about racial loyalty and betrayal that one only hears today in the rhetoric of the extreme right. But for me, at least, its very ambiguity makes it interesting. With immigration once again at the top of the national agenda, it's a novel that still has the power to thrill and disturb, performing one of the signal services of fiction, forcing the reader to inhabit other realities, other possibilities and perspectives, making the present order seem less fixed and immutable than before.

PART ONE

I

The reading room seemed warm when one first came in from the outside, but the impression did not last. To stretch fuel stocks as far as possible, the burners had been set at their lowest working point. Cold settled from the room's high dome on to the figures huddled in front of the desks, bundled into overcoats, painfully making notes or turning pages with gloved fingers; their legs, in some cases, wrapped round with blankets. From time to time, someone would get up and seek to restore circulation, arms beating, booted feet stamping against the polished wooden floor. The rest paid no attention but concentrated on their books, with the greedy sad determination of a man facing death, or the end of a love affair.

Pausing to look at them, Andrew Leedon rubbed his hands against the silver Victorian muff-heater Madeleine had given him. She had found it in an antique shop and presented it to him on his birthday, along with a supply of the small charcoal by which it was fuelled. But even charcoal had become impossible to obtain, and its brief usefulness, after the many idle years, was almost at an end. He blew through the small holes in the side and watched the red glow brighten. A chair scraped, and his attention turned back to his fellow readers. He felt pity for them, but it was mixed with envy. The future was a current which soon, very soon now, must drag them down into the maelstrom; for the moment they bobbed like corks in this eddying backwater, but the deep tug of the undersurge was there and none would escape it. Yet they were indifferent. The red-eyed, grey-haired man across the aisle, with his pile of volumes on King Arthur – he had always been there, in the same place, with the same books. When the end came to him, in however strange and incalculable a form, it would be irrelevant,

3

as irrelevant as the pneumonia, or heart attack, or cancer, which would otherwise have rendered his seat vacant. Soon all the seats would be vacant together until, as must happen, marauders broke in to rip out the wood and carry away the books that were left for fuel. Some of the rarest books had already gone, to the libraries in Cairo and Accra, in Lagos and Johannesburg, and more would go in the next few weeks, but there would still be enough to draw the mob. The people reading here were not so foolish as to expect a reprieve; for the library or for themselves. It was that he envied.

The main lights were off, conserving electricity. There were only the small reading lights and, high up, the greyness that filtered in from outside. He thought of Africa; of sunshine, long beaches by a blue ocean, the green of trees and grass. It was hard to believe that in just ten days they would be there: impossible to imagine it. But it was true. Soon they would be travelling high over the frozen lands to the warm south. Things might be difficult, but there would be warmth and safety. There were only one or two moments in a man's life when he really needed to be lucky. This was one.

A man with a greasy blond beard, wearing a dirty raincoat, came along the aisle and stopped beside Andrew. He said, in a courteous gentle voice:

'Would you by any chance have a match that I might borrow?'

'Smoking's still prohibited, isn't it?' Andrew asked. 'They haven't relaxed that rule?'

He shook his head. 'I don't smoke. To start my fire, at home. I have the means of striking.' He fished in a pocket and brought out an empty matchbox. 'One match would be enough.'

'I'm sorry.'

He could have lent him his lighter; he would not need it before he got back, and Madeleine had one of her own. But it might not be returned, and a butane lighter with an almost full cartridge was too valuable a thing to take a chance on.

4

The man said: 'I'm sorry for troubling you. Thank you all the same.'

He walked away towards the exit. Andrew saw him stop twice more and ask, with the same negative result. At the door he paused again, looking round the room in hopeless inquiry. Then he went out. As the door swung to behind him, Andrew had an impulse to go after him with the lighter. Even if it were not returned, they could manage with one for the relatively few days remaining, while that poor devil had to go back to a freezing room, and to a future equally devoid of warmth and hope. But he did not, when it came to the point, rise from his chair. Madeleine might lose her lighter, or the charge might fail prematurely. One took no chances these days. It was too cold for charity.

Andrew turned back to his study of the thick file of *The Times*. As one of the Associate Editors of the programme, he was not usually required to do the menial job of research, but things, after all, were running down. This was to be the last documentary that *Late Night Final*, that popular television feature, would present – a final analysis of what had happened, and why. And a day or two later the transmitters would fall silent, the small screens go blank. But by that time . . . Africa.

The light was poor, the bulbs glowing dully on the inadequate voltage. He ruffled the pages back awkwardly, peering at dates and headlines – back through the early days of scientific reports, dubious prognostications, tucked away in inconspicuous places, with headings like: NEW SATELLITE PROBE CONFIRMS SOLAR RADIATION DECLINE. The beginning was before that; in the intervals, people had died and loved, killed and been born and been betrayed. Between the world's catastrophes and those of the individual man, relationships were mostly coincidental. The day of Hiroshima was a birthday or a wedding anniversary, or the day an old dog, dying in the sunshine on the lawn, took a childhood with it.

He found what he was looking for at last: the report of an

obscure speech by an obscure Italian scientist at an unimportant conference. There was no main headline, but a small side-head said: *Radiation Cycle in the Sun Suggested*. They had given Fratellini's speech five lines; the rest of a long paragraph was devoted to something on polar magnetic fields.

It was a small signpost, he reflected with irony, to point to such large things – to the world's wreck and to his own cuckoldry.

It was difficult to tell, looking back, how good a summer that had been. The records gave a statistical answer – at Kew, the century's fourth best for dryness, the third best in hours of sunshine. But all those previous seasons, that had matched this one or even surpassed it, were blurred in the memory by other springs, other summers. This was different, a C Major crescendo that lingered in the heart, a recollection of love across the dry divide of age. There were brief spells of poor weather, one in July, another early in September. For the rest, what breaks came in the continuation of warm blue days were no more than pauses, preparing for still more brilliant skies. From Sicily to the shores of rocky Norway, Europe basked in the heat.

In Andrew's life, too, as he saw it at the time, it was a season of brightness. His job filled the three criteria for satisfaction: he enjoyed it, he had confidence in his ability to do it well, and his work was appreciated in the right quarters. Behind this lay a family life which offered him, he thought, all that a man needed.

The Leedons had been married for eleven years and had two children, boys of ten and eight. Carol had been, when Andrew married her, a girl of startlingly good looks, and in her early thirties she was still beautiful. She had heavy chestnut hair and blue eyes, a clear skin touched with rose, and features that, apart from the obvious qualities of regularity and proportion, showed contentment and, for men, a promise of peace. The promise, Andrew had found, was misleading: there was more selfishness and laziness in her nature than generosity. But her faults were moderate. They did not make her too difficult to live with; and she had an ease, a naturalness, both in crises and in the everyday tension of life, which, he felt, more than compensated for them. He was fond of her, and still capable of being excited by her body. Perhaps more than that he was proud of her beauty and her presence; a little surprised, even after eleven years, at his own triumph in having captured her, but no longer questioning the fact of his achievement. He had never, for a moment, regretted his marriage, nor wanted another woman with anything but momentary desire. Had he ever put the question to himself, he would have said that he loved her; but the question would have embarrassed him.

For his children, he felt a detached, clear-eyed affection. The elder boy, Robin, was an aggressive uncertain child, brilliant in his studies in part, but contemptuous of whatever failed to interest him. He took after Andrew physically, and was already tall and thin, with more than a hint of the same slight stoop. Andrew recognized loneliness in him, but any impulse to comfort it was held in check by an awareness of the difficulties, and of his own probable inadequacy in such an undertaking.

Jeremy was quite a different boy: broad-shouldered, slow moving, purposeful, good-natured, and a little dull. He had Carol's brow and eyes, and hair that renewed its blondness every summer. Adults generally liked him, and boys of his own age automatically accepted his leadership.

Both were now at boarding school. Andrew looked forward to their return at the term's end, and for a few days after their departure for school found the unaccustomed tidiness and silence of the house unsettling; for the remainder of their time away he settled quite happily into his routines of television work and normal social life. Carol wrote the weekly letters to them; occasionally Andrew added a postscript.

About a week after the boys had gone back for the Michaelmas term, McKay, Andrew's Editor-in-Chief, dropped in to his office while he was dictating notes to one of the programme's secretaries. McKay was a ferret-faced, slimly built man, with red hair and conspicuous soft blond eyelashes; he had an aggressive manner which perhaps was meant to offset his physical slightness, but was amiable enough. Andrew found him easier to work with than most of his previous superiors in television producing because he made decisions quickly, and did not interfere with a job once delegated.

McKay said: 'Mind if I break it up? Nothing important?'

Andrew said: 'Notes on the Thorpely business.'

Thorpely was a small Suffolk village in which there was currently a scandal about drains that the programme was proposing to investigate: two different local authorities each imputed responsibility to the other and refused to do anything. Meanwhile some of the local people had been driven from their homes and were living in shacks at the far of the village.

'We can't use it this week anyway. Too soon after Little Shipton. O.K., Sue, I think you can pop off.' He watched her with mild interest as she gathered up her things and left; she was a quiet sinuous girl who dressed effectively. To Andrew, he went on: 'We're going out to a party.'

'Who and what,' Andrew said, 'and how long? I'd better ring home if we're going to be late. This was my evening off, remember?'

'Winston & Peck. Five thirty to seven, but you don't need to stay for more than half an hour.'

Winston & Peck were a middle-rank publishing firm, with a reasonably impressive non-fiction side and a small and select fiction list. Andrew creased his forehead in inquiry.

'Anything worth while? I didn't know anything good was on their stocks.'

'Lord Benchitt's memoirs.'

'Nothing we can use, is there?'

'I did think of putting him on and getting Curly to savage him, but even bad publicity's too good for the old bastard. No, there's someone going to be there I want you to meet. A fellow called Cartwell, from the Home Office.'

McKay had great confidence, Andrew knew, in his ability to get on with people and to get things out of them. It was an art in which McKay felt himself, with good reason perhaps, to be particularly weak, and he had utilized Andrew on earlier occasions as a contact man. He wondered what McKay had in mind this time.

'For general purposes,' he asked, 'or something in particular?'

'Both. He's the kind of man who might always be useful. For a starter, I thought you might angle and see if he knows anything about this.'

He was carrying an evening paper which he held out to Andrew, his thumb marking the story in which he was interested.

'I saw it,' Andrew said. 'So we're going to have a cold winter. Is it worthwhile, and would he be likely to have anything, anyway?'

'The sun producing less heat. It might be a story.'

'The difference is very small – only detectable with precise instruments.'

'It's the *idea*. We depend on the sun absolutely. We could get in some interesting speculation.'

'Do we need a Home Office opinion for that?'

'There might be something there.' He stared at Andrew for a moment, and then shrugged. 'Perhaps not. But it's worth your getting to know him, anyway. We haven't got a proper Home Office contact now that Price has gone into industry.'

He made the last comment with some annoyance. Andrew grinned.

'Thoughtless of him, just for twice the salary, a gold-plated expense account, and a top-hat pension. No consideration.'

McKay smiled also. 'No consideration,' he agreed.

'Glad to come, in any case,' Andrew said. 'The drinks were very good at the last Winston & Peck do.'

'They always are. Though for Benchitt, hemlock would be more appropriate.'

Winston & Peck, having been bombed, like so many of their rivals, out of Paternoster Row, had taken premises at three temporary addresses before settling, with an air of finality, into their present office. They now occupied a house in a quiet street in Mayfair, roughly equidistant from Curzon Street and the Park, with only a small tasteful brass plate to indicate that the house was other than residential. Many of the surrounding houses had similar small plaques;

none, in fact, was a private dwelling. Drinks were served in the L-shaped room on the first floor which had once been the main drawing room and now, with removable partitions, provided offices for the three chief directors. The office furniture, except for the grey metal filing cases, had been removed, and a dozen Regency chairs and two sofas brought in. The room was already quite full when Andrew and McKay arrived. Most of the guests looked like authors, Andrew thought, and the urgency with which they clutched and downed their drinks bespoke either the unsuccessful or the alcoholic.

McKay said: 'Ah, there you are, Cartwell! Someone I'd like you to meet. Andy Leedon – he works on the programme.'

He completed the introduction with a nervous brusqueness which quite justified his lack of faith in his own ability to handle people socially.

Cartwell said: 'Glad to know you. I've already told McKay I watch your thing when I get the chance. One of the three television programmes which rarely induce the vomit reflex: the best of the three, I should say.'

He was a small dark man, with a quick smile and a look of alertness. He was wearing a lounge suit which was well cut but, Andrew thought, a shade too light. He was also wearing a bow tie, a practice of which Andrew, in general, disapproved.

McKay, having introduced them, seized an opportunity to move away. It was the sort of thing he had done before, and Andrew found it partly touching, partly irritating. He said to Cartwell:

'Ian tells me you're Home Office?'

'Did it need telling? Doesn't the Civil Servant shine through the grosser flesh?'

Andrew smiled. 'I wouldn't say so.'

'Thank God.' He plucked drinks from a passing waiter. 'I'm starting to get defensive about it, though. Something I must watch.'

'Does that mean you don't like the job, or that you think you ought not to?'

'Not quite either, I fancy.' He looked at Andrew with interest. 'I like the comment, at that.'

Instead of circulating, they stayed talking to each other until it was time to leave. David Cartwell was, Andrew found, a good talker who was still capable of listening with intelligence and attention. More than this he had a gift for intimacy without obtrusion. On the point of leaving, Andrew said:

'We must meet again some time.'

Cartwell nodded: 'I'll tell you what – come round for a drink on Sunday. About eleven? With your wife. 17 Denham Crescent – do you know it?'

'Round the corner from South Kensington tube station?'

'That's it.'

'Well, thank you. We'll be very glad to come.'

It was only after they had parted and he was walking towards Park Lane to get a bus that Andrew remembered McKay had wanted him to sound Cartwell on the matter of the solar radiation drop which was thought to herald a cold winter. He was a little annoyed with himself for having forgotten; he liked to think of himself as methodical. It was a consolation, he reflected, that the matter was so unimportant a one.

Carol raised some objection to his having accepted the invitation on such brief acquaintance, and of involving her on social terms before she had had an opportunity of appraising the other people. On the Sunday morning she toyed with the idea of crying off, leaving Andrew to go on his own and present excuses for her. What finally decided her in favour of going, as she frankly explained, was that she had always admired the houses in Denham Crescent – Regency in white stucco with Italianate porches – and wanted to see what they were like inside.

They were admitted by a dark, rosy-cheeked girl, who seemed a little more than maid, a little less than au pair, and who showed them into the sitting room overlooking the road. It was a bright morning, and sunlight gleamed on the dark glossy leaves of the shrubs in the small paved courtyard below the windows.

Carol examined the furnishings of the room.

'Some quite good stuff,' she said. 'That bow-fronted chest in the corner . . .'

She broke off as a thin blonde girl came in. She appeared to be in her middle twenties. She was quite plain, Andrew decided, and this surprised him. He would have expected Cartwell to have a more decorative wife.

In a nervous, somewhat harsh voice, she said:

'Mr and Mrs Leedon? I'm Madeleine Cartwell. David will be down in a moment.'

She turned with a quick smile, snatching herself from them almost before she had finished speaking, at the sound of rapid foot-steps from outside. David Cartwell entered the room. He looked dapper in grey slacks and a dark red silk shirt. As with the bow tie, it was the sort of thing Andrew did not particularly favour. Nor did Carol. He hoped it would not put her off too much; she had a tendency to let first impressions of people harden into prejudices.

'You found your way,' David said. 'Good boy, Andy. And this is Mrs Leedon?'

'Carol,' Andrew said. 'This is David.'

He looked at her closely, intently, as he took her hand. He turned to Andrew.

'Do you realize you have a beautiful wife? I suppose you do. Probably not well enough, though. You get too used to things by having them.'

Carol smiled faintly. She seemed amused. Madeleine said:

'Don't let him embarrass you.'

Carol smiled more openly. 'I won't.'

'Ah, but she is a beauty,' David said. 'Don't you agree, Maddie?' His glance went to Andrew. 'I do a little colour photography. I'd like to borrow her for that. You don't mind, do you?'

Andrew was amused. 'Of course not. Should she take her clothes off here, or do you have a studio upstairs?'

David laughed. 'My line is faces. That's one I did of Maddie over there.'

Andrew went to examine it. It was a full-plate study of

Madeleine in three-quarter profile, against a soft brown out-of-focus background. It did not contrive to make her beautiful, or even pretty, but it caught a fine distinction of features, a delicacy of brow and jaw and throat which, now that the photograph had drawn his attention to it, Andrew could see in the woman herself.

'Yes,' he said, 'borrow her by all means. And I want a copy of the result.'

'It will be arranged,' David said. 'Now, what are you people drinking? Teacher's or Haig? Gin or vodka? I think there's some sherry kicking around as well, a remnant from last Christmas.'

Carol, in due course, manoeuvred Madeleine into showing her round the house, and the two men were left alone. The girl who had let them in brought a silver bowl containing mixed nuts and put it down on a Georgian occasional table. Andrew commented, as she went out again:

'Extraordinarily rosy-cheeked, that girl.'

'Effect of high-altitude living,' David said. 'She comes from some tiny village up in the Italian Alps. You get that sort of thing above the fifteen-hundred metre level. The small capillaries rupture – I'm not sure if it's the low pressure or the cold winters. Perhaps both.'

'Now you mention it, I remember seeing a lot of glowing complexions at Zermatt.'

'That's it. She's a pleasant morsel, don't you think?'

Andrew nodded. 'Very pleasant.'

'Tempting, too, but quite apart from her simple Catholic virtue, which I suspect is still unspoiled, it would be embarrassing for Maddie.'

He spoke with a matter-of-factness that caused Andrew to revise the opinion he had begun to form of him. Among his acquaintances, he had summed up the men who were as openly attentive to women as David had been to Carol as purely verbal performers: the philanderers used a less direct, even secretive approach. But the comment on the maid, its tone in particular, put things on a different level.

He said, partly in evasion of the turn the conversation was taking, partly in challenge: 'I should think Madeleine is a very nice person.'

'A great girl,' David agreed. 'One way and another, I don't know how she puts up with me.'

The same theme cropped up a week or two later, when the two men met for a lunchtime drink. In the interim, the Cartwells had been for drinks to the Leedons' house in Dulwich, and they had made up a foursome for the theatre. It looked as though they were likely to see a fair amount of each other. Andrew liked David well enough in mixed company, but found him better with the women out of the way. He was more relaxed, less emphatic in tone. They drank and put their pint tankards of bitter back on the polished brown counter, and Andrew thought, with surprise: this man could be a friend. It was a feeling which had not occurred to him in more than ten years – since his middle twenties, since his marriage, he had made many new acquaintances but no new friends.

David said: 'I like this pub. Perhaps because there's always a man behind the bar, instead of a woman.'

'Do barmaids bother you?'

He grinned. 'Maddie calls it my atavistic streak. The old deep-down need to get away from the female sex from time to time. The Freemason in all of us.'

'Well, yes. I can't say I mind female hands drawing my beer, though.'

'The protest is exaggerated? Yes, I think you're right. I find women too fascinating too much of the time; hence the compulsive need for occasional lay-offs.'

It was a simple confession, neither rueful nor boasting. Andrew said:

'I suppose there are worse obsessions.'

'Worse, but none stronger. Do you feel like going on to a proper lunch, or can you make do with a fattening snack? They have a tolerable line in bangers.'

'That will do me.'

David signalled to the barman, and ordered sausages and rolls and butter. He looked at the level of beer in their glasses.

'Better double up on those, too.' He fumbled in his pocket for silver. 'Everything degenerates into habit – nausea, vanity, everything. For a year after I began drinking beer, I couldn't stand the taste of it. All I was getting was the satisfaction of being one of the boys. And even when I'd grown to tolerate it, I'd always had enough at the end of the first pint. Then I got to like the taste. Now I don't even notice it going down.'

'I wouldn't altogether agree with you,' Andrew said. 'Many things have lost their savour as far as I'm concerned, but a glass of good bitter isn't among them.'

David smiled suddenly. 'They don't keep a bad cellar here, do they? No, write that last one down to the disillusionment of middle age. The ordeal of too much pleasure and too few kicks.'

'It suits me.'

'It suits me, too. That's what I dislike about it.'

It became a habit for them to have a midday drink together, two or three times a week. From time to time, in addition, David persuaded him to stop off at Denham Crescent in the evening, for a drink and sometimes a meal. This was on Tuesday or Friday, when *Late Night Final* was broadcast. Andrew wondered, at first, how Carol would take this. But when he made a tentative, semi-apologetic approach on the subject, he said:

'My God, Andy, why should I mind? I like the Cartwells.' She smiled. 'And I don't suspect you of running after Madeleine.'

'No.' He smiled in return. 'That would be a little improbable.'

'Yes. Just a little.'

It was a week later that David, meeting Andrew at lunchtime on Friday, said:

'You were planning to drop in tonight, weren't you?'

'If I'm invited.'

'What do you want, a gold-engraved card? Thing is, I shan't be able to be there myself.'

'That's all right. I can find something else to do.'

'No,' David said, 'you must drop in. Maddie will be expecting you.'

'If I find myself round those parts, I will, then.'

David said earnestly: 'I wish you'd make it definite.'

With surprise, he said: 'Does it matter?'

'Well, this is something that's turned up unexpectedly – my not being able to get back till late. It would cheer the girl up to have company.'

Andrew shrugged. 'If you think so.'

'I haven't made my marital excuses yet. I'll be giving her a ring when I go back to the office. I'll tell her you're coming.'

The Crescent was cool, cream and green from the painted houses and the shading trees, when he turned into it from the glare and noise of Denham Street. Madeleine opened the door to him. She was wearing white slacks and a pale blue blouse and her hair was drawn tightly back. Andrew was conscious again of her lack of beauty, but conscious, also, of her freshness, of the delicate emphasis of bone beneath the skin.

'Come right in, Andy,' she said. 'Nice to see you.'

She led the way to the sitting room. 'Gin and something?'

'What are you having yourself?'

She picked up her glass from the coffee table. 'Just Cinzano and soda.'

'That will do me very well.'

He watched her pour his drink. She went to the kitchen and he heard the refrigerator door open and slam. She came back and eased the square of ice out of its plastic container into his glass.

'Are you sure it's not a nuisance,' he said, 'my dropping in like this?'

She shook her head, smiling. 'You saw David at lunchtime?'

'Yes.'

'And he told you he wouldn't be able to get back himself until late?'

'Yes. I was going to cry off, but he insisted you wouldn't mind.'

'Did he say why?'

'Why you wouldn't mind?'

'Why he wouldn't be here himself.'

'Well, no. I assumed it was something that had cropped up at the office.'

She brought the glass to him, and he took it, thanking her. She stood by the chair, looking down at him with an expression whose significance he could not fathom. There was some wariness in it.

'I used to think once,' she said, 'that men always confided in each other. I got it from a boy-friend I had when I was about nineteen. He certainly had, as I found out.'

'Confided? About their womenfolk, you mean?'

She sat down in a chair opposite his, and crossed her legs. She was wearing heel-less leather slippers with an intricate gold-stamped design.

'Womenfolk is a lovely expression,' she said. 'That's one of the things I like about you, Andy – you're just a little bit old-fashioned.'

'Now,' he said, 'tell me what I've done wrong.'

'David really didn't say anything?'

Andrew said awkwardly: 'Is there anything wrong between you two, then?'

'I *do* like you for being old-fashioned,' she said. 'No, I suppose he wouldn't, under the circumstances.' The last phrase carried a shadow of emphasis. 'There's nothing wrong – nothing basically. He's meeting . . . a woman.'

With surprise, Andrew asked: 'Did he tell you that?'

'No. He doesn't, at this stage. I've never been sure whether it's because he genuinely thinks he's deceiving me, or just because he finds it embarrassing to talk about.'

Andrew was embarrassed himself, and a little resentful. It was not his affair, and he objected to being forced to discuss it. It would have been understandable if Madeleine had taken her troubles to Carol, he thought, but not that she should ventilate them among David's male acquaintances. He stayed silent, and Madeleine said:

'You find it the same, do you? I don't usually talk about these little affairs, Andy.' She hesitated, on the point of saying something else. 'Oh, never mind it.'

He was touched by her unhappiness. 'I'm sorry.' He paused. 'What did you mean – at this stage?'

She shrugged. 'He tells me about them afterwards, once they're safely over. It's his kind of honesty. And his way of getting absolution, I suppose.'

'And you forgive him, of course.'

'Of course.' She spoke with faint irony. 'There couldn't be any doubt about that, could there?'

'It's a childish way to carry on, but people do childish things. They don't mean anything.'

'Don't they?' She gave him a hard look. 'Don't they?'

'Not in any real sense.'

'Tell me, Andy, have you ever been unfaithful to Carol?'

'No,' he said, 'I haven't. Do we need to discuss me and Carol?'

'No.' Her voice had misery in it. 'We don't have to discuss you and Carol. I'm sorry, Andy. I ought not to inflict things on you. Knowing, when you can't do anything about it, is the worst part. I just wish he could be a bit clever in disguising things. Happy ignorance is something to be envied.'

The resentment he had felt against Madeleine was transferred to David; he pictured him taking some girl out, at this moment laughing and talking with her, and was angry with the picture on her behalf.

He said: 'Would you like me to talk to him?'

'Talk to him?' She stared. 'About his carrying on? I don't think that would do any good.'

'It might.'

She gave a small laugh. 'I'm sure it wouldn't. Forget about it.'

'There must be something I can do.'

She considered him thoughtfully, and then smiled. 'Yes. I've nothing to offer you but *pastasciutta* or a scrappy salad. You can take me out for supper, if you like.'

Andrew nodded. 'I'll be glad to do that.'

3

The weather broke in mid-October, and the Fratellini hypothesis came back into the headlines, swept there by the blizzards that ranged over continental North America and continued unchecked across the Atlantic to Europe. In London, the first morning, there were three inches of snow, soon churned into mud and slush by the rush-hour traffic, but augmented, as the leaden morning wore on, by fresh falls. The wind was cold, from the north-east. Before midday, the evening papers were talking of Fratellini's winter. The following morning, with snow still coming down, there was fuller coverage and more speculation. McKay called Andrew into his office where, Andrew observed, the large print of the Utrillo snow scene in Montmartre had been replaced by a Renoir of a girl in the long summer grass. McKay valued art for its thermal effects.

'I've been looking at your notes,' McKay said, 'for the Fratellini thing. I thought we might rush it through for Friday.'

McKay had assigned it to him, as a low priority project, some weeks earlier. He objected:

'We're short of a lot of background material still.'

'Such as?'

'We wanted film of Fratellini himself, and of the Observatory. The team that's gone out for the new Vatican excavations was going to handle that as well.'

McKay wagged his thin face in negation. 'We shall have to do without them. Topicality comes first. Next week the whole thing may be forgotten. Can you make up ten minutes?'

'I should think so. How long do we give Wingate?'

'Christ, do we have to use him again?'

'We've paid for him.'

'These term contracts are a mistake. There are some faces and voices that just don't wear well. Wingate's got one of each. All right, give him three minutes – and make sure he doesn't overrun.'

'He knows his stuff.'

McKay said gloomily: 'I despise that kind of mind. We're all a knowing lot of bastards in this trade – we have to be – but at least we only claim to know things on a superficial level. These science journalists talk as though they know the lot. I'd like to see him drop a really monumental clanger.'

'It wouldn't do the programme any good.'

'Well, he could drop it in his weekly sermon in the Sunday press. Can I leave all this to you, Andy?'

'Yes. Do you want a cancellation cabled to the team in Rome?'

'Cancellation?'

'Of the Fratellini interview, since we shan't have time to use it.'

McKay considered this. 'No, I should let it stand. We may be able to use it some time. In the spring, maybe. A retrospect on the Fratellini Winter.'

'If there is one.'

McKay shrugged. 'On "What Happened to the Fratellini Winter", then. We can use it either way. Besides, Bill Dyson's got a girl-friend in Milan. He'd never forgive me if I lost him a chance of looking her up.'

Over the week-end, the snow stopped falling. There was a thawing rain on Saturday afternoon and Sunday, and on Monday it was clear and cold, with small clouds skating over a chill blue sky. In the pub where David and Andrew met, by contrast, it was warm and stuffy, apart from occasional piercing draughts when the street door was opened.

'A whisky chaser,' David suggested, 'against that Fratellini Winter?'

'Just this one, then. I've got some work this afternoon.'

'So have I, but I'll see it better through a slight haze. I saw your programme on Friday.'

'Did you? Any comments?'

'You were spreading a certain amount of alarm and despondency, weren't you? Talking about ice ages.'

'Did it worry the Home Office?'

'Not officially. Quite a talking point, though. And I'm told Harrods had a run on skis the next morning.'

'Trevor Wingate's the trouble. We've contracted for a dozen appearances and we have to use him or forfeit the money. It would be better to forfeit, but the accounts people would never stand for it.'

'I don't like that grin of his,' David said. 'Too much of the sneer in it.'

'Not telegenic at all, but it took us several programmes to realize that. It does sometimes. All we can do is feed a line into him that will capture audience interest on its merits. So we gave him the new ice age hypothesis to put over.'

'You probably scared some timid viewers.'

'We did say it was extremely unlikely.'

'In small type. What really came over was the pictures of glaciers rolling down the Welsh mountains and polar bears sunning themselves on the ice in the Pool of London.'

'We've always prided ourselves on our impact value.'

'I've been looking things up,' David said. 'There seem to be a number of different theories as to what caused the ice ages, but the fluctuation in solar radiation one is among the healthiest. A bloke called Penck worked it out. Do you realize that an overall drop of about three degrees really could bring the glaciers back to northern Scotland?'

'I've done some homework, too, remember,' Andrew said. 'Precipitation counts for more than temperature levels in producing ice caps. Siberia's as far north as Greenland, and as cold, but there's no Siberian ice cap. The moisture-bearing clouds don't penetrate so far into the land mass.'

'Well, hell's flames, we're not likely to run short of moisture-bearing clouds in these offshore islands, are we?'

'Anyway, the drop's inconsiderable. Fratellini figures on a fall

22

of between two and three per cent in the solar energy reaching the outer layers of the atmosphere. There's a normal variability of about three per cent due to local and temporary fluctuations in the sun.'

'But we are going to be colder. That's definite, isn't it?'

'A white Christmas or two, perhaps. We might even roast an ox on the Thames again. Most authorities seem to agree with Fratellini that the fluctuation's likely to be short-lived – less than six months probably.'

'But it might last longer?'

'In the last six and a half centuries there have been two advances and two retreats by the European glaciers. They increased in the western Alps at the beginning of the fourteenth century, and retreated again in the fifteenth. Towards the end of the sixteenth century they advanced again, in both the eastern and western Alps, and in Iceland. They went on advancing up to the first half of the nineteenth century, and then turned tail. The icepacks have been retreating all over the world since then. It might be time for them to make another small advance.'

'Worth a flutter in home heating appliances on the Stock Exchange?'

'As long as you understand that it's a flutter. If it's only a temporary downward swing, as the climatologists think, there may be an upward swing to follow. Sunburn lotions may pay off better. The trend has been towards higher temperatures for the last century.'

'I preferred the programme,' David said. 'Not polar bears, perhaps, but think of a cold clear frozen Thames, voices hushed in the quiet air, the tinkle of sleigh-bells, maybe, along the Embankment.'

'I didn't know you were such a sentimentalist.'

'All we cynical realists are. It's our only defence against ourselves. I used to keep a collection of Christmas cards: the kind with snow scenes – peasants gathering firewood against the sunset, cottages on the edge of the woods, coaching inns . . . You know.'

'And robins.'

'No, no robins. One has one's standards.'

'What happened to the collection?'

'I got discouraged. My elderly aunts died, or went religious and sent artistic Nativity scenes. All I get now are classical reproductions and would-be humorous things. It didn't seem worth going on.'

'I'll look one out for you this year.'

'That's a kind thought.'

Andrew looked at his watch. 'Time I was getting back. I suppose you don't feel like a bachelor evening tonight – a quiet pub-crawl? Carol's going over to Ealing to visit a rather revolting woman she used to go to school with.'

David shook his head. 'I can't make tonight. Why not drop in on Maddie – you could cheer each other up.'

'Perhaps. I'll see.'

In the end, though, he did not. Instead, he came across one of a party of young Nigerians, who were over as a television study group, wandering aimlessly about the studios. He asked Andrew directions, in cultured English and a voice somewhat melancholy in tone, and on impulse Andrew asked him to come and have dinner. He took him to his Club, chiefly in the hope of encountering the Secretary, an Anglo-Indian who disliked the black races as much as Andrew disliked him. The hope was unfulfilled, but the young Negro's naïvety and gratitude were pleasant, and the evening passed well. Carol was not yet in when he got home. He went to bed, and was almost asleep when he heard her opening the front door.

4

Andrew had to spend a week in Sweden, planning one of the special half-hour programmes which they did, from time to time, on different countries. He had sent a card to the Cartwells, giving them the address of his hotel, and on the morning he was due to leave there was a card in reply from Madeleine. It expressed the hope that he was having a good time, and ended: 'Come and see me, when you get back.' The injunction puzzled him slightly – it implied some kind of urgency without making it explicit – but he put it in his pocket and then forgot about it in the confusion of departure.

Carol always met him at the airport after trips of this kind. He went to the Bar to find her, and saw her sitting at a table by herself, looking towards the door. Her face had a tense look, and he wondered if she were angry about something. He would need to find out the trouble, delicately, and jolly her out of the mood.

'Hello, darling,' he said. 'Good to be back.'

'Had a good time? You look well.'

'Fairish. Too much food and drink. Would you like another here, or shall we push on home?'

She disliked airport buildings and was usually glad to get away. He was surprised when she said:

'Get me another, will you? I'm drinking gin and peppermint.'

Andrew got himself a whisky and brought the drinks over. It was probably best to behave normally, and follow her lead. Whatever it was would come out soon enough. He saw that her blue eyes had fixed on his with a probing steadiness that disturbed him; he picked his drink up, and looked at that.

She said: 'I'm going to leave you, Andy.'

He was aware of a slight shiver that ran across his shoulders and down his spine; he hoped the tremor had not shown. The girl behind the bar called something to a colleague at the back, and her voice grated on him, raucous, almost unbearably harsh. He tried to look back into his wife's eyes, but found he could not.

'I'm sorry,' Carol said. 'I think it's best to be direct about it.'

He looked at her hand, at the dull red polish of the fingernails, and thought of the times he had watched her paint and dry them; and of all the other small intimacies of their life together. From now on, for him, she would be groomed and clothed – friendly or hostile but always a stranger.

He asked her: 'Who is it?'

'David.'

He was not too numb to be amazed.

'David? David Cartwell?'

'Yes.'

'It's you he's been seeing these past weeks?'

She spoke with some impatience. 'Yes, of course.'

'But . . .' He choked back the trite pointless words which came automatically to his tongue. In a level voice he said: 'Sweetheart, you want time to think things out.'

She shook her head. 'No, I don't.'

He had felt no jealous resentment when she mentioned David's name, but now he began to resent him on her behalf. For him this was just one more in a series of adventures; Carol had taken it more seriously. He wanted to explain this to her without hurting her. It was not easy.

'David,' he said, '– I don't want to run him down or anything, but I told you what Madeleine said about him . . .'

'You mean, that he's made something of a practice of this? I know that. In the past.'

'And you think it's going to stop?'

In a dry voice, she said: 'One takes chances on people, doesn't one? You did, on me.'

'It was a good bet for eleven years. I'm not prepared to write it off yet, either.'

Her eyes searched his, and again he looked away.

She said: 'You're not going to make trouble, Andy, are you – about a divorce? I'm not asking you to do anything yourself; just divorce me on the evidence I provide.'

Andrew said: 'We need another drink.' She made no reply, and he took their glasses to the bar for replenishing. This time he got himself a double. When he brought them back, he started off on a prepared line:

'David's a fascinating character. I can see that myself, and I suppose the sexual angle adds quite a bit. His technique looks impressive, too. And we've been married a long time. It's not so surprising that you should have gone temporarily overboard.' She tried to say something, but he overrode her. 'I know it seems serious to you. Perhaps it is serious, for him and you. Perhaps you'll make a reformed character out of him. But let's wait and see about that, shall we?'

She said, with the first signs of anger: 'Don't try so hard to be so bloody reasonable. What's the next thing – that I go off by myself somewhere to get it all straightened out in my mind?'

'I can't see it would do any harm.' He was a little angry himself. 'It's not so funny from my side, either, remember.'

'I want David,' Carol said. 'I'm asking you to co-operate.'

'And the children?'

'I want to keep them if I can, and I don't think you would really want them for the whole of their holidays. You can have any reasonable access, of course.'

The calculation infuriated him. He said:

'And when David realizes that you're getting too serious, and backs out the way he's done before – what do you do then?'

She sighed wearily. 'We're in love. Can't you understand that?'

'I can see that you are. And that he's wanted you to believe that he is.'

'Look,' Carol said, 'I know David. I probably know him better than I've ever known you. We're the same type.'

He thought he knew what she was referring to. 'Leading a bit of a wild life before we were married doesn't make you the same type as David,' he told her. 'Being as good-looking as you were, and mixing in that crowd, it was inevitable. But that's nearly twelve years ago.'

'Is it?'

'You probably have a bit of a hankering for your youth. We all do. That doesn't mean you would really go back to that kind of life if you had the choice.'

'All right,' she said. 'I have to tell you, don't I? To think I used to worry at one time about your being suspicious. Of George Price, particularly.'

'George Price?'

'And others. That kind of life, Andy – I never did abandon it. There's no harm in your knowing now.' She sat back, putting her hands together on her lap. 'It might make things easier for you, I suppose.'

He felt the involuntary shiver again, and the clamminess of sweat down his back and along his legs.

'How many others?'

'Three or four. None of them was important, before David. That's how I recognize the difference.' The blue eyes stared at him. 'I never turned you out of my bed before, did I? But I couldn't sleep with you now.'

His legs were trembling; for the moment he wanted only to end this nightmare, to get away. He said:

'What do you want me to do?'

'For the present, you could go to a hotel. Or I'll move out, if you prefer that.'

'No,' he said. 'I'll go. That's all right.'

'Did you get my card?' Madeleine asked. 'I wasn't sure that it would arrive before you left.'

Andrew nodded. 'Yes. I got it.'

'It was difficult to know what to say. I knew from David what was waiting for you, but I couldn't mention that, of course. I

28

thought you might not want to come here afterwards, so I wrote asking you.'

'I would have come anyway.'

'I'm glad. What are you doing – where are you living, I mean?'

'I've booked in at a hotel for the time being. I haven't had time to look around yet.'

She smiled sadly. 'I suppose it wouldn't do for me to take you as a lodger. All sorts of possible trouble with the Queen's Proctor.'

'David?'

'A friend of his who's gone to Spain has lent him his flat. It's just off the King's Road.'

'Madeleine, I don't understand.' He looked at her; it was as easy to look into her eyes as it had been hard with Carol. 'Did you know it was Carol when you told me there was another woman?'

'Not for certain, but I was pretty sure.'

'She's told me that – this isn't the first time.'

'I guessed that, too. I guessed that when I realized David was interested in her.' She spoke with faint bitterness. 'It's not the chaste women that appeal to him. I suppose it should be counted in his favour.'

'And the appeals don't last. All right – tell me how long it's going to be before this one peters out. You know how he operates, and I think I have a right to the information.'

'He's asked me to divorce him, too.'

There was a silence. Andrew said:

'Why should he be serious now?'

'Why, indeed? I had thought, some day, it might happen – I could hardly feel secure, could I? But one expects it to be a younger woman. Carol's six years older than I am.'

'Seven. She was thirty-two in June.'

'David said thirty-one.' They looked at each other, and Madeleine began to laugh. 'It's silly, isn't it? As if a year matters, or seven years.'

'Can I get myself a drink?'

'Yes. Get me one, too. Scotch, I think.'

From the sideboard, he said to her: 'I understand it up to a point. They've both been cheating for years, so there was every reason for them to get together. It went well. I was as ignorant as I'd always been, and you were as prepared to turn a blind eye, and take him back when he got tired of it. Then what happened?'

'Calling them cheats doesn't help, does it? And even cheats have feelings. I don't know Carol well enough to know why she fell in love with David — except that I know he's lovable. As for him, well, she's very lovely. Lovelier than any of his other conquests. And then, if she fell for him . . . As I said, he's never pursued chaste women. It was always kept very much on the physical level, on both sides. He was so busily concerned with demonstrating that he could master their bodies that their hearts just didn't enter into it. Carol's the first one who's really gone after him. He would feel guilty if he didn't love her in return.'

'What about you? Doesn't he feel guilty about that?'

'There are degrees in guilt, aren't there? And I've queered my pitch by being too understanding before. With me, the guilt is blunted by all those confessions. If he leaves me for Carol, he only sees it as wronging me a little more than he has done in the past — wronging her would be a different kind of betrayal. And he can always tell himself that it's better for me, too — that I'm well rid of a bad husband.' She tried to smile. 'In fact, he's told me that already.'

'Yes, you know him,' Andrew said. 'And it's true enough, I suppose.'

'And you,' she said, 'are rid of a bad wife. A stroke of good fortune for both of us. We should be properly grateful, you to David and me to Carol. We might have gone on for years otherwise, mightn't we? For a lifetime.'

He said: 'I don't know what I'm going to do. When I came here . . . I still didn't think it was serious — on his part. I'd got used to that idea.'

After putting their drinks on the coffee table, he had sat down in an armchair. Madeleine got up from her place and came over to him. She put cool dry hands on his forehead and sat on the arm beside him.

'Poor old Andy,' she said. 'It's really hard for you, isn't it? You're losing innocence, as well as a person. I wish I could help.'

He had come to her, consciously, for sympathy, but her physical closeness, reminding him of his loss, distressed him. Restless, he got up and walked to the window to look out.

'I cry at nights,' she said. 'Women are luckier than men, I suppose?'

He turned back to face her. 'Go on talking.'

'About what?'

'It doesn't matter.'

She smiled sadly. 'No. It doesn't matter.'

5

David was already leaning against the bar when Andrew got there. He said:

'Hello, Andy. The usual?'

Andrew hesitated, then shrugged. 'Thanks.'

The tankard was set down in front of him, and he lifted it to drink. David raised his own.

'Health and wealth,' he said. Putting it down, he went on: 'I'm glad you came along. I wasn't sure you would.'

'Not for the pleasure of seeing you.'

David smiled. 'Well?'

'I suppose there are some practical details we shall have to sort out.'

'The lawyer can see to them. Andy, I'm sorry things have happened like this. You may find it hard to believe, but I truly am.'

Andrew said, with cold anger: 'The trouble with you is not so much a matter of being unprincipled as of being irresponsible. You can't admit that your actions have effects.'

'I think I do admit that. But I also think it's a good idea to rescue what one can from the debris.'

'On your terms.'

David shrugged. 'On the best terms that can be agreed.'

'For weeks you were sleeping with my wife and meeting me seemingly as a friend.'

'Nothing seeming about it. It started with Carol when I hardly knew you – that first time you came round for drinks. And bear in mind that I sensed things about her which, for all the time you'd been married to her, you failed to see.'

Andrew said bitterly: 'You're very frank about your future wife.'

'Yes. I'll be frank about myself, too. Even if you had been my friend then, I don't think it would have made any difference.'

'No. You take what you want, don't you, whoever it belongs to?'

'A human being isn't a possession. We're all free agents, Andy. I'm as much against rape as anyone.'

'They voluntarily make contracts. They incur responsibilities.'

'You take people too seriously.'

'You think that's a bad thing?'

'It depends how you look at them, I suppose. When it was a matter of immortal souls, and the risk of an eternal sizzle, one had to take oneself seriously. Aspects have changed.'

'Aspects aren't standards.'

'They affect them. And the moment you stop believing in the Jealous God and the Laws of Moses, you lose sight of land. After that it's every man his own navigator. You talk of responsibility. We're responsible for ourselves, to ourselves, and no one else. And for any children we may happen to have – a marginal responsibility, anyway. Putting the kids first has done far more harm to far more kids than it's ever done good. I know all about that one. I had a self-sacrificing mother.'

'You're something of a bastard,' Andrew said, 'aren't you?'

'In both senses of the word, as a matter of fact. That's probably what made her so self-sacrificing. I'm also something of a realist.'

Andrew said stiffly: 'I couldn't be expected to know . . .'

David laughed. 'I wasn't trying to embarrass you. And I'm not trying to make excuses. The kids didn't come calling after me in the street. She's fairly well off, and she passed as a young widow. I didn't know the truth until I was at Oxford, and I wasn't particularly impressed by it when I was told. After a careful weighing up of the odds, I've decided that it's not just bastards who are out for themselves. The practice is universal.'

'There are rules, and some people stick to them.'

'Maybe. But no two people follow the same set. And where do the rules come from? There can't be many who still swallow the idea of the golden tablets on the mountain. We make our own up.

And we respect the laws of the land, of course. But take the policemen off the streets, and what happens?'

'Some people will behave badly. So the rest, the majority, have to form another police force.'

'Yes. To keep their quiet life. To make sure they can sleep peacefully at night. Not for the abstract good, Andy.'

He had a frankness, a sincerity, which was disarming; it was impossible, in his presence, to persist in disliking him. He looked at Andrew now, almost with a boyish innocence, and said:

'I am going to go on seeing you, aren't I? Not just for sorting out the practical details.'

There was something else. David was his sole link with Carol – to cut adrift from him was to lose any possibility of having news of her.

He said: 'McKay reverted to the subject this morning. He's heard rumours that the Government is taking the Fratellini Winter more seriously. He asked me to see if there was anything I could get out of you.'

The motivation behind McKay's introduction had come out at an early stage in their acquaintance.

David said: 'As long as we carry on meeting, I don't mind what the justification is. I think the rumour probably refers to the Fuel & Power boys. They're anxious to make sure there's no repetition of the '47 crack-up. We're buying American coal to stock up with.'

'Is there any more news of the drop in radiation?'

'Nothing exciting. It is dropping. The Americans are hoping to get some information from their new series of satellite probes.'

'But no one's worried?'

'I believe the Coal Board's delighted. They had a very heavy overstock and they've just about worked through it with extra orders. And have you noticed the way Oils have jumped?'

'It's an ill wind, isn't it?' With a faint reversion of bitterness, he said: 'That cold's only unpleasant when you're out in it unprotected. I suppose it's quite fun when you're looking out from a nice warm room at the poor shivering devils outside.'

There was a pause before David said: 'I don't think it's like that, Andy.' He lifted up his tankard to show that it was empty. 'How about buying me the other half?'

The children came home for half-term, and Andrew took them out two afternoons; the rest of the time they spent with Carol. It was only in seeing them off from Waterloo station that they joined forces.

Boys from a public school were going back on the same train; the windows were crowded with young male faces, from eight to eighteen, the platform studded with groups of parents. Andrew, who had himself gone to a grammar school, from a poor home, remembered seeing such a train-load when he was about thirteen, and noting their pink-and-white confidence. Now his sons conformed to the pattern: a triumph for environmental moulding. He wondered if they were happy; he supposed they were.

Carol said: 'You have my letter to give to Matron?'

'I think so,' Robin said. 'Somewhere.'

'Better look.'

He searched his pockets and produced it.

'Toffee,' Carol said. 'No, it won't wipe off. Keep it in that envelope till you get to school and then put it in a clean one.'

In a resigned tone, Robin observed: 'She'll think I've been spying on what you've written if the envelope has my handwriting on it.'

'Of course she won't. There's nothing private in it. It's only about your booster shots.'

Jeremy said: 'Matron's a living horror.'

'She's devious,' Robin explained.

'Show her the toffee-stained envelope,' Andrew said, 'and explain it all.'

'Probably make her even more suspicious,' Robin said. 'Still, one can but try. I *think* we're about due to go.'

Carol put her face up and was dutifully kissed. Andrew's hand was shaken.

'Be good,' Andrew said.

'You, too.' A spasm of inquiry crossed Robin's face. 'I suppose we'd better write to both of you, hadn't we? I mean, separate letters?'

'You can drop an extra line to me when you find time,' Andrew said. 'To the studios, since I'm still unsettled.'

Robin nodded. 'Sure thing.'

As they left the platform, Andrew said: 'We're lucky to have such understanding children.'

'Yes.'

He handed in the platform tickets. 'Do you feel like a drink, before we go our ways?'

She looked at him with some uncertainty. 'Well . . .'

'It's all right. I promise not to drug your gin and tonic.'

She smiled. 'All right.'

They walked separated by a distance that had to be consciously gauged: far enough apart, but not so far as to be conspicuous. His hand touched hers accidentally, and he choked down an apology as he pulled it back. All this was good training, Andrew reflected, in grasping the essential ridiculousness of life.

He brought their drinks to a small table near the door of the Buffet. It was not very clean, and carried an overflowing ash-tray. At the next table, a large woman coped noisily with three large children.

'Is there any British Railways terminus that has a place where one can sit and have a drink in civilized comfort?' Andrew asked. 'I think I hate railway stations.'

Carol said: 'I hope we can be friends eventually, Andy. It's just that I feel that depends on the break now being a pretty sharp one. If we see much of each other at present, you're bound to show you resent things.'

'And not seeing you stops my resenting?'

'No. It stops you showing it.'

'That makes a difference?'

36

'I can reproach myself better than you can reproach me. Not as harshly, perhaps, but better from the point of view of my going on admiring and liking you.'

'That's very important. You've no idea how important that is.'

'Now,' she said, 'you're showing it. I am being selfish, aren't I?'

She was wearing a blue jersey suit that matched her eyes; it was high-necked and clung softly to the outlines of her breasts. The scent she had on was an unfamiliar one. Presumably David had given it to her. Each day her life took a step away from the one they had shared; each day the pattern shifted further.

'I'm seeing David. Isn't that where the resentment would come out most? Or do you think in this happy future you have planned I can be friends with you and not with your husband?'

'I leave that to David to sort out. But I don't think resentment would bother him as it would me. And I don't think you would be able to keep it up against him for very long.'

Andrew recognized the truth of that.

'Unprincipled charm,' he said. 'What every woman wants.'

'There you are. If I reacted to that, it would be angrily. David would be able to make a joke out of it. He'd probably make you laugh, as well.'

There had been some idea in his mind of making an approach to her. Nothing explicit or emotional – a sounding-out as to whether passion might not be dropping a degree or two from its high fever; a reassurance, no more than hinted, that there was still a way back. He saw how useless this would be, and remained silent.

Carol said: 'I'm glad you and he are seeing each other. And that you're seeing Maddie.'

She was using David's diminutive for Madeleine; just another small thing gleaned from the closeness which left him outside. He was not sure if he loved her, but he had never wanted her more than at this time. He thought of the first time he had seen her, at a summer party, wearing a red organdie dress, and flirting with Steve Wiltshire who was, someone had told him, her lover. He

37

could remember desire, and the bitter jealousy, and the awareness that, in every way he could imagine, she was out of his class. It was far worse now.

With dull sarcasm, he said: 'Everything's working out for the best, isn't it?'

Carol got up, pulling on silk net gloves.

'This doesn't do any good, though, Andy. I must be going. Thanks for the drink.'

6

There was a blizzard early in November and, while the snow still lay unthawed in gutters and gardens, another, fiercer and colder. Later the snow was gentler, less urgent, but more persistent. Towards the end of the month there was a fall which lasted, with very little intermission, for forty-eight hours. The temperature fell below zero, and stayed there. The rush-hour trains and buses crawled painfully in and out of London over ribbons of snow and ice. Stocks of coal dropped sharply, and there were exhortations, in the press and on television, to economize on fuel. December began with a week almost free of fresh falls and lit for brief spells by a watery sun; but only a surface layer melted during the afternoons, to freeze once more with the grey fall of evening. After that the snow came down again.

Once over the initial shocks and discomforts, people got used to the new conditions. Traffic began to move more freely: for the roads an operation was launched which brought gravel-scattering trucks into the cities in the early mornings, while on the railways mobile gangs kept the lines clear and the points and signals free from frost. Oil shares boomed on the London Stock Exchange as the laid-up tankers put to sea again, siphoning the world's oil surplus northwards. In their lunch-hours, office workers skated on the Serpentine and the lakes in the royal parks; officials who tried to stop them were brushed aside. Christmas approached and the song, 'White Christmas', plugged at first, was quietly dropped. Even at the lowest level of commercial sentimentality, there was no magic left in the idea of snow. The new pop favourite, which surged to the top of the Hit Parade and stayed there, was a translation of a German ballad, resurrected from the dark days of the Second World War:

All our troubles are rolling,
Rolling, rolling away –
Although there is snow in December,
There'll always be sunshine in May.

One heard the wistful little tune everywhere.

Carol was to have the boys for Christmas, and Andrew for the New Year. Until the morning of Christmas Eve, he thought she might ask him to join them for the day itself, for the dinner anyway, but there was no message. During the afternoon, though, Madeleine telephoned him at the studios.

She said: 'If you have any other plans, don't hesitate to say so, Andy, but if you aren't doing anything better, what about coming here tomorrow?'

'You'll be on your own?'

'Well, yes.'

'It's nice of you, Madeleine. I think we should warm each other with the season's cheer. But there's no need for you to get tied up with cooking. We can go somewhere. How about the Dorchester? I'm told they do a very fair Christmas dinner.'

'No, we'll have a heavy lunch here. The bird is bought and prepared. Come round about twelve.'

'I'll be there.'

There was a small hesitation, before she said: 'If you want to cancel – if anything crops up – just give me a ring.'

'I shan't want to cancel. See you tomorrow.'

Andrew took two bottles of champagne with him. The door was, as usual, on the latch, and he went in. From the direction of the kitchen, Madeleine called:

'Who is it?'

He found her busy in an apron, her pale face slightly flushed.

He said: 'Sorry if I'm early. I thought I'd better give these time to cool.'

She smiled. 'Lovely. Pop them in the fridge and then go and find yourself a drink. I'll be clear in half an hour.'

'I'll bring drinks in here for both of us.'

She said warningly: 'I'll probably find things for you to do.'

'I'll risk that.'

When he came back, he said: 'Yesterday – you knew I wasn't going round to Dulwich?'

Madeleine took the drink from him. She looked at him directly, her brow creased in a slight frown.

'I'd spoken to David. He said Carol was planning to be on her own with the children. He suggested that if you weren't coming here, he should.'

Andrew put his drink down. 'You could have cancelled this, you know. I wouldn't have minded.'

'This was *before* I rang you. I told him I'd asked you to come.' She smiled. 'Isn't it strange? I find I can lie to him now. I never could before.'

She returned to her preparations. Andrew said:

'Was it wise, do you think?'

'Lying to him?'

'Refusing to have him come here. It was an approach, after all.'

'The first sign of weakness? He might have tried to take me to bed, do you think? I'm almost sure he would. And that after that he might have stayed. And then Carol would have taken you back, and everything would have been as it used to be.' She shook her head. 'I've no illusions left about David and me. He hates the idea of being lonely over Christmas. And after being separated, he would find a spice in seducing me. He could do it quite easily, too – we both know that. But it would have made no difference. He would have gone back to Carol.'

'If she'd taken him. You might have told her . . .'

'Andy darling, don't you understand? He would have told her. You still don't know them, do you?'

He said heavily: 'I suppose not.'

'If I have any chance of getting him back, it's not by letting him make love to me. As it is, he's just that little bit more uncertain. It isn't enough to make a difference, but it's something.' She smiled at him. 'And I have you. That's quite a lot, you know.'

'Why did you lie to him? Wouldn't it have made your point better simply to refuse him and tell him you were going to ask me instead?'

She said gently: 'Lying is always a sign of some kind of weakness. As it was, he suggested I should put you off.'

'I suppose he would. But you didn't agree?'

'I was strong enough for that. I'm glad I was.'

Standing behind her, he touched her arms lightly.

'So am I.'

After the meal they stacked the dishes in the machine and took coffee into the sitting room. Already, at half past two, there was a dimness of approaching dusk in the air; through the windows they could see the shrouded white shapes of the other houses, on which more snow was falling out of the grey sky. They sat together on the long sofa, and he kissed her. They had kissed from time to time, quite innocently, and on this occasion, too, it started like that. But they were more alone, it seemed, than they had been before, and the world was quiet and sad, matching their loneliness.

'No,' Madeleine said. 'No, darling.'

Her voice was drowsy, a gentle complaint. She was wearing a grey jersey frock that buttoned down the front. Her hand checked his for a time, and then fell away.

'Please, Andy . . .'

Her breast gleamed with the snow's whiteness. He put his lips down to it. She lay still, unmoving; a moment or two later she put her hands up to his head. He thought she was going to push him away, but instead they curled round, pulling him more closely against her flesh. The pulse of her heart beat under his lips. It was a moment of assurance, with no need of haste or impatience. They were locked in peace and comfort; even the distant sound of the telephone bell did not, at first, break this.

When it had been ringing for perhaps half a minute, Madeleine stirred. She said:

42

'I'd better go, darling.'

'Let it ring.'

She eased him from her and got up, buttoning her dress.

'I won't be long,' she said. 'I promise.'

He put a hand up. 'Leave the top one undone. Another promise.'

She smiled and nodded. 'All right.'

He listened to her steps going away to the hall, to her voice, remote, the words indistinguishable, and to the footsteps returning. She came into the sitting room but stood away from him, on the far side of the coffee table.

'David,' she said. 'He asked if you were here.'

'What does he want?'

'He asked if he could come and have coffee with us.'

Her hands, as though automatically, went to her dress and fastened the remaining button.

'Damn him,' Andrew said. 'Damn him to hell and back. Why did you say yes?'

'I'm sorry.' She spread her hands. 'What else could I do?'

'How long before he gets here?'

'A few minutes. He was calling from South Ken station. Please be nice, Andy. I won't let him stay long.'

'No. But from one particular point of view, it makes no difference now whether he goes in a quarter of an hour or stays all day. Does it?'

'We were being silly,' Madeleine said. 'Both of us.'

'It's all right for you.'

'Is it?' she said. 'Is it?'

She came to him, in an embrace not of passion but of desperation. She did not release herself until they heard the front door open and David's voice calling. She brushed her hair back with her hand; she was even paler than usual.

David, entering the room, said cheerfully:

'Hope you can put up with me for a spell. I feasted myself with poached eggs on toast, but I lost heart when I reached the Nescafé stage.'

43

'There's plenty of cold turkey,' Madeleine said. 'I could warm up some vegetables.'

'Just coffee for the moment. I may try a turkey sandwich later.'

Madeleine left the room and returned with the coffee jug and a cup and saucer. She said:

'I suppose you still like it almost cold. I could make fresh.'

'You know how I like things.'

Madeleine said: 'Andy and I have plans for the rest of the day. We supposed you weren't staying long.'

'A gentle supposition, a broad broad hint. No, I won't impose on your kindness.'

He looked at her, smiling. Madeleine started to say something, checked, then started again. Andrew cut across her words.

'That's all clear then, isn't it, David? Or are you starting to get jealous?'

'If I were,' David said, 'I hope I should be able to feel ashamed of myself. As a matter of fact, I did have another motive in coming round, ulterior but not inferior. I want to give you both some good advice.'

Andrew said: 'Do you really think we're likely to benefit from any advice of yours?'

'I don't know. It depends whether you act on it.'

Madeleine said: 'What advice is it, David?'

'To emigrate. Somewhere south. Somewhere within the Tropics, for preference.'

Andrew said contemptuously: 'I thought that particular panic was over.'

David said quietly: 'It hasn't begun yet. I suppose I'd better give you the information that goes with it. It comes out of a file that was marked "Cabinet Only" until yesterday. It's only been cleared now for certain officials who may be concerned, at top level, in planning precautions. I scraped in on my last year's promotion.'

Andrew said: 'Are you trusting me with this confidential information? Despite my job and – shall we say, personal background?'

'Yes, I'm trusting you. I want you to persuade Maddie. And

what do I lose if there is a leak and they trace it to me?' He smiled wryly. 'My pension?'

'What is it, David?' Madeleine asked.

David took out his wallet, and produced some jotted notes on a piece of scrap paper. He said to Andrew:

'When I spoke to you about the programme you did on the Fratellini Winter – you told me you'd done your homework on the subject.'

'I don't remember it all now.'

'I'll refresh you. Insolation – that's the term for exposure to solar energy: there's an accepted figure for it. The income for the outer layers of the atmosphere averages 1.94 calories per square metre. And it varies' – he glanced again at the scrap of paper – 'within limits of about three per cent.'

Andrew nodded. 'I remember that.'

'And the drop predicted by Fratellini was rather less than the normal variation.'

'Yes. That, too.'

'Ten days ago, an American weather satellite took a reading.' David tapped the paper. 'The new figure was a little higher than 1.80, something like 1.805. That represents an overall drop of seven per cent. Fratellini's maximum, allowing for unfavourable fluctuation, was six.'

'An extra one per cent,' Andrew said. 'Is it something to worry about?'

'That was ten days ago. Three days ago they got another reading. It was 1.80 exactly.'

Madeleine said: 'I don't follow all this. Does it mean it's going to go on getting colder – indefinitely?'

'It will probably bottom out in due course. But it's still going down. Fratellini said two to three per cent, and the figure is now four plus. I think it's been worked out that during the ice ages the overall temperature was only nine or ten degrees lower than it is now.'

'But there's probably no exact correlation between a drop in solar radiation and air temperatures – there are all sorts of factors to be considered. Cloud cover and so on. And our mean temperature is only about fifty anyway. Four per cent of that works out at two degrees.'

David said: 'Four per cent if you're counting in the normal fluctuation. But seven per cent from the average. And still going down. That's the sole and basic point. Still going down. Fratellini's calculations are out of the window. All guesses are equal from this point on.'

'And what do you guess?' Madeleine asked.

'An ice age,' Andrew said. 'London blanketed by the eternal snows. A new *Daily Mail* London to Paris race, on skis and skates only. Have I got it right?'

'There are fifty million people,' David said, 'living on this island. The east coast of Greenland, which stretches for twice the distance from Land's End to John o' Groats, supports two villages. But it doesn't need an ice age to make life uncomfortable. How much food will the farmers grow if winter lasts into May, and starts again in September? What's going to happen to the Canadian wheatlands? The overwhelming bulk of our food comes from the temperate lands. What happens when they become sub-temperate?'

'You're talking,' Andrew said, 'as though the radiation drop was going to be permanent.'

David said slowly: 'We have no reason now for thinking anything else. Fratellini predicted six to nine months, but Fratellini also predicted a maximum of three per cent; and we're through that already. We just don't know how things are going to turn out.'

'Then surely it's a bit premature to leave the country?'

'Later on it may not be so easy.'

Madeleine looked at him. 'Is that out of the confidential file, too?'

'No. It's what is known as intelligent anticipation, a characteristic which should be possessed by all senior Civil Servants. And there's something else you may not have thought of. That immigration countries may impose restrictions, too.'

Madeleine asked: 'What countries were you thinking of?'

'The Americans are going to move down into South America, in so far as they're able. Some of them have started already. Property values in Rio and Montevideo have jumped more than a hundred per cent in the past month. I think Africa's a better bet. One of our own ex-colonies – Nigeria, Ghana, somewhere like that.'

'Are you serious?' Andrew asked.

'Yes. I'm serious.'

'Are you going yourself?'

There was a pause before David replied. 'The rat with a private lifeline can take his time before leaving the sinking ship. I'm one of Them, remember, not one of Us. I can plan things and take my time. You're not so happily placed.'

'And Carol?' Madeleine asked.

'I haven't spoken to her about it yet. I only saw this report last night. I hope I can persuade her to go. I didn't want to break it to her over Christmas, with the boys there.'

Andrew said quietly: 'Yes, what about my sons? Where do they fit in?'

'I hope Carol will take them with her, and make a home in Africa.'

'And take them away from school? Have you thought what kind of schools there are likely to be in Nigeria and Ghana?'

'She could try Algeria or Egypt, or even South Africa. My own feeling is the nearer to the Equator the better. And I think the future's more promising in the Negro countries. One can't really tell, of course. If the worst comes to the worst, God knows what will happen.'

Andrew said: 'So far I've been very co-operative. I've agreed to the divorce, and I haven't asked for care or custody of the boys. But I don't mind telling you that the moment my solicitor's office opens the day after tomorrow, I shall be round there.'

'Telling them all this?'

'I don't think I should need to do that. Simply asking for an injunction against their being taken out of the country without my consent. I don't need to give reasons, and I don't think I should have much trouble in getting it, do you?'

David drained his cold coffee and poured more from the jug.

'No, you'd get it. Andy, no one's trying to take the boys away from you. I think you ought to go out there, too. And Maddie.'

Madeleine said: 'You're being a bit unreasonable, David. We should all look rather silly if this turns out to be just another hard winter.'

'I was up at the Pool of London yesterday,' David said. 'There are chunks of ice floating. You can cross the river above Chiswick.'

'There have been other winters as cold, though, haven't there?'

With flat determination, David said: 'It's going to get worse. A lot worse.'

'But there's not such an urgency, is there?'

'The financial side has to be considered. Leaving now you could realize capital – sell both the houses, and so on. And convert sterling into whatever currency you want. Later, it may not be possible.'

'Why not?'

'Because the kind of panic I'm thinking of could make a London house worthless overnight, and make sterling a currency without value or meaning.'

'Can I use that?' Andrew asked. 'It would make a good slant in a programme.'

'They wouldn't let you use it. Try it, and see. We're too close to the edge already.'

Andrew said: 'Madeleine and Carol are free agents. There's no reason why they shouldn't take your advice if they see any sense in it. I don't, myself. And I'll make sure that, if Carol leaves, the boys stay. I'll get that court order.'

David shook his head. 'You're making a mistake.'

'Possibly. I think it would be a bigger mistake to trust you in anything, though.'

7

January and February were savagely cold. The Thames froze almost up to Tower Bridge; beyond that the Pool and the estuary were thick with floating ice. One of the evening papers promoted a Winter Fair on the river, but it was not a success. The wind rose in the night, and many of the flimsy structures that had been erected on the ice were blown down and scattered. It was too bitter, in any case, to encourage people to venture far from shelter.

March opened on a comparatively milder note, but there was still no thaw. Food prices, which had been rising for some time, began to rocket, and there was a wave of strikes throughout the country. They culminated in a general strike, which lasted three days: during those days prices doubled and re-doubled. The Government, which had proclaimed a State of Emergency and taken necessary powers, showed no sign of yielding them again. There was strict censorship, and the police were armed. Rationing and price controls were introduced for a wide range of foods; patient queues lengthened in the grubby snow outside provision shops. Press and television called on the people to endure, to show their ancient phlegm. 'If winter comes,' quoted the Prime Minister in his clipped and confident voice, 'can spring be far behind?'

Andrew had gone to his solicitors after Christmas, and they had approached Carol. She had not proved difficult. She had agreed to the children being made wards of Court, pending a decision on care and custody at the time of the granting of the divorce. The hearing had been set down for the beginning of April.

Meanwhile, at the end of March, there were to be the Easter holidays, and it was arranged that Andrew should meet the boys at Waterloo. The taxi which took him there, in a snow storm, carried chains on its wheels. Andrew realized that very little gravelling was being done now, and that little in a perfunctory manner.

'Shockin' wevver,' the driver said. 'Don't get no better, neiver, do it?'

'No,' Andrew said. He glanced at his watch. 'We're going to be late.'

'Shouldn't worry. Not as late as the train'll be.'

At the station, Andrew went to the indicator board. A ninety-minute delay was signalled. He turned away to go in search of a snack, and found David coming towards him.

David said: 'Hello, Andy. Hoped I'd find you here.'

He had been away from the studios all morning, and presumed Carol had been trying to get in touch with him. It crossed his mind that the school, which was five miles from its railhead, might have been cut off by the latest blizzard, and that the boys might not be able to get to London for the time being.

'About the boys?' he asked.

'Yes.' David took his arm. 'Something I want to draw your attention to first, though.'

He pointed. There was an armed sentry guarding the gate at Platform 9. Other soldiers were on duty elsewhere in the station.

'What's all that about?' Andrew asked.

'The Army,' David said, 'is standing to. Not just here, but in strategic places all over the country. England is now under martial law.'

'Do they expect trouble?'

'A cut in the ration scale will be announced this afternoon. A very large cut.'

'That reminds me,' Andrew said. 'I missed breakfast. I was going to get a sausage roll.'

'I'll come with you,' David said. 'You can have mine as well.'

The rule in snack bars had been one item of food per person for some time. As they approached the door of the Buffet, Andrew saw another familiar sign: SORRY – NO BEER.

50

He said: 'What was it, about the boys? Are they keeping them at school for the present?'

'I have a letter for you,' David said.

The envelope was blank. Andrew opened it and took out a sheet of paper. The letter was in Carol's handwriting.

Dear Andy,

By the time this reaches you, the boys and I will be in Africa. I'm sorry to have to let you down again, but it's the best thing for every-body. David is quite right: things are going to get worse. If you have any sense at all you'll get out yourself while there's time. I may say I've sold the house, forging your signature on the con-tract. You won't have expected me to draw a line at that, will you? I only got £3,200, and was lucky to get it. I've also cleared out my account and cashed the Savings certificates. My total capital is just under £4,000. On David's advice, I've chosen Lagos as our best bet. I'll send you an address as soon as I have one. I really think you ought to come out yourself.

Yours,
Carol

'You've read it, I expect,' Andrew said. David shook his head, and Andrew gave him the letter. 'You'll know what's in it. It was your idea, wasn't it?'

'Basically,' David said. He handed back the letter. 'Will you go out there?'

'To Lagos? And find she's taken them to Cairo, or Salisbury, or Johannesburg? I'd be a fool to trust anything she writes or you say, wouldn't I?'

'They've gone to Lagos, all right,' David said. 'The idea in your going out would be to bring them back?'

'What else?'

'Things are a bit chaotic there. It would take you some time to get a court order. By the time you got one, I don't think you would want to use it.'

'Why not?' David nodded towards the soldier with an automatic rifle, patrolling a few feet away from them. 'Because someone has called out the military?'

'Glasgow,' David said, 'has been in the hands of a mob for the past two days. By some accounts a communist mob, by others just a mob. I don't think it's an important point.'

Andrew looked at him. 'I would have heard that – through the news room . . .'

'Security is now very *tight*. But you probably will hear it soon. And a few other items. If you do leave the country, you'll be surprised how different things look from out there. I know a bit about it. I've had access to the foreign press.'

'More propaganda for emigration?'

Andrew was a little surprised at the mildness of his own reaction; he would have expected to feel anger at David's part in this new betrayal. It made him realize how greatly things had changed, how his own apprehensions about the situation had unconsciously sharpened. There was relief in his mind as well as resentment. He thought of the children in the strong safe sunshine of Africa, and was not altogether unhappy about it.

'I think you should go,' David said. 'The insolation figure, by the way, is down to 1.74.'

'That's a slower rate of decline. It was 1.75 at the beginning of the month.'

'Yes, it is slower.'

'So it looks as though it's bottoming out. We may be over the worst.'

David shook his head, in a gesture of negation and certainty.

'We're not over the worst. We haven't reached it yet.'

The London mob erupted on Easter Monday. The morning was bright and by midday one could hear small trickles and gurgles of water as ice and snow melted from roofs and gutters. In the afternoon, Andrew and Madeleine walked to Knightsbridge and the Park. They were not alone in seeking this outing; the streets suddenly were full of people, and so was the Park itself. Children snowballed each other along Rotten Row. Young men and women skated under the Serpentine bridge.

As they came in sight of Marble Arch, Andrew said:

'It's even thicker up this way. Shall we turn back?'

Madeleine looked at the crowd ahead of them.

'The orators,' she said. 'It might be fun to go and listen.'

He objected: 'We'd never get near the speakers. There must be thousands there.'

'If we can't hear them, we'll come away.'

'All right.' Andrew nodded towards the sky. 'It's clouding over.'

A cloud took the sun and, as though this were a signal, things changed in front of them. It was confusing at first, a formless whirl, a savage ripple in a hitherto motionless pool. Madeleine clutched his arm.

'What is it? Are they running away?'

'Towards us.' He looked behind them to see if there was any obvious focus for the movement, but saw nothing. 'Trouble with the police, perhaps?'

Later he learned what had happened. The mob had collected, chiefly from Paddington and North Kensington, and had been harangued by its leaders. Men had a right to food, and there was food in the shops. It was there for the rich, who could buy on the black market:

'My week's ration!' shouted one speaker. He waved in the air a single rasher of bacon. 'There's the Dorchester down the road. Do you think they're living on one rasher of bacon in the Dorchester?'

There were now two authorities – the police and the military. The officer commanding troops had wanted to move in and break up the meeting from the start, but the police chief had overruled him. He preferred defensive to offensive action. Machine-gun posts had been set up at the Arch and along Park Lane and Oxford Street, and he did not think the mob was desperate enough to rush the defences, or strong enough to break through if they did. He was right in the first conclusion and may have been right in the second, but he had failed to anticipate what actually happened. There were no defences in the open spaces of the park itself. This was something the mob's temporary leader and spokesman had realized.

'They've put the police on to stop us,' he yelled, '– the police and the bloody soldiers. If we go to the Dorchester, or the Ritz, or Fortnum and Friggin Mason's, to take what's our due, they'll shoot us down. But we don't have to go that way, brothers! What about a little run across the Park? What about Harrods, say? The rich buy their food there, too. You don't pay cash in Harrods. You give them a cheque, and to hell with the coupons! Let's go and give them a cheque, then. We'll write one out on the Bank of England. What do you say?'

As the crowd moved and surged forward, there was a moment when it might have been scattered by a few shots, but the movement had taken place too quickly, and in the wrong direction. It was a different matter ordering men to fire on their unarmed fellow citizens when they were, to all intents, running away, than it would have been if they had been advancing against the guns. A minute or two later an order was given, and a few shots were fired over their heads, but the only effect then was to quicken the charge.

Andrew took hold of Madeleine's arm as it burst over them.

'Go with it!' he said. 'Whatever's happening, don't try to stand against it. You would be knocked over and trampled.'

They were swept several hundred yards before they succeeded in easing their way to the edge and, finally, out of the stampede. They watched the mob move on towards Knightsbridge, leaving fallen figures in its wake. A boy about seven sat in the snow, weeping. He would not be comforted when Madeleine spoke to him and at last, still sobbing, picked himself up and ran after the others.

'Should we stop him?' Madeleine asked.

'No.' He had a sense of helplessness. 'I don't think it would do any good.'

They made their way back through the side streets. They heard shots, and distant shouting, and at one point, seeing Harrods in the distance, had a glimpse also of the rioting crowd round it and heard the crash of glass. The sun was still hidden by clouds and there was a cold wind. In these parts the streets were empty, apart from occasional figures who came to their doors to look and listen, but did not stay long in the open. Andrew and Madeleine did not say much until they reached her house.

Then he said: 'I'm going to move in with you, Madeleine. It's the safest thing.'

She nodded. 'Yes. Please do.'

8

McKay said: 'I've forgotten – were you with us in the Ally Pally days?'

'No,' Andrew said. 'I was still in Steam.'

'The moving finger writes,' said McKay, 'and having writ, turns back. We're moving up there at once.'

'Why?'

'In two words, compactness and defensibility. All under one roof, and we shall only need a company or two of soldiers to look after us. It's not as though we're worth looting.'

'And how do we get there and back – armoured car? Or are we expected to sleep there?'

'Not yet. You'll get escort between Alexandra Palace and the tube station.'

'That's something.'

'Yes. Anything strike you about it?'

'Needing escort? I'm not surprised. I nearly got caught up in the Harrods riot.'

McKay looked at him thoughtfully. 'If I were you,' he said, 'it might occur to me to wonder how long one could rely on the Underground keeping going. Yes, ask me how long you can rely on the Underground.'

'All right. I'm asking.'

'And I'm not supposed to tell you, but it's being prepared for tonight's News, so it would be a trifle ridiculous to stand on the niceties. The Underground is being closed tonight apart from the Piccadilly line. And that will have three stops only: Piccadilly in the centre, Wood Green, for Alexandra Palace, in the north, and Heathrow Central in the west.'

'Heathrow Central?'

'The nearest tube station to London Airport.'

The significance did not penetrate. He said, conscious of his stupidity: 'Why the tube?'

There was a large-scale street map of central London on McKay's desk. He picked up a thick blue pencil and began to draw a line northwards from a point on the river.

'From the chilly plush of Cheyne Walk,' he said, 'up the Earl's Court Road; then, in a long and nearly straight line, Holland Park Avenue, Bayswater Road, Oxford Street, and High Holborn. Up Clerkenwell and Old Street to take in the bulk of the City, down Bishopsgate, and a small diversion along Leadenhall Street to take in the Mint and the Tower and a few wharves in the Pool. And what does that give you, with the river as its southern boundary?' McKay looked up, eyes sharp in his thin face. 'It gives you the London Pale. The name isn't official, but it's apt. Inside those lines, order – outside, chaos and barbarism. Except for our little oasis at Alexandra Palace and, of course, the airport.'

'Is this serious?'

'Very.'

'You mean – they're abandoning the whole of Greater London? What's going to happen to the people outside the Pale? What about those who come in to the centre to work?'

'Essential enterprises have already made their own quiet arrangements for essential personnel. The others will be turned back. What they do then is their own business.'

'And in the rest of the country?'

'Similar arrangements. Strongpoints will be held.'

'They can't abandon people like that.'

'That was my own reaction. But they can't protect them, either. If they try to stretch the armed forces over the country as a whole, the whole country will go under. This way, they can preserve order at the centre.'

'For how long?'

'I gather there's another side to the calculation, also,' McKay said. 'When things get back to normal, it will be that much easier to go out and re-impose order. The ranks of Tuscany will have thinned in the meantime.'

'My God.'

'It would be appropriate to thank Him. You're to be one of the lucky ones. Your digs are inside the Pale, aren't they?'

Andrew nodded. 'South Ken.'

'I'm bringing my lot down from Hampstead,' McKay said. 'We're being billeted at the Savoy, I understand.' He smiled, a cold unhappy smile. 'I would never have imagined that. By the way, keep mum about this until after the News. It's probably getting around fast, but there's no need to make it faster.'

'All right.'

There was a knock at the door, and McKay called:

'Come in!'

A boy entered, carrying a framed print. It was the Utrillo snow scene. McKay said:

'What the hell's that?'

'It's after Easter, sir. You change the pictures over at Easter.'

'Not this year, I don't,' McKay said. The boy stood uncertainly by the door, holding the picture. 'Bring it over here. On the desk.'

He stared for a moment at the bare white outline of the Parisian streets. To Andrew, he said:

'Any offer for this inspiring study of winter? I thought not.'

Leaning forward, he scrawled with his blue pencil across the canvas, dragging with such violence that the point finally tore it. He pulled the pencil down again, this time deliberately and obviously ripping. He tossed the pencil into the metal wastebox, and pushed the picture off his desk.

'You take it, son,' he said to the boy. 'It will burn. Keep yourself warm on some cold spring evening.'

Andrew took a couple of camera-men along on the north patrol three days after the Pale was established. McKay, in suggesting this, had been careful to stress that it was entirely voluntary.

'I'm not sure whether we can use the stuff if you do bring it back,' he said. 'I rather feel it would be held to encourage alarm and despondency, even if it's no worse than long shots of empty streets. But as documentary material for the future . . . all the same, don't unless you feel keen yourself.'

The patrol consisted of two armoured cars. Andrew and the camera-men went in the first. The officer in charge was a Captain Chisholm, a tall lean fair young man in his early twenties. He gave an impression of imperturbability and spoke with a slight Yorkshire accent. Andrew asked him what route was laid down.

'There's nothing laid down precisely,' he said. 'It's just a matter of making a sweep. My idea is north along Baker Street, up round the top of Regent's Park, Camden Town, King's Cross, and back along Pentonville and Aldersgate. We could vary that if there's some place you're particularly interested in. The only thing is, we try to stick to the main thoroughfares as far as possible. It's too easy to get trapped in narrow streets.'

'I can't think of anything at present,' Andrew said. 'What's the idea behind the patrols, anyway? They seem a bit of an unnecessary risk.'

'Showing the flag, I suppose,' Chisholm said. 'And I suppose they think it may encourage the more dangerous mobs to move out rather than cluster round the Pale.'

'Are people moving out?'

'I doubt if the gangs are. There have been big treks out to the country, but my guess is that those are the more law-abiding citizens panicking. I should think the dangerous ones will stick around in the hope of getting into the Pale. There was a nasty attack from Fulham last night. We had quite a few casualties.'

'Poor devils.'

Chisholm looked at him. 'Ours, or theirs?'

'Both.'

'My folks are in the Leeds Pale,' Chisholm said. 'I hope they are, anyway. How long do you reckon it will be before things quieten down again?'

Andrew shrugged. 'A month or two. Maybe longer.'

'I'll tell you,' Chisholm said, '— I'm glad this isn't my city. I suppose I'd still do the job if it were, but I'm glad it's not.'

The cars rattled along Baker Street at rather better than thirty miles an hour. There were a few signs of life — some figures skulking away into doorways as the patrol reached them, others calling out in entreaty, in some cases running after them as they passed. One man, coming out into the street in front of them, stood in their path, both arms raised in appeal.

'Don't swerve,' Chisholm said to the driver.

The car plunged towards him; at the last moment he fell backwards. Looking back, Andrew saw him picking himself up out of the frozen snow. The second car ran past within a couple of feet of him, but he made no move or sign towards it.

Just past the Marylebone Road intersection, Chisholm pointed up at a window. A black cat could be seen sitting on the ledge behind the glass. It looked content, and quite plump.

'There's a dinner someone's overlooked,' he said. 'I doubt if they'll go on overlooking it for long. Pussy's living on borrowed time.'

They had a glimpse of Regent's Park on their right.

Andrew said: 'What about the Zoo animals?'

'They killed them off the day before things were closed down. They brought the carcases of everything that was edible into the Pale.'

'Who decided what was edible?'

Chisholm laughed. 'That's a point, isn't it? Standards are changing fast now. I suppose there will be a few chewing rattlesnake and porcupine — raw as like as not.'

His brash insensitivity was probably enviable. In any case, for the job he was doing, it was essential. Andrew saw one of the photographers focus on a body that lay huddled in the gutter and swung the camera round to hold it as they drove past. It was the luxuries of illusion and self-deception that were enviable: there had never been a sensitive butcher, and very few vegetarians who did not wear leather shoes. Enviable, and lost forever.

They passed the deserted terraces of the Zoo. From somewhere among the buildings, smoke rose – too thickly to be a small cooking fire. One of the buildings must have caught. Fires had sprung up, since the setting up of the Pale, in various parts of Greater London; at night one could see the distant smudges of red on the horizon. But none of them so far had turned into a major conflagration. Luck; or possibly the omnipresent snow and ice helped to douse them.

Trouble came in the stretch of road facing King's Cross station. Their car had reached the junction of the Caledonian Road and Pentonville when one of the men gave a shout. The second car, twenty-five or thirty yards behind them, had stopped. The lead car swung round in a tight circle and headed back. The driver drew up alongside.

Chisholm called: 'What's up?'

There was a Sergeant in charge of the second vehicle.

He said: 'She cut out, sir. Briggs is having a look.'

The driver had the bonnet up and was busy underneath it.

He called something about plugs without looking up from what he was doing. Chisholm said, to his own driver:

'Better get down and give him a hand, Sandy.'

Without the reassuring sound of the engines, the silence all about them had a disturbing note. And here, at the confluence of five roads, one had a feeling of being exposed. Andrew mentioned this to Chisholm.

'Yes. Better this way, though, after all. We're not overlooked.' He stared at the silent buildings surrounding them. 'Seems very peaceful, doesn't it?'

It continued to look peaceful after figures had begun to appear. There were a few of them at first, inconspicuous in the doorways or standing at corners where it would be an easy matter to dodge away. As the numbers grew, there were more signs of boldness. A man stepped out into the road, some twenty yards from the cars, and shook his fist. He shouted confused angry insults at the watching soldiers. Beside him, Andrew heard Chisholm draw in breath, but he gave no orders.

Surprisingly, the shouting man was stopped by the others. They called to him to be quiet, and after a short time he went silent, and walked awkwardly away. As though this were a signal, the others began moving in towards the cars. They looked entirely peaceful; in fact, friendly.

A little man in a ragged overcoat said: 'Can I give you a hand, guv'nor? I know a fair bit about motor engines – used to work in a garage.'

Chisholm said, trying to keep the stiffness out of his voice:

'Thank you, but we can manage.'

There were at least three women in the crowd. One of them, a strapping woman in her late forties, called out cheerfully:

'How about a lift into town, laddie? There hasn't been a bloody bus along all morning.'

There was a titter of laughter, in which some of the soldiers joined. She went on:

'You can squeeze me in, then, can't you? I don't mind sitting on someone's knee. Come on, boys – I'm all yours for the price of the bus fare. You don't want to pass up a chance like that. I won't be on offer for long.'

Chisholm stared in front of him, his face blank. For the rest it was still a joke – a conspicuous triumph for the English sense of humour in adversity. It was another woman who caused the atmosphere to change. She was five or ten years older than the first, a grey frozen wisp with staring blue eyes.

She said: 'Take me in with you, mister.'

There was no reply. The laughter died away. She moved closer until she stood only a yard or two from the side of the car.

'I'll come out again afterwards,' she said. 'I'm not asking to stay in there. My girl's in there. She's having a baby; it's about due now. I only want to see she's all right. I'll come out again after that.'

Chisholm still said nothing.

She said: 'I promise I'll come out again and cause no trouble.'

There were murmurs from the others. A man called: 'You can

take her with you, can't you?' The woman moved still closer and others followed suit. In a hard voice, Chisholm said:

'Stand back, all of you. This is a military patrol. Get back.'

The man who had previously spoken now said: 'When I was in the Army we fought for our own folks, not against them. What kind of military turns women and kids out to starve? You ought to be protecting them, not turning them back.'

Chisholm said: 'We have to obey orders.'

The compulsion to offer some justification, Andrew thought, must have been almost overwhelming; nevertheless, it was a mistake. It provoked an immediate outcry of anger and protest, and a general surge forward from the crowd. Chisholm shouted to them again to get back, but they paid no attention. He had shown himself as something other than a uniformed figure, and they feared him and respected him less as a result. There was a difference in their attitude; it was harder, more openly self-seeking, and more hopeful. A big man at the back shouted:

'Get those bloody guns off them! We could use those guns.'

Chisholm ordered them again to stand back, to be greeted this time by a general shout of derision. The little blue-eyed woman clung to the side of the car and tried to haul herself up.

If the men were ordered to fire, at this close range, it would be a massacre; and it was far from certain how the massacre would end. As it was the troops were outnumbered about three to one, and the other side was still being augmented as more came in from the side streets. But if they were not ordered to fire, the conclusion seemed as certain. Concentrating on this, Andrew did not at first hear the new command Chisholm gave. It was in a different tone, the voice of a man confident of his response:

'Masks on.'

It was only as he saw those around him slipping theirs on that Andrew took this in, and began to fumble with the mask which he had been given before leaving the Pale, and which had since hung uncomfortably against his chest. He was still struggling with it, as Chisholm's next command came:

'Bombs away!'

Vapour wreathed up, grey against the white of snow. Most of the people round the cars turned and ran, stumbling and falling over each other in their urgency. A few came on for a time and then, clutching their eyes, staggered away. Andrew got his mask on at last, but not before the tear gas had reached him. He sat with streaming eyes, staring out at a blurred scene. They were all in retreat; even the blue-eyed woman, doubled up, was crawling away across the snow. In a harsh muffled voice, Chisholm said:

'Fixed that yet, Sandy?'

'Not yet, sir. And I can't see what I'm doing properly with this damn thing on.'

It was another ten minutes before they were ready to move. During that time, no one approached the cars. Andrew had thought there might, at least, be insults shouted from a distance, things thrown, perhaps, from the windows of the houses; but nothing happened.

Taking his mask off as instructed, he said something of this to Chisholm.

'We were lucky,' Chisholm said dispassionately. 'Lucky it happened in a wide street. Lucky there's no one in that little lot with either guts or initiative.' The engines of both cars were revving, and now theirs began to pull away. 'All the same, next time I'll give them the gas a bit sooner.'

Andrew said: 'I wonder what will happen to her.'

There was a moment's silence before Chisholm replied:

'We know what, don't we?' His voice was cold, deliberately ugly. 'The only question is when. The sooner the better, I should think.'

They did not speak again until after the cars had turned south at the Angel: they were on the home run now. As they passed a traffic light, blank and dripping icicles, Andrew remembered a run along there in a B.B.C. van more than a year before. They had been doing a hospital programme; they had been late, and at this intersection the lights had been against them for a long time.

64

He said, almost to himself: 'I wonder what's happened to Bart's?'

Chisholm said: 'Nothing that I know of.'

'Did they evacuate into the Pale?'

'Couldn't be done. Most of the doctors and nurses stayed on. They had some provisions; I don't know how much.'

'Can we . . . ?'

'Go round that way? It's slightly off course.' He considered briefly. 'O.K., if you want to.'

Red Cross flags had been hung from several of the windows of the hospital; the windows themselves had a blank and empty look from a distance – some of them were broken. As the cars approached, though, there were some signs of life; here and there a face looking out, a hand waving. Above the noise of the engines it was possible to hear thin cries, the words indistinguishable. At the main entrance, the door lay smashed and awry. Bodies, some half dozen crooked heaps, dotted the snow. Some of them seemed to have fallen, or been thrown, from the upper windows.

'I wonder how many of them got away,' Chisholm said. His face was white, angry. 'Bloody fools. It was bound to happen. And what good has it done?'

The cars stopped. With the engines idling, the cries, of pathetic greeting or for help, were clearer. There was one more urgent, a piercing immediate cry of agony. It did not come from the hospital but from a side street.

Chisholm nodded to the driver. 'Up there, I reckon, on the left. Take it slowly.'

The car swung round the corner and they saw it: four figures struggling in the snow in the centre of the street. Three of them disengaged and began to run away, awkwardly, slipping and stumbling. The fourth lay there; her hands moved feebly to drag down the nurse's uniform that was rucked up to her waist.

'All right,' Chisholm said. 'Get them.'

Andrew saw one of the men fall to the volley of fire from the cars; the other two got away, apparently unharmed. Chisholm had vaulted down from the armoured car, and he ran across to the nurse. He helped her to her feet. She came back with him, his right arm supporting her. She looked very small beside him, a little thing not much above five feet with a dainty face and a mass, dishevelled now, of auburn hair. There was some blood on her face, and the beginnings of severe bruises.

She was helped up into the car, and room was made for her. She drew shallow sobbing breaths, but did not say anything and looked down at her hands, clasped together in her lap. Her skirt was badly torn, specked with frozen snow. She had a fur boot on her left foot, nothing on her right.

'You'll be all right now,' Chisholm said. 'Get you to bed – a warm drink . . .'

The cars raced along deserted streets, with St Paul's dome ahead of them. They halted in front of the tangled barbed wire fence that marked the edge of the Pale. There was a gate here, and a guard post. The driver of Chisholm's car gave three blasts on his horn. In a little while, an officer appeared with two soldiers. The gate was opened enough for them to get through, and they came out.

Chisholm called down: 'North patrol returning. Open up, would you?'

The officer, a lieutenant, flicked a salute.

'Carrying any civilians, sir?'

'Television personnel. They have passes.'

The lieutenant said slowly: 'And the young lady?'

'We picked her up at Bart's. She was being attacked. She needs attention.'

It was a moment before the lieutenant spoke. Then he said: 'New orders this morning, sir. No admissions to the Pale without specific authorization from G.H.Q. I'm sorry.'

'Look,' Chisholm said, 'she's a nurse. We're going to need people like her. She can pull her weight.'

The lieutenant was about the same age as Chisholm, but dark, moon-faced, melancholy of expression. He said:

'Orders, sir. Nothing I can do.'

Chisholm leaned down towards him. 'She's a nurse. She stayed behind at Bart's to look after her patients. The gangs have wrecked the hospital, and we found her being raped in the snow outside. I'll take the responsibility for admitting her to the Pale.'

The lieutenant shook his head. 'You can't do that, sir. The responsibility is mine.' There was some anger in the sadness of his face. 'Good God, what sort of sights do you think we have to see here?'

Chisholm vaulted down from the car. He took the lieutenant to one side and talked to him earnestly, quietly. They saw the lieutenant shake his head.

The girl spoke for the first time. She said to Andrew: 'Could you help me down, please?' Her voice had the slightest touch of Irish brogue.

Andrew assumed she wanted to add the weight of her presence to Chisholm's plea; he did not see how anyone, under any kind of orders, could refuse her entry if she asked. He got down from the car himself, and helped her down. She began to stumble away.

'No,' he said, 'this way.'

She paid no attention but walked on, away from the gate leading to the Pale. Chisholm saw her, and called:

'Nurse! Come back. We're still talking things over.'

She did not stop. Andrew made a step to follow her but halted, checked by the small figure's resolution. Had she hesitated at all, or looked back, he would have gone for her; perhaps he would have done so if she had run. But she went with undramatic determination, limping through the snow, and they watched her until she reached a side road, and disappeared.

Then Chisholm said: 'I'm going after her.'

The lieutenant barred his way. 'No, sir.'

The two men stared at each other, in anger and self-disgust. Then Chisholm shrugged his shoulders.

'You win.' He climbed back into the car, and Andrew got up after him. He looked in the direction the nurse had taken, and looked away. To the lieutenant, he said:

'All right. Open up.'

67

9

Ironically, summer time, as far as clocks were concerned at least, had come in the previous week-end. The evenings were an hour longer. Andrew and Madeleine sat muffled up in clothes, drinking weak coffee – she had managed to stock up before coffee disappeared from the shops but even so they only drank it two or three times a week – and talking quietly together. They had both read the evening paper, a single sheet printed both sides, and anyway it was too dark for reading. The use of electric lights in private homes was not permitted before nine o'clock at night.

Apart from the cold, and the slight nausea of hunger which by now was an almost constant companion, Andrew felt contented and at ease. Here, in this room, with Madeleine, it was possible to forget the agonies beyond the Pale, and the uncertain future within. One had to forget them; they were unbearable to live with.

David had said he would call round about nine. They sat on in darkness and eventually he came just before ten.

Madeleine asked: 'Do you want the light on?'

'Not if it's going to disturb you,' David said.

Andrew got up. 'We might as well.'

The arrival was an intrusion, and he wanted it to be marked as such. The light came on, and David blinked his eyes. His face was drawn; he looked tired. Madeleine saw this too.

She said: 'Sit down, David, and I'll get you a drink.'

'How is the situation with the Scotch?' he asked.

'Simple. There is none. I brought up a bottle of the Cockburn instead. Do you mind?'

David shook his head. 'A very sound idea. I put it down the year after we were married – when we came back from Brussels. Two dozen, at 27s. 6d. a bottle. How many are there left?'

'I'm not sure. About a dozen and a half.'

'We'll kill a couple, then. This is the time to drink them.'

'You look worn out,' Madeleine said. 'Are things hectic with you?'

'Tolerably.' He yawned, and looked at Andrew. 'Have you had a letter from Carol lately?'

'I had one this morning.'

'She sounds O.K., doesn't she?'

Madeleine carefully poured the port into three glasses and brought them over on a tray. David picked his up.

'Well, here's to summer. The temperature on the Air Ministry roof was three degrees above freezing at midday today.'

Andrew said: 'That's something.'

'Too little, and too late. Do you have any idea how fast we've been liquidating our overseas investments? And did you know we've been trying to negotiate the sale of B.P. in the Middle East to Iraq? Concessions, equipment, plant – everything.'

'Grim – but we should be able to live for a while on the proceeds.'

'The negotiations broke down. Iraq no longer recognizes the British Government, which it says, with some reason, can no longer exercise sovereignty over its own territory. They've taken it all over without compensation; supposedly in self-protection.'

Madeleine said quietly: 'What is going to happen?'

'Here?' He nodded to Andrew. 'Andy's going to be out of a job in a few days' time, for one thing.'

'Why?'

'They're closing television down. It's a wasteful means of communication for an area the size of the Pale, and as a gesture it's no longer impressive.'

'And then?'

'The idea is to try to hold out. There are stocks of food – more than one would think. That part's been well planned. If things pick up, if the sun warms up . . . there will still be next winter to get through, but after that it may be easier.'

'And if things don't pick up?'

David made a gesture of resignation. 'We go under. It's a fair chance that we shall anyway. They're getting very hungry outside and very desperate. I wouldn't care to guess how long the military will hold them out.'

There was a silence. David went on:

'I can get you two seats in the outward plane next Wednesday. Lisbon – Timbuktu – Lagos.'

With gentle firmness, Madeleine said: 'No. Not for me, anyway.'

David sipped his port and looked at her. The look was one which excluded Andrew: an appeal, to which his obvious fatigue gave something of desperation.

'Maddie,' he said, 'I don't want you on my conscience. Please go.'

'I don't want to be on your conscience,' she said, 'but I want to stay.'

David smiled wrily: 'You're not often stubborn, but I can never force you when you are, can I? The seats are available now, but I won't be able to renew the reservation.'

'I know. I shan't blame you.'

'If things crack up, they'll crack up fast. There's an evacuation plan for those who count. I count, because I'm helping to draw it up. I can get on one of those last planes myself, but I couldn't get anyone else on. Do you understand?'

'Of course.'

'And I couldn't go and leave you here, Maddie. Could I, now? I don't know what will happen here eventually, but if you refuse this flight you're condemning all three of us to it. Whereas, if you go, we can all spend our declining years in the African sun.'

'Carol's out there already.'

'I know. She seems very far away, doesn't she?' He emptied the glass and put it down. 'I'm not going without you, Maddie. There's nothing more certain than that. And I can't go with you. I wouldn't be allowed to. Being useful is what makes me certain of getting out in time if the worst happens, but it's equally certain that I can't get out before that.' He shrugged. 'It's your choice.'

She tilted the bottle very carefully as she refilled the glasses. The wine was a soft gleaming red. She handed the men their glasses and raised her own. Her face was calm, still, sad in recognition of the inevitable.

'All right, David,' she said. 'We'll go. Let's drink to our African future.'

PART TWO

Besides arranging the flight itself, David had also dealt with the currency question. Under present conditions there was no hope of selling the house in Denham Crescent, nor of obtaining a mortgage on it, and most other goods were similarly unnegotiable. He did manage to get three hundred pounds for Madeleine's fur coat. Her final liquid assets worked out at just over seven hundred pounds, to which David himself contributed a further five hundred. He smiled when she protested that he might need it in London.

'Not in the Pale. The new currency is power, and I have enough to get by. You can invest it for me in Nigeria, and I'll collect it with interest when I come.'

Andrew found that two hundred and sixty pounds was all he could raise himself. The rest was tied up in equity shares, and the Stock Exchange had suspended trading for an indefinite period.

'I can get a bank draft through for Maddie,' David said, 'as my wife. But a separate one for Andy would be too tricky. If he's willing to trust you, I can have the whole lot credited to your account at a bank in Lagos. You can take a tenner apiece in notes to cover your incidental expenses until you get to the bank.'

They booked in at the newly built Hotel Africa. That, too, had been arranged by David. The hotel was very full and they had to accept rooms on different floors: Andrew took a room on the fifth floor at the back, Madeleine's, on the third floor, overlooked the Marina and the lagoon. It was evening when they arrived. Beyond the lights of the Marina itself, the lagoon was dark. Further off, on the mainland, they could see the bright flash of neon.

They found, on going down to dinner, that while most of the diners were black, all the waiters were white-skinned. They were served by a tall thin grey-haired man. He came from Frankfurt and handled the plates with some awkwardness. He apologized for his clumsiness. He had, it appeared, been a shopkeeper.

'What's it like in Frankfurt?' Andrew asked.

He looked at them with a cold remote smile.

'The buildings still stand, the fine new American buildings, and the fine new roads are still there, under the ice. I went back to Frankfurt in 1945, to the ruins. It was alive then. Now it is dead.'

'How long have you been here?' Madeleine asked.

'Three weeks, madam.'

'No regrets.'

'But of course not. Where we live, it is a little primitive, perhaps, for my family. But I have a good job: the *dash* is very good.'

'The *dash*?'

The waiter smiled. 'The vernacular for tips. The wage itself is not high, of course.'

With the coffee, he brought a note for Andrew. It read:

Dear Andrew,

David tells me you're arriving today and staying at the Africa. If you would like to see me, I shall be at the Island Club from about half past nine onwards. Or you can leave a message for me there.

Yours,
Carol

'The Island Club,' Andrew said to the waiter, '– is it far from the hotel?'

'Not very far, sir.'

Andrew showed the note to Madeleine. 'Shall we go along there?'

'Only one of us is invited.'

'That doesn't matter.'

'I think it does.'

'David may not have mentioned you were coming today as well.'

'More likely she wants to talk over private matters. There must be things to discuss.'

'You're part of my private life,' Andrew said. 'Private, if not intimate.'

Madeleine smiled. 'Not of Carol's, though. Anyway, I think I would like an early night. You go along, Andy. You can tell me all about it in the morning.'

Andrew felt a tingle of anticipation as he walked to the Club. It was months since he had seen Carol – the occasion had been the boys' return to school after the Christmas holidays – and there was the strangeness of meeting her here, in a foreign land, their old lives splintered behind them and everything new, uncertain, difficult, promising. He gave his name to the doorkeeper, a Frenchman by his accent, and was conscious of a feeling of guilt that Madeleine, preparing for bed in the loneliness of the hotel room, had so completely slipped his mind.

'You will find Madame in the lounge bar,' the doorman told him. 'Through that door, sir, and on your right.'

The room was roughly circular, with the bar cutting an arc across the top. The walls had been painted with continuous murals, a series of huge concave panels. Around the bar they depicted snow and ice, from which projected broken fragments of masonry, towers, domes, pinnacles of brick and steel. These scenes changed, as one's gaze continued in either direction from the bar, into seas at first iceberg-laden, then empty, then calm and silvered by the sun. Past the seas, along the section of the wall directly facing the bar, were the golden sands and palm-fringed shores of a warm and happy land. Carol was sitting over there, at a table by herself. Andrew saw as he approached her that there were quite a number of white women in the room, but he only saw two white men. There were a lot of Nigerians. The noise of their chatter marked the difference between this and a similar establishment in a European capital.

'Hello, Andy,' Carol said. 'Nice to see you. Do sit down. What will you drink?'

'Can I get them?'

'No. Members only.'

'You are a member?'

She nodded. 'They do have European liquor still, if you want to break me, but I'm on South African brandy. I find it's not at all bad.'

'Thank you,' he said. 'I'll have that.'

She called the waiter, a white again, and ordered the drinks. Andrew watched her and considered his own reactions. The *frisson* of anticipation of meeting her again had faded; and to his surprise it left no successor. She was still beautiful, and attractive in a more colourful way than he remembered – the black dress splotched with large hibiscus blossoms, and the twisted skein of heavy costume jewellery round her neck, were not things she would have worn before – but there was no recognition; her beauty no longer spoke to him as it had once done. He had a quick moment of relief, blending into a warm remembrance of Madeleine. There had been two ties, he knew, which held Madeleine from him – her own with David and his with Carol. One of them, at any rate, existed no longer.

Carol gestured towards the murals. 'What do you think of them?'

'A little cruel. Or insensitive, anyway.'

'It's not a sensitive country. There's a practical point to it, too: the people here tend to hug the bar, and this persuades them into the outer spaces. It was only opened last week.'

'You come here a good deal?'

'Now and then.' Skipping over the point, she went on: 'The whole Club's been more or less torn down and done over again in the past six months.'

'A bit gaudy.'

'One gets used to that. I quite like it. There's a lot of money here now. Mind you, one needs a lot, to live.'

'The children,' Andrew said, '– how are they?'

'They're at school at Ibadan. It's the best school in the country according to repute. Very few white boys are there.'

'I don't suppose that matters.'

'Matters!' She stared at him, and laughed. 'My God, Andy . . .'

'Are they well, happy?'

'Both, I think.' She fished inside her handbag, and brought out a letter. 'Have a look.'

It was from Robin. Andrew read through it, and handed it back to Carol. It was like any letter from any boy at any boarding school.

'Yes,' he said. 'They seem happy.'

'They should be. The fees are sensational.'

He sipped his brandy; Carol poured ginger ale into hers. She watched him with a curious, half smiling, half defensive look.

Andrew said: 'David saw us off.'

She made a murmur of assent. After a pause, she said:

'How is he?'

'Under strain. The pressure's pretty heavy. But well enough, I think.'

'Poor David.'

'When he does leave, it will be practically without warning, I gather.'

'Yes. He told me all that. I think he ought to have got out earlier.' She spoke objectively and dispassionately. 'He could have done it. He had enough pull.'

'Perhaps he will now, if you persuade him.'

She did not reply immediately.

'Europe's a very long way off,' she said, '– emotionally, not just geographically. One's recollections fade. Places, people. Or perhaps just mine.'

He saw the implication, and was slightly shocked. She leaned forward on the table, her breasts pressing together between her folded arms.

'I'd almost forgotten what you looked like, Andy. It's like seeing you with fresh eyes.'

It might or might not have been provocatively intended. He was confused, suddenly aware of the fact that she was still, legally, his wife, that he was still responsible for her. If her infatuation for David was over, she might well think it worthwhile resuming their old relationship: it had not been an unhappy nor unsuccessful one. The thought disturbed him, but in a different way from that which he would have imagined.

He said awkwardly: 'David will be coming eventually. Meanwhile, I want to look after Madeleine.'

Carol gave a small laugh. 'Some things are familiar! Well, that's good. How are you going to go about it, by the way? Do you have any idea?'

'I should be able to land some kind of job. Journalism or television . . .'

She said briskly: 'You can forget them. Europeans not wanted. In fact, Europeans not wanted in any of the professions. There are some branches people got into early, but those two weren't among them. And there's even a glut of white doctors, now. The porter at my block of flats had a medical practice in Vienna.'

'I hadn't realized it was as bad as that.'

'There's one profession that's still open. You had a commission in Tanks. You could help them train for the war.'

'What war?'

'Against South Africa. As far as I can see, it's expected to break out in two or three years' time. You might get a commission. They allow white officers up to the rank of Captain, on short service commissions.'

'No,' Andrew said. 'I don't think so.'

'How much money have you brought with you?'

'Two hundred and fifty. Madeleine's got over a thousand.'

'Put it together then,' she said, 'and start some kind of a shop. It doesn't matter what kind. The blackies are still tickled pink at having their goods served with white hands. And you might not do badly, if you pick the right line and place. As I've said, there's money about.'

'Thanks for the advice.'

'Don't wait too long before you act on it. It's easy to fritter money away, especially in Lagos. Ibadan's as bad. It might be better in the north – Kaduna, perhaps. It's more primitive, but there might be more scope.'

'In a short time here,' Andrew said, 'you've become very well-informed on the country.'

Carol smiled. 'I have my sources of information.'

'You yourself,' he said, '– are you all right?'

'I manage.'

'Have you got some kind of a job?'

'Yes. A kind of job.' She glanced at her watch. 'Do you feel like another drink?'

The watch was new; the face was set round with chip stones that flashed as her hand moved. Simultaneously he realized that the heavy necklace was not costume jewellery; the heavy strands were gold, set with large semi-precious and precious stones.

'So I needn't worry about you, need I?' Andrew said. 'No, thanks. I think I'd better be getting back. It's been an exhausting day.'

'I'll give you my address,' she said, 'in case you want to get in touch.'

She excused herself at the door of the lounge, and they said good night. At the door, Andrew paused to speak to the porter; it was an impulse which would remain and grow stronger, to salute the fellow white, to give form and recognition to a shared loneliness.

'What part of France?' he asked.

'Dijon. I ran an *agence immobilière*.'

Andrew nodded. 'I remember motoring through one evening in winter. I had a meal. I can't remember the name of the restaurant, but the food was good.'

'In Dijon the food was always good.'

'And walking through the streets afterwards. It had been raining and they gleamed in the lamplight. And the shops – the *pâtisseries*, the little jewellers', the butchers' shops with deer and wild boar hanging up outside.'

'I remember those, *monsieur*. And the milling crowds outside the Pauvre Diable, and the hum of talk in the *brasseries*. And other things.'

Two heavily built Nigerians came in with two women, and he turned to attend to them. The men wore brightly coloured robes and turbans. The women were white. As Andrew left he glanced back into the Club and saw Carol again. She was returning to the lounge, escorted by a Nigerian in evening dress.

On his way to breakfast next morning Andrew picked up a newspaper, the *Times of Nigeria*, in case he had to wait for Madeleine to come down. But she was already at the table, and smiled to him as he entered the room. He sat down and laid the paper, still folded, on the table.

Their hands touched lightly. She said:

'I feel ashamed of myself. I've ordered a double bacon and eggs.'

'It's always a good idea to share a sense of shame. I'll have the same.'

'How was Carol?'

'Very comfortable.' He paused. 'She appears to have got herself a rich black boy-friend.'

Madeleine looked at him, and said quietly: 'She might have kept it from you, at least.'

'She didn't flaunt it. I only saw them together by accident. It makes no difference to me. It will do to David, though, won't it? And to you.'

'I don't know.'

'About David or about you?'

'About either. But you – does it release you?'

'It didn't need that. When I saw her again it was quite different. It helps, that she can look after herself.'

'And the boys?'

'They're in a very expensive boarding school at Ibadan. They seem to be happy. She showed me a letter from Robin.'

'Ibadan?'

'A hundred and ten miles up country. It's the capital of the Western Province and twice as big as Lagos.'

'I thought it was on the Persian Gulf.'

'Abadan. We've got a lot to learn, haven't we? And we'd better learn it quickly. After all, we're refugees.'

'Are we? I suppose we are. What else did Carol say?'

'She gave me good advice.'

'What kind?'

'She thinks I might get a job in the Nigerian Army, training them for the war they expect to make on South Africa when they're ready. In conjunction with other African states, I suppose; it's difficult to see how they would get to grips otherwise.'

Madeleine smiled. 'You weren't keen on that.'

'No. Her alternative suggestion was that you and I should pool resources and open a shop. White shopkeepers are popular, it seems. And they still have some kind of scarcity value.'

'Military training or shopkeeping. Things aren't going to be awfully easy, are they? What shall we do – newsagent and tobacconist, pots and pans? I suppose we'd need qualifications to run a chemist's shop?'

'Of a kind. I passed a hole in the wall last night which had a sign hanging outside it. It said Sincere Medicine Chamber.'

She shook her head. 'We can't compete with that.'

Andrew said: 'Carol took four thousand with her when she left England. I suppose I have a right to some part of that. But . . .'

Madeleine said quickly: 'No, we don't need it. Please. I'd rather not.'

'It means I can only put up a fifth as much as you.'

'Does that matter?'

'It might do. When David comes over.'

'We aren't going to fall out over money, whatever happens.'

'Not over anything, I hope.'

'No.' She put her hand out to his. 'I'm sure we won't.'

Their fingers pressed together in the small reassuring contact of flesh.

Andrew said comfortably: 'I think that's our bacon and eggs arriving now.'

They ate their breakfast with relish, savouring plenty after the privation of rations. Filling his coffee cup for the third time, Andrew remembered the newspaper he had bought and which had lain unregarded on the table. He opened it out to the front page: it was garishly printed on cheap-looking paper, but it was impressive after the London news sheet. The main headline concerned South Africa: ATROCITIES AGAINST WOMEN AND CHILDREN. The sub-heading said: BANTU LEADER'S REVELATIONS. It was a lip-smacking eye-rolling horror story which Andrew found unconvincing. His eyes turned to another headline, lower down the page and on the other side. This said: EUROPEAN CURRENCIES – GOVERNMENT DECISION.

The story below was brief and factual. A meeting of African Finance Ministers at Ghana had unanimously agreed to a moratorium on all transactions involving the currencies of nations with capitals lying north of the 40° line of latitude.

Andrew gave the paper to Madeleine, marking the place with his thumb.

'It looks as though we only just made it in time,' he said.

She read the account with care. Looking up, she said:

'Have we made it? The moratorium's from today.'

'Our draft's already through.'

'But it hasn't been cashed. Does that make a difference?'

'I don't think so. But we'd better go and find out.'

The clerk at the Foreign counter was a tall refined-looking Negro. He listened patiently to Andrew, and directed them to the Assistant Manager's office. This was along a corridor and opened out of a small waiting room. There were magazines and newspapers strewn on a table by the wall, from the bulky latest issue of *Drum* to the flimsy single page of the London news sheet, dated about a week earlier. A chocolate-coloured girl in a white pleated dress, wearing upward-curving diamanté spectacles, took them through to the inner office.

The Assistant Manager was a squat fat man with kinky grey-white hair. He rested his elbows on the desk and held his hands up with palms facing outwards; the palms were exceptionally pale, almost white.

'Well now,' he said, 'what can I do for you, Ma'am? And you, Boss?'

The vocatives were sardonically stressed; he sat behind his pale hands, smiling.

Andrew said: 'Your clerk directed us here. Mrs Cartwell has had a remittance sent from London.'

The Negro nodded. 'This here is Mrs Cartwell?'

'Yes,' Madeleine said. 'I'm Mrs Cartwell. I have my passport with me.'

'And you – Mr Cartwell?'

'No. My name's Leedon.'

He shook his head very slowly. 'White folks have their own ways of living.' He looked at Madeleine. 'White but comely. You know the Song of Solomon, Mrs Cartwell? Welcome to Lagos. No reason why you shouldn't be happy here.'

Andrew said shortly: 'Thanks for the good wishes. Now perhaps you could arrange to pay Mrs Cartwell the money due to her.'

'You came in yesterday?' the Assistant Manager asked. 'How was London, Mr Leedon? I hear it's cold up there.' His face split in a toothy smile. 'Mighty cold, I hear.'

'We're here to do business,' Andrew said. 'We haven't the time to stay chatting.'

'You've got more time than you think. I reckon you've got a lot of time.'

'That's for us to decide.'

There was a pause before he replied. 'I'll tell you something about myself, Mr Leedon. I'm Bantu. I was born in a tin shack in Jo'burg.'

'Some other time. Not now.'

'I got away from that country. I went to London. I studied at London University. I didn't get my degree, Mr Leedon – that's why I'm just a bank clerk. Still, I had sense enough not to go back to the Union. I came here instead. I live in a house an Englishman used to live in, quite close to the golf course. I play golf, Boss.'

Andrew said: 'Is this necessary? I take it you don't like South Africa. But you got an education in London, and you came then to a black country which the British made independent. As you say, you're doing all right.'

The smile was renewed, even more widely. 'I'm glad you spoke like that. I must confess I was hoping to provoke you into putting me in my place, Boss. Or should I say, into trying?'

'I'm not trying to put you into any place. We came here simply for Mrs Cartwell to draw the money due to her.'

'When I was little, I went to the Mission school. One thing they taught me was that you don't have to expect justice in this world. Justice comes later on, in Heaven. I'm not so sure about Heaven now, but they were certainly right about justice on earth. It may be that you will find being white a disadvantage here in Africa. That's not the way things ought to happen. But I hope you're going to be philosophical about it, Boss. What can't be cured must be endured. They taught me that slogan in the Mission school, too. That's a really good motto to have, Boss. Very consoling when you hit hard times.'

Madeleine said: 'If you'll forgive me – the heat, after London . . . Could we . . . ?'

There was an electric fan on his desk. He stretched a hand out and switched it on. It moved round and round like a blindly questing face, whining at a low pitch.

'Anything to keep you happy, Ma'am. I guess you're more sensitive than we black folks.'

Andrew said: 'We realize our position as guests of your country. We don't want to be difficult. But I think we've had enough of this. If you aren't prepared to deal with Mrs Cartwell's remittance now, without delay, we shall have to look elsewhere. Is the Manager available?'

The hands closed gently, showing black knuckles. He leaned his face on these and looked at Andrew.

'He's available, Boss. To valued clients, whatever colour their skin happens to be. But I'll deal with the remittance now, if that's what you want.'

'If you don't mind.'

'I don't mind at all.' He pulled over a folder and opened it. There was a sheet of paper on top, which he pushed across the desk. 'There you are, Boss.'

A typewritten note said:

'Credit to the account of Mrs Madeleine Cartwell the sum of £1,470 (fourteen hundred and seventy pounds sterling) on due presentation of credentials.'

CANCELLED was over-stamped in thick blue letters. A handwritten addition said: 'Authority withdrawn under Govt Order 327 (S).'

Andrew said: 'This remittance came through before the decision about European currencies.'

The Assistant Manager nodded. 'That's right, Boss.'

'Then it should be paid.'

'I don't think you understand. The credit was in sterling. That currency no longer exists on the continent of Africa.'

'But it was to be paid in Nigerian money.'

'The note doesn't say that. A bank can't exceed its authority, Boss. Mrs Cartwell might have wanted to collect in some other currency. In Boer money — or maybe cowrie shells.' He smiled again. 'Sorry, Boss.'

Andrew stood up. 'I think we'd better see someone at the Embassy.'

The Assistant Manager nodded cordially. 'Go right ahead. Outside the door and turn left. Only a couple of blocks along.'

As they came into the street, a dilapidated truck, overladen with women in the blue Yoruba wraps and brightly coloured head-ties, sprayed petrol fumes at them. On the side of the truck, huge yellow capitals said: TRUST IN GOD. The women were chanting some kind of song, audible above the din of traffic. Even so early in the day, it was hot and clammy.

'What happens now?' Madeleine asked.

'The Embassy should be able to help.'

The Embassy foyer was crowded with people: there were perhaps a couple of dozen. They had to wait for some time, before being ushered into the office of a Junior Secretary. He was red-haired and thin-faced, with a small moustache. He had a look that was in general evasive but occasionally, for several seconds at a time, embarrassingly direct; as though he had worked himself up to a staring point. He took a propelling pencil to pieces while Andrew told him what had happened at the bank.

'Yes,' he said. 'I'm sorry. It's really hard lines. It's a bit of a blow altogether. We had no idea they were going to do this, of course.'

Madeleine said: 'Then there's no way of getting the money?'

He said unhappily: 'The money doesn't exist, Mrs Cartwell. He had no cause to be rude to you, but the legal position is quite clear: the issuing bank in London will already have been notified and the sum credited back to their account.'

Andrew said: 'So we're penniless. Is that the position?'

'Unless you have something you can sell.'

'Our clothes. Nothing else.'

'It's most unfortunate. You're not alone in this. Though I don't suppose that is any consolation.'

'Can the Embassy give us any help?'

His eyes focused on Andrew; they were very light grey and rather small, fringed by silky lashes.

'I wish we could. But this has hit us, too. To be frank, we shall have to depend on some kind of charity from the Nigerian Government to keep going at all.'

'Advice then, if you can't help.'

'You might be able to get into the Army, Mr Leedon, if you have some military background.'

'To help them prepare for a war of extermination against the whites in South Africa?'

'One has to be realistic. And fair. There has been considerable provocation, from the point of view of the black Africans as a whole. There's something of a parallel with the Moors in Spain. And I doubt if you would be required to take part in military operations; you would have a training function solely.'

'And that should satisfy my misgivings.'

'Loyalties are not so clear cut. One thing you may care to remember is that Nigeria is inside the Commonwealth, while the Union of South Africa is not.'

'Is that comment intended seriously?'

'Why shouldn't it be?'

He had begun to reassemble the pencil; he took the chromium-plated nose-cone and blew through it. Andrew said:

'Apart from the Nigerian Army?'

'The only other jobs would be – menial.'

'And accommodation? We're in the Hotel Africa at present.'

'I think you will find that the hotels will be requiring cash settlements from Europeans as from today. Have you enough to pay your bill to date?'

'Just about.'

'That's a good thing. If you hadn't, they would probably hold your luggage.'

'So we move out,' Andrew said. 'Where?'

'I wish I could suggest something. I'm afraid rents have been sky-rocketing here lately.'

'There must be somewhere,' Madeleine said.

The Junior Secretary sighed. He brought a visiting card out of his desk drawer.

'There's this fellow. I don't much like him, or what I've heard of him, but he's supposed to be knowledgeable. I suppose it would do no harm to go and see him.'

The card said: *Alf Bates, Estates & Properties Handled*, and gave an address. Andrew put it in his pocket.

'Thank you,' he said.

'Sorry I can't do more.' His gaze fixed on Andrew again, unblinking. 'Let's hope things pick up.'

The address Carol had given him was in the old colonial sector. The house was a low-lying ranch-type brick structure, surrounded by lawns over which hovered a fine mist thrown in the air by sprinklers. It drifted in a slight breeze and wet the petals of the ranks of red roses that lined the drive. As they approached the house, Andrew saw that there was a sun-dial set in the wall over the door. He wondered if the sun-dial in the garden at Dulwich was still coated with ice.

Madeleine, at his side, was silent. She had been opposed at first to the idea of coming to see Carol, and then had wanted him to come on his own. They had tried telephoning but the line appeared to be out of order. In the end, she had agreed to come, on Andrew's insistence. She was clearly unhappy as she watched him press the door bell.

The door was opened by a very tall, very fair-skinned man in a scarlet uniform with gold piping. He said: 'Can I help you, sir?' It sounded like a Scandinavian accent.

Andrew said: 'I would like to see Mrs Leedon.'

The blond head was shaken slowly. 'I regret that Mrs Leedon is not in, sir.'

'When will she be in?'

'I regret I do not know that, sir.'

'Can I leave a message?'

'I doubt if that . . .'

He broke off as a woman's voice, with a different, softer accent, called from inside the house:

'Carl! Who is that calling?'

Half-turning, the butler said: 'For Mrs Leedon, Ma'am.'

'Ask them to come in.'

The woman met them in the hall. She was a Negress, of medium height and aged about thirty. She was dressed in European style, wearing a soft red silk dress and gold-embroidered silver slippers. She was not beautiful, but had a grave impressive air.

'Mr Leedon,' the butler announced, 'and Mrs Cartwell.'

Andrew said: 'I'm sorry if we're disturbing you. My wife gave me a card with this address. I had no idea anyone else lived here.'

'That's perfectly all right, Mr Leedon. I am Maria Arunawa. Mrs Leedon is my husband's social secretary. She did not mention that?'

'No.' Andrew shook his head. 'She didn't mention that.'

'Come in to the sitting room, and have some tea. Or something cooler, if you would prefer it.'

The sitting room had lime-coloured walls and a sage-green fitted carpet, apparently with a thick sponge rubber underlay. Chairs and two couches were covered in white satin, studded with golden buttons. Venetian blinds kept out the sun's rough glare, and there was the soft whirr of air conditioning.

'Please sit down,' their hostess said. 'Can I help you in some way?'

'It was my wife I wanted to see,' Andrew said. He hesitated. 'Is she expected back soon?'

'Not soon, I'm afraid.'

Her look was friendly, sympathetic. He told her of their experience at the bank. She shook her head slightly.

'How dreadful. So many dreadful things are happening. I wish there was something one could do.'

'My wife and I,' Andrew said, 'had agreed to divorce. But I thought she might be in a position to help us out – at least, if she had room, to let us stay with her for a few days while we found something for ourselves.'

'I wish I could ask you to stay here, Mr Leedon. But my husband makes strict rules. I cannot invite guests to stay without his sanction.'

'I wouldn't dream of asking you,' Andrew said. 'I suppose my wife is with Mr Arunawa now. In Lagos?'

She smiled. 'I must correct you. He is Sir Adekema Arunawa. He is anxious that his title should be properly understood. That is another rule.'

'Lady Arunawa,' Andrew said, 'I must apologize.'

She shook her head. 'Please. The rules are not for me. Unfortunately Sir Adekema is not in Lagos. He left this morning on a business trip to Mombasa. Mrs Leedon went with him, of course.'

'For how long?'

'He did not say. There was some talk of a vacation following that. He does not like committing himself on these things. He will probably go to Victoria Falls. It is a place he likes, and Mrs Leedon has not been there yet.'

'I see. Do you have any way of getting in touch with him?'

'Not directly. There is nothing which would justify that, from my point of view. But I have the address of his business contact in Mombasa. You could write to your wife there. They would forward it, perhaps.'

'Thank you. I would like to have that.'

A fluffy blonde girl came in with a trolley which had a silver tea-set on top and an assortment of cakes underneath.

'Thank you, Molly,' Lady Arunawa said. 'You can leave it with me.'

She poured tea into delicate Spode cups and handed them to the others. Then she offered them cakes. Madeleine, with a quick glance at Andrew, took a large one. They had lunched, as an economy measure, off dates and some kind of soft orange drink.

During tea, Lady Arunawa spoke in general regretful terms of the havoc caused by the Fratellini Winter. Her sadness over it was as obvious as her ineffectuality. Andrew was reminded of an aunt of his, a country vicar's wife, talking about the Arab refugees at tea-time in the rectory, her words punctuated by sounds of cricket from the field outside. He wondered what had become of her.

She left them afterwards to get the address she had promised them. They were alone in the quiet well-proportioned room.

'Take a good look,' Andrew said, 'at the way the rich live. It will have to last us a long time.'

Madeleine got up from her chair, and came swiftly across the room to him. She knelt on the carpet and put her face up to be kissed.

'What is it?' he asked.

'Because it's true – we shan't have anything like this, shall we? And because it would be silly to think it doesn't matter.'

'Kiss me again. It may not matter so much.'

She shook her head, and stood up. 'Lady Arunawa's coming back.'

She gave them the address, written on the back of her own card, and they prepared to leave. She said:

'I've been thinking – it's going to be very hard for you. This is a hard city anyway, and you are white. Have you any money at all?'

'Just a little,' Andrew said. He spoke stiffly, ashamed of the urge to beg which suddenly dominated his mind. He did not look at the Negress.

'I do wish I could help,' she said. 'But Sir Adekema keeps very strict control of the household accounts. He does not permit – does not like me to handle money myself.'

'Thank you for the thought,' Andrew said. 'We shall manage all right.'

'I hardly know how to say it,' Lady Arunawa said, 'but if you had thought, perhaps, of picnicking this evening? – restaurant meals are so expensive these days, and generally not good. We have plenty of food in the house – cold meats and such. Would it offend you if I suggested your accepting a packed meal to take with you? I would like to ask you to stay to dinner, but Sir Adekema's instructions are quite definite there. I may not ask guests even for a meal.'

Andrew was about to decline the offer, but Madeleine spoke first.

'We should be very grateful,' she said. 'Thank you.'

Lady Arunawa smiled. 'I hoped you would say that. I've already asked for the food to be got ready.'

They left the road and walked south along the beach. It was early evening and the sun was flat and red on the horizon, but the fine white sand was still hot when one reached down to touch it. It gave beneath their feet and found its way into their shoes. They took them off, and Andrew pushed them into the top of the carrier bag which contained the food. The sand was warm and yielding to the bare feet.

'Far enough?' Andrew asked.

Madeleine nodded. 'Far enough.'

They had walked about half a mile from the road. A grove of some kind of fir came down to the edge of the beach here, and had cast small cones into a hollow between two dunes of sand. There was no sign of anyone, no sound but that of the long rollers breaking to north and south.

Madeleine took the carrier bag and set out the food; there was even a disposable paper table-cloth to lay things on, and two cardboard plates. There were slices of cold beef and tongue, a cold chicken, potato salad in a plastic bag, oddly shaped tomatoes, a small bottle of black olives and one of some kind of chutney, and sliced white bread wrapped in white muslin. There was a large bottle of lemonade and two small bottles of beer; and two peaches. Tucked in with the bread she found screws of salt and pepper.

'No butter,' she said. 'It would have run, of course. Anyway, the bread looks appetizing. Are you having the beer, Andy?'

He nodded. 'We did well, didn't we, in our first shot at panhandling?'

'She's a nice woman. I hope she doesn't get into trouble over this.'

'Over giving us a little food? How is he to know anyway?'

'He probably has the servants spy on her. I didn't care much for the look of Carl. Well, let's hope not, and enjoy our meal; she would want us to do that.'

Madeleine finished laying things and surveyed the result.

'No knives and forks: I suppose he counts those.' She lifted the bag and shook it, and another small package fell out. 'Plastic spoons,' she said. 'That's something. And cigarettes and a box of matches.'

When they had eaten, she packed away the food that remained. Andrew lit cigarettes for both of them, and gave her one.

'Bicycle,' he said, studying the packet. 'A new brand. I suppose one will get used to it. If one can afford the luxury of smoking.'

'How much money have we got?'

'One Nigerian pound. Some shillings and pence.'

'We'll have to find something tomorrow. Some work to do, somewhere to live.'

Andrew lay back, looking up at the sky. It was almost dark enough for stars but although he thought he caught glimpses in the corner of his vision, they disappeared when he looked for them.

'Will we see the Southern Cross from here?' he asked. 'I suppose so.'

'Tonight,' Madeleine said. 'We haven't thought about what we're going to do. We can't go back to the hotel.'

'They might let us sleep on the floor at the Embassy.'

'At least, it's warm here.' She reached out and touched his arm. 'We can sleep out here, on the beach.'

'It won't be very comfortable.'

'Clean, though, and quiet. I don't like the idea of going back into the city.' She pointed to the carrier bag. 'And there's enough left for breakfast.'

'All right.'

'Did you ever want to do this,' she asked, 'when you were a child, at the seaside? I did.'

'Yes,' he said. 'But I'd forgotten that.'

They sat talking quietly for an hour while the stars came out in the indigo sky. Then they kissed good night and settled themselves, by unspoken agreement, in their separate hollows in the sand. A dog howled for a time in the distance, but otherwise there was only the surge of the breakers.

Andrew went to sleep quite soon. When he awoke there was light from a half moon, just lifting clear of the branches of the trees. Madeleine seemed to be peacefully asleep. He got up quietly, so as not to disturb her, and walked up into the grove. It was somehow lonelier there than on the long deserted beach. He stretched himself; his back and shoulders were stiff and cramped.

He went back to the beach, but to the other side of the dune. Although the night was still warm, he found himself shivering. He was conscious, in this penetrating shadowless brightness, of all that he had lost. His job, and England itself, seemed unreal when he thought of them. For the boys, who, he now saw, would inevitably drift from him into whatever chequered difficult lives lay before them, he felt a mild regret. For Carol, none; not even disgust. In this night's limpidity, the things which had belonged to him – which he had thought important – lost all meaning. He had no longing for them.

What he felt was not, he knew, a sense of loss. It was worse than that: a sense of nakedness, of being stripped down to the poor bones of self and circumstance. The things that had gone had been illusions, but he did not see how he would survive without them. The pain he felt was worse than the pain of love; because in love, always, some hope lingers. He knelt on the sand, leaned forward. It was an attitude of prayer, but he had nothing to pray to or for. He had nothing to offer, either. All he was aware of was the clinging misery of emptiness.

He did not hear Madeleine until she touched him. She put an arm over his shoulder.

'Andy,' she said, 'are you all right?'

In a dry voice, he said: 'Yes. Quite all right.'

'I was frightened. I woke up and found you gone.' He made no reply. 'Being alone in the night, one becomes a child again. At least, I do.'

He stayed silent. Her hands went to his face, and he felt her trace the wetness of tears on his cheeks. He would have pulled away, but lacked the will to do anything but stare, blindly, at the waves and the moonlit sand. He did not resist when she pulled him down beside her, cradling him to her against the slope of the dune.

'Darling,' she said, 'everything's going to be all right. Don't cry, Andy darling. Please, don't cry.'

He was shivering again, more violently than before. She kissed the tears from his face, and chafed his hands with hers. After a time she released them and sat up away from him. There was a rustle of clothing before she came back to him. She lay with her head above his now, her cheek against his hair. She had undone her blouse and removed her brassiere: the softness of her breast was against his neck, a warm slow tide of flesh that pulsed across his own. The gesture of maternity, he thought dully, so much more natural to the woman who has suckled no children.

But the warmth was real, and the softness; the pulse was vivid. Her hands touched his body, moving gently, lovingly, the finger tips counting the lines of rib. His body stirred in the end and he caught her to him, pulling her face down, kissing and being kissed.

He shelled her from her blouse: shoulders and arms and small pointed breasts had an unearthly beauty – her body was silvery, black and white but all silver. In the pause of watching her, he said:

'Out of pity?'

She shook her head. In a low voice, she said:

'Perhaps loneliness.'

'It isn't necessary.'

'It is,' she said. 'Darling, it is!'

They swam afterwards, and then walked on the beach until they felt dry enough to put their clothes back on. After that they lay together on the sand and went to sleep. Andrew woke again to a brightening sky, and Madeleine pulling at his arm to wake him.

'Someone coming,' she said.

He sat up. Three men in uniform were approaching along the beach, one of them with an Alsatian straining at a leash.

'Stay quite still,' he said. 'We don't want them to turn the dog loose.'

'Police?'

'I think so.'

As they got near, the one slightly in advance called:

'Stand up, boss. And you, lady.'

They stood up. The man was a Sergeant, Andrew saw. He was tall, thin, with sharp nose and mouth and a small moustache. He planted his legs apart and stared at them.

'I guess you know you're breaking the law, boss,' he said.

'Surely,' Andrew said, 'there's no law against sleeping on the beach?'

'There's a law against white vagabonds, boss. You can sleep any place you like so long as you've got ten pounds in your pocket. Do you have that money?'

'No. Not with me. I didn't know there was such a regulation.'

'You new to Lagos?'

'We got in the day before yesterday.' He hesitated. 'We had a draft of money to be cashed yesterday, but the currency restriction came first.'

The Sergeant nodded. 'I heard about that. And we've picked up some others.'

'We have some things at the Hotel Africa – clothes, suitcases. They would fetch ten pounds.'

'Maybe.' He grinned sardonically. 'It's a poor market right now, boss.'

Madeleine said: 'Do you have to arrest us, Sergeant? We didn't know we were breaking the law.'

He looked at her for a time before answering. Andrew thought at first that the gaze was insolent, possibly lecherous, but when the man spoke it was with a surprising and reassuring softness.

'I know that, lady,' he said. 'The law, now – it may seem hard, but there's reasons. We have a lot of white folks around Lagos these days, and a lot of them don't have money. Some of them have been breaking into houses, stealing and such. They have brains and nerve, and they don't care what happens. We had a lady badly beaten by a white house-breaker only the night before last. That's why we have the law, and patrols.' He nodded towards the Alsatian. 'And the dog. He was trained on hunting black men – he was a guard dog in the diamond fields up in Sierra Leone – but he finds no trouble in switching colours. He's a good dog.'

Andrew and Madeleine were silent. The less one said, Andrew felt, the less likelihood there was of giving offence.

The Sergeant said: 'Better not sleep out any more. We have to keep the laws from being broken. You understand.'

'Yes,' Andrew said. 'We understand. Thank you, Sergeant.'

'We're on our way back to the station,' the Sergeant said. 'It's about a mile, mile and a quarter. Could offer you a cup of coffee if you feel like walking along that way.'

'We'd be grateful,' Madeleine said.

'Come right along, then.'

As well as the coffee, they got a lift into the city on a police truck. They had also been able to wash and tidy themselves up at the police station, but Andrew was not able to shave: his kit was with the luggage at the hotel. Their pressing need was for accommodation and work, and it seemed worth trying the man whose name had been given at the Embassy; he might have ideas on the second point as well as the first. The address was in a new office building in the Ikoyi district, but it was only just after eight o'clock when they found it, and there was no sign of the day's activity having begun.

They were forced to walk around. Newspapers were on sale, but at sixpence they were too dear to buy. They contented themselves with reading the headlines as they passed. They seemed to be chiefly concerned with an internal scandal in one of the Nigerian political parties, but the Bantu atrocity story was still being carried.

They returned to Bates's office about nine fifteen. It was a small place on the second floor: basically one room, divided by a lath partition topped with frosted glass. A dark Jewish-looking girl with a small white face was typing in the outer part. She listened to Andrew, and said:

'I'll see if Mr Bates can see you.'

She had a middle-European accent; possibly Viennese. She knocked on the door of the inner office and went in. When she came out, a few moments later, Alf Bates was just behind her. He was a short red-faced man, in his forties, with a look of stupidity and cunning. His hand held the girl's shoulder intimately; he gave her a little push as he greeted his visitors.

'Come right on in,' he said. 'Glad you called. Nothing like starting the day early. That's where we'll beat the blackies yet. They've learned a lot, but they're still damn lazy.'

He ushered them to seats, and sat himself behind his desk on a broken-down swivel chair. The desk was badly worn and one side was splintered. Bates brought out a small pad and unclipped a fountain pen from the breast pocket of his shirt.

'Names,' he said. 'Let's get those right for a starter.' Andrew told him. 'Mr Andrew Leedon,' he repeated, 'and Mrs Madeleine Cartwell.' Small grey eyes stared at them inquisitively. 'But you're in harness – that right? You don't want a place each?'

'No,' Andrew said. 'We don't want a place each.'

'Don't mind me,' Bates said. 'Live as free as you can. There's not much free, and less every year. You want a little place? Nothing fancy?'

'I want a job,' Andrew said. 'Our money was caught in the sterling freeze.'

'All of it?'

'Yes, all.'

'Ah,' Bates said. 'That puts you in a special category – among the dead unlucky. Could be worse, though, couldn't it? You could be gathering chilblains up in the frozen North.'

'Have you any suggestions?' Andrew asked him.

Bates looked at him. 'For you, it isn't going to be easy. Apart from the Army there isn't a hell of a lot you can do.'

'I don't mind what I do.'

'Nor do most of the whites here – and they got here first.'

'There isn't something around the television studios? Anything at all?'

Bates laughed. 'They've got Chiefs' sons sweeping the floors there. Television mighty powerful juju. No, you can forget that one.' His gaze was speculative. 'I don't think you've got the right build for a labouring job, especially in this climate. It's supposed to be a few degrees cooler these days, but not so as you'd notice.'

Madeleine said: 'Is there something I could do?'

'Well now,' Bates said, 'I've been giving that a little thinking over. I might be able to fit you in across the water.'

'Across the water?'

'The night spots are on the other side of the lagoon. There's a call for white women, provided they're young and' – he grinned at her – 'attractive.'

'To do what? I can't sing or dance, I'm afraid.'

'You can shuffle round a floor. You can sit at a table and let someone buy you a drink.'

'A Negro?'

Bates raised his eyes briefly to the ceiling. 'Who else can afford to buy drinks? I might get across and buy you one once a fortnight, but it will mean eating light that week if I do.'

'And the pay?' Madeleine asked.

'Five pounds a week.'

'Judging from the prices I've seen here, one couldn't live on that.'

'It's nominal. You get a commission on drinks, as well. And tips. And so on.'

She said slowly: 'In other words, what you're really suggesting is prostitution. There's a certain demand for white female bodies. That's it, isn't it?'

'Mrs Cartwell,' Bates said, 'I'm not suggesting anything. I'm putting you in the way of a job. After that, it's up to you. Some women like it over there, some don't. No one forces anybody to like it or dislike it, and no one forces anybody to take the job or to stay in it. It doesn't worry me, either way.'

Andrew stood up, and Madeleine followed suit.

Andrew said: 'What about losing your commission, Mr Bates? Doesn't that worry you?'

Bates smiled without annoyance. 'I get a flat rate for introductions. They can leave the same day, and I'm not hurt.'

'Flat-rate pimping,' Andrew said. 'Less remunerative, probably, but less trouble as well. And quite reasonably profitable providing the turn-over's high enough.'

'If insults upset me, Mr Leedon, I'd have retired with stomach ulcers ten years ago. I take it you don't want the job, Mrs Cartwell?'

'No,' Andrew said, 'she doesn't. Thank you for the offer. Good-bye.'

'Sit down,' Bates said. Andrew halted by the door. 'Come back and sit down. It's a big city in a big country, and you're on your own in it. No jobs and nowhere to live. It's worth putting up with my company a little longer.'

It was Madeleine who came back first and took her seat.

'That wasn't hurt pride, Mr Bates. I thought we'd exhausted the possibilities as far as you were concerned.'

Bates opened a packet of Bicycle, and offered it across his desk. 'Cigarette? Go ahead. Bought out of the property side, I guarantee, not the white slave traffic.'

When they had lit up, he went on: 'I think I can get you a job at the hospital, Mrs Cartwell.'

Her face brightened. 'I've had some nursing training . . .'

He took his cigarette out and pulled a shred of tobacco from his lip before answering.

'Benson & Hedges I used to smoke. I like a good cigarette. The job wouldn't be nursing. There's no shortage of nurses. It would be ward-maid or cleaner.'

Madeleine looked at him steadily: 'And the pay?'

'Roughly eight pounds a week.' He shrugged. 'Not a fortune. And no *dash*. The nurses get the *dash*. I'm told it used to be a penny a time for fetching a bed-pan. It's a shilling now, and that's the minimum. It goes up to half a crown, where they can afford it and the need's urgent. There's inflation for you.' His eyes came back to Madeleine's face. 'But, as I said, you wouldn't be in on that. They fetch the bed-pans and get the *dash*. All you do is clean them. And scrub floors, and so on.'

'Have you anything else to suggest?' she asked. 'Private domestic service, for instance.'

'No. They only keep white people for show, and not all of them like doing that. And there's an over-supply. The rich blackies are rich enough, but there aren't as many of them as you might think.'

'All right,' Madeleine said. 'I'll take the hospital.'

Bates scribbled a few words on the back of a visiting card.

'Give this to the Secretary,' he said. 'I'll have a word with her first on the blower.' He grinned. 'No commission on this one: just for the goodness of Alf Bates's heart.'

Madeleine said: 'Thank you.'

Andrew said: 'I'd rather there was something for me. I don't mind what.'

Bates pushed his tongue round the front of his teeth.

'Sure,' he said. 'But not easy, as I told you. And you want somewhere to live?'

Madeleine said: 'Yes.'

'I hope you can take it straight. You're going to have to live in a poor quarter. A very poor quarter. You can't even afford one of the little places at Sbute Metta or Yaba. For the time being it's going to be Ikko itself.'

'Ikko?'

'That's the vernacular for the island. Lagos: the city. The place I'm going to direct you to is going to cost three pounds a week – it was thirty bob a month not so long ago – and when you first look at it, you aren't going to believe anyone could live in it. But you're going to live in it because you have no choice. You'll think you'd rather live out in the open, but you can't do that because the police won't let you.'

'We've learned that much already,' Andrew said.

'That's good. You're better off knowing where you stand. This is a slum you're going to live in; Johannesburg has the only place in Africa that comes near it. The shack that's offered for rent is ramshackle and dirty and it stinks. There'll be open drains nearby. I'm told it has one advantage over Johannesburg: no flies. The flies can't take it.'

Andrew said: 'You paint a powerful picture of the property.'

'I like to get things clear from the start: it saves disappointments. You're going to have to live in a nigger slum, and I want you to get used to the idea. There are quite a number of whites living there now, and some of them have cleaned their areas up a bit. Nothing to stop you doing the same with yours, but you won't get any rent reduction if you do. In fact, you may get it put up.' Bates shook his head. 'No, I'm not the owner. I just collect the rents.'

'Is this the only place you have?' Andrew asked.

'No. It's not even the only place at the price you can afford. It's the best. It's closed at both ends. Some of them people use as passageways to go from street to street.'

'How do we get there?' Madeleine asked.

'I'll draw you a map. If you decide to take it, just move right in. It's supposed to be rent in advance, but I'll trust you till the end of the week.' He looked at them genially. 'In fact, I can lend you a couple of quid if you're strapped.'

'Thank you,' Andrew said. 'We'll manage, though. There are a few things we can sell.'

Bates nodded. 'Come back and see me if it gets too rough. Not that there's much I can do.'

They walked through the jostling streets, under the blue oppressive sky. Madeleine said:

'We can make do for a time. Something will turn up.'

'Yes,' Andrew said.

They were passing a dilapidated white building, its windows covered with heavy iron grilles. He halted by the steps leading to the entrance, and she followed his glance upwards. A billboard had been placed above the door, and it was covered with posters. One, showing an idealized Negro soldier with rifle and bayonet at the ready, was headed: PROTECT OUR BELOVED COUNTRY. Another had, overprinted across a tank rolling through scrub country: THE CRUSADE FOR AFRICA IS ON! Large red capitals at the top of the board said:

NIGERIAN ARMY RECRUITING CENTRE

'It's not that desperate,' Madeleine said.

'I think it is.'

'We're white,' she said. 'One has some loyalties.'

'I'm just beginning to realize how narrow mine are.' He pressed her arm. 'Wait for me here. I'll try not to be long.'

'Not yet,' she said.

'Don't they give you a bounty for joining?' he said. 'Maybe we'll sleep in a decent bed tonight.'

A Negro Sergeant behind an Inquiries sign directed him upstairs. Room 17 had a sign saying: Recruiting Office: Whites Only. There was another Sergeant behind a desk, a fat placid-looking man who chewed something while he talked. His lips were fleshy and unnaturally red.

He said: 'Anything I can do for you, boss?'

'I was thinking of volunteering for the Nigerian Army. I've had experience in Tanks.'

The Sergeant chewed silently for a moment, before saying:

'How old are you, boss?'

'Thirty-seven.'

'You look all of that. And we aren't accepting men over thirty. Except as training officers.'

'That's what I had in mind.'

'You'd better go and see Captain Lashidu, boss. Room 22 – right along the corridor.'

'Thank you.'

'O.K., boss.'

Captain Lashidu, by contrast, was a slim alert man, with thin straight eyebrows and a high forehead. He looked more Indian than Negro; there was probably, Andrew thought, a white branch or two in his family tree. He said, in a brisk, pleasant, only lightly accented voice:

'Your name, please.'

'Andrew Leedon.'

'Age?'

'Thirty-seven.'

'Place of origin?'

'I've come from London. I was born in Kent.'

'Military experience?'

'I held a National Service commission in the Royal Tank Regiment.'

Lashidu nodded. He had been writing the answers on a pad; now he put down the pencil. It was an ordinary red pencil, with a badly chewed end. There had to be stress, Andrew thought, beneath that kind of calmness.

'You wish to join the Crusade, Mr Leedon?' Lashidu said.

'If that's what it's called. I want to join the Nigerian Army as a training officer.'

'Why?'

'There aren't many careers here which offer any scope for a white man.'

'That is true. You are not distressed by the thought that you will be training an army to fight white people in South Africa?'

'Has war been declared?'

'Not yet. You are not distressed by the possibility, shall we say? By the probability, rather?'

'I am distressed by the thought of having no job,' Andrew said, 'of having to live in a slum, of not being able to look after – a person I'm responsible for. Those are the things that distress me.'

'One has to ask this question,' Lashidu said. 'Your attitude is the correct one, I think, Mr Leedon. Egocentricity is the natural state of man, but insupportable by reason of its loneliness. I can accept the Trinity more easily than the strictly monotheistic conceptions of deity. One extends oneself, to a wife, children, friends, and relatives. It is a mistake, I believe, to continue this process, which goes on, if unchecked, through villages, provinces, countries. And races, of course.'

'You may be right,' Andrew said. 'I wouldn't argue against it.'

'Your military experience,' Lashidu said, '– you have no means of establishing that, I suppose?'

'Only through the Army Records Office in England.'

Lashidu smiled. 'I gather it is snow, not dust, that gathers on those files now. It would scarcely be practicable to refer to them.'

'I don't know – I suppose there's a chance you might already have recruited someone from my old Regiment . . . that's slim, I imagine.'

'Most slim. But I think we can get over that difficulty. You will be required to swear to your past military background. Should the facts subsequently be found to be incorrect, you become liable for court-martial. You understand this?'

'Yes.'

'Then there is no real obstacle. All we need now is one hundred and twenty-five pounds.' Lashidu smiled. 'Cash, naturally.'

'For what?'

'As *dash*.'

'*Dash* for volunteering for the Army?'

'For accepting you as a recruit in a profitable and promising career.' He picked up the pencil. '*Dash* is a part of our way of life. If you have not already learnt this, you must do so, Mr Leedon. In accepting the protection of a new country, you accept its way of life. There is no alternative.'

'*Dash* is one thing. I should have thought buying Army commissions was quite different.'

'As to that, we have good precedents. In your English Army, not only were commissions bought at one time, but regiments also. For many thousands of pounds.'

'That was quite a long time ago.'

'Yes,' Lashidu agreed. 'In the days of old England's glory. Perhaps the world has taken a step backwards; or even several steps. Is that a bad thing, do you think? I am told that the Americans and the Russians still have scientists working in remote places, trying to devise ways of using nuclear power to warm their chilly continents. At any rate, they are too busy to think of throwing hydrogen bombs through space at each other.'

Andrew said: 'Spare me the philosophical rigmarole. In an Army, one can always go to a superior officer.'

'To report me for seeking *dash*?' Lashidu smiled. 'Do you think he doesn't get his share? Look, Mr Leedon, I am willing to leave my own share in abeyance. But he is not. You will still have to pay seventy-five pounds before your application can be passed. There are no exceptions to this.'

'And if I take this story to the opposition press?'

'The crime of libelling the Armed Forces is quite severely punished. You may try, with pleasure.' He paused. 'Come, Mr Leedon, you are a man of sense, not emotion. The *dash* is not excessive. It is worth something for a white man to be an officer and a gentleman in Africa.'

'I'd worked that out already.'

'Had you? Then why quibble, in Heaven's name?'

'Because I haven't the money.'

Lashidu raised his thin eyebrows. 'How much do you have?'

'Nothing at all.'

It was a moment before Lashidu replied. He said:

'The moratorium, I suppose? I should have checked on that point earlier. I regret that I have been wasting your time, Mr Leedon.'

Andrew stood up. 'And I yours.'

'Of less importance. The Government pays for it. I am sorry to hear of your misfortune. This is not an easy country in which to live as a poor man.'

Andrew nodded. 'So I understand.'

'I have never felt inferior to the English,' Lashidu said, 'and so I have nothing against them. Their present situation here is an interesting one. I am most curious as to how it will develop.'

'Thank you,' Andrew said. 'One appreciates the interest. I'll drop you a postcard.'

'They have a sense of humour.' Lashidu smiled. 'No doubt that will help.'

Despite Bates's frankness in preparing them for it, the sight of the shack they were renting came as a shock. An old Yoruba mammy, wearing a patched blue robe and a new red silk scarf round her head, yielded the place up to them; she had been acting as caretaker. She gave them a torn sheet of paper, headed Inventory. A badly typed list indicated the items of furniture. 'Bed' appeared on it, but had been scratched out. They were too stunned by the picture the interior presented to query this point.

There was only one room; the boards at the end apparently divided this shack from the next, because a mélange of jazz music and human voices in heated conversation came through with little or no diminution. The room had one window, a small square to the left of the door, and unglassed. The board walls had been painted yellow at some time, but the paint was stained and chipped; further decoration was offered by pinned-up pages torn from an old Swiss calendar – there was a rare incongruity in looking at the familiar scenes of glaciers and snowy mountains and Alpine meadows in this setting. An old chest-of-drawers, with one drawer missing, stood against one wall. There was a broken-down cane easy chair, and two wooden upright chairs painted blue. The floor was of rough boards, engrained with dirt. To one side a piece of matting, six feet by about four, apparently filled in for the missing bed; at any rate, it had four or five old Army blankets stacked in a heap on it. In the far corner stood a wooden table, carrying some pots and pans, a few bits of crockery, a paraffin lantern, and a primus stove. There was a large metal jug underneath the table and a red plastic bowl, the rim frizzled and distorted by some chance application of heat, beside it. To one side, a round can presumably containing paraffin – the pungent smell defeated all the other smells, though without disposing of them.

The mammy saw him look at it.

'I filled it up for you, boss,' she said. 'You got that right full of blue paraffin. Twelve shillings.'

They had managed to sell a few items of their personal belongings, at ridiculous prices. Andrew counted the money out to her. He was fairly sure she was charging at least double what it had cost, but he felt there was no point in arguing. The main thing was to get her out and face the thing on their own.

But she was less eager to leave.

'You got a fine house there,' she said. 'Good neighbours. Next door, that's my cousin and his family. You want anything, just give them a knock. They look after you.'

'Yes,' Andrew said. 'Thank you.'

'They'll maybe even rent you the radio, you being lonely and just the two. Only five shillings a week, I should think. Six, maybe. You want me to ask them?'

Andrew shook his head. 'We can't afford that.'

'Maybe four shillings. Three even. They put a new battery in right last week.'

It was almost tempting, if only to stop the din that clearly was likely to go on as long as there was a radio transmission available: except that they would obviously use the money to rent or buy another, and probably even noisier, set for themselves. He said:

'We have no money to spare for radio at all.'

Her fat black face split into a smile. 'I guess you can listen to their radio, can't you, boss? Maybe you'll want to help pay when they get the next new battery. But I'll leave my cousin and you to talk about that.'

Madeleine spoke for the first time since they had come into the shack. She said:

'Where does one get water?'

'Why, child, there's a tap right at the end of the street. You don't have to walk more than fifty yards – seventy-five, maybe.'

She nodded. 'I see.'

'You got a fine house,' the nanny repeated. 'Come on over here.'

They followed her to a position close by the table which served for a kitchen. Squatting down, she pulled up a loose board and pointed to the space beneath it.

'You don't have to carry no slops outside,' the mammy said. 'Times, that's a real help.'

Andrew looked where she had pointed. It was possible to see, despite the darkness, that an open drain ran under this corner of the room. He thought he saw a rat scramble away. As he bent down the smell, concentrating in nose and throat, made him want to retch. He took the end of the board from the mammy's hand, and pushed it back into place. She watched this complacently.

'See what I mean,' she said. 'Just no trouble at all.'

Madeleine had gone to the other side of the room, and was staring out through the window.

'All right,' Andrew said. 'Thank you for showing us everything. We can manage ourselves now.'

'The lady will want to know which shops to go to. Some of those shopkeepers are rogues, but I've got a nephew who's . . .'

'Another time,' Andrew said. 'Not just now.'

She grinned. 'O.K., boss. Then you just give me the *dash* and I'll leave you two folks in peace.'

'*Dash?* For what?'

'For looking after the house, boss. Only one pound, that's all. You just give me that, maybe twenty-five shillings if you're feeling kind-hearted, and off I go.'

'The landlord pays you for that. It's his property you're supposed to be looking after.'

'As God's my judge, boss . . .'

In the end, he gave her five shillings, as the only means of getting rid of her. She went, with a final threat of returning to take

Madeleine to her nephew's shop, and they were alone. Jazz thumped relentlessly at them and voices – quarrelling, laughing, singing – but they were alone. Andrew went and stood behind her. He touched her neck with his lips.

'We'll get out of this,' he said. 'Can you stick it for a little while?'

She turned and faced him. 'You're a comfort, Andy,' she said.

Her voice was dry, strained, and at first he thought she was mocking him, mocking his failure in bringing her to this. But her face, damp with sweat in this close evil-smelling heat, was also wet with tears. It was her moment of desolation, he recognized, as his own had been at night on the beach. He kissed her, and found her body stiff, withdrawn, yet desperate for comforting. He put his arm on her waist, and led her towards the mat. He spread out one of the blankets over it; they did not look clean, but they at least were not stained and greasy as the matting was. He thought she might protest, revolted by the sordidness of their surroundings, but she lay down obediently. She stared at the ceiling as he lay beside her. It was a piece of corrugated iron, supported on two shaky joists; rust stains covered it and at one point a hole provided a glimpse of the sky's hot blue.

His hand holding the thin bones of her wrist, he said:

'I'm going to write to Carol. There are limits to pride, you know.'

There was a pause, before she said: 'Yes, there are limits.'

'She'll be able to do something for us – or get Sir Adekema to do it.'

'I'm sure she will.'

'And it's only what's due, after all. The money from the house, from our bank account . . .'

Madeleine said fiercely: 'Stop it! What's the point in justification? We'll beg her, if necessary. Can't you see? A few weeks of this and I'll be pleading with Bates to fix me up in one of those places on the other side of the lagoon.'

They were silent, the din of their neighbours continuing all round them. A woman passed along the street, laughing uncontrollably. Bing Crosby and Frank Sinatra sang the party duet from 'High Society'. A dog began howling monotonously. There was heat and the smell of decay and corruption.

Her gaze had turned from the roof to the nearest wall, and his own followed it. She was looking at one of the plates torn from the Swiss calendar. It was a colour photograph of the Jungfrau, taken from just above Kleine Scheidegg. The bright Alpine flowers bloomed in the foreground; beyond lay the white slopes of the mountain, cradled in the cool blue silk of air.

She said: 'We stayed there once.'

His hand slackened on hers. It was Madeleine then who turned to him. Her eyes searched his face slowly. Then she brought her mouth close to him, whispering.

'I'm glad I've got you, Andy. So glad.' He kissed her and she responded fiercely. 'The door,' she said, '– does it have any kind of lock or bolt?'

Andrew got up and went to see. There was no key to the lock. The bolt socket had a nail missing and would scarcely have kept out a vigorous child. He shot the bolt anyway, and turned back to look at Madeleine. Seeing her there, lying on the grey torn blanket, her dress crumpled, blonde hair disarrayed, face clammy with sweat, he knew all the bright impossible conviction of love.

When the first rain came, a week later, they lay awake listening to it drumming on the iron roof in thankfulness and relief. But the relief was short-lived. Before long they were conscious of the leaks, and that a spreading pool of water had reached the mat on which they were lying. They had to get up, light the paraffin lamp, and arrange the bowl and jug beneath the worst of the drips. It was impossible to sleep after that.

The rain continued heavily all night and most of the next day. By the time it stopped, the whole floor was soaking. Madeleine was out working at the hospital, and Andrew dried up as best he could, taking the opportunity first to scrub the boards again; they had done this on the second day of their tenancy, but he felt it couldn't be done too often. Fortunately it had been possible to keep the matting and the blankets reasonably dry by stacking them on the table. He managed to get the place into something like order by the time that Madeleine returned. He also had a meal ready for them: cereal and fruit, and weak coffee, with bread and goat cheese to follow.

She looked exhausted, as she always did after the day's work. She would not say much about what it was like, but it was obvious that it drained her to her last resources of energy. As she came in, she took off her shoes with a small gesture of despair; they were heavily caked with mud, which had also splattered her legs.

'It's a quagmire out there,' she said. 'How long does the rainy season last?'

'Three months, I believe. Sit down, and I'll wash your feet. You'll feel better then.'

She produced a package from her string-bag. 'Something from the kitchens.'

It was cooked rice in a plastic bag. Andrew took it and put it with the rest of their provisions, in the net-swathed box he had hung from one of the joists. She sat down, sighing.

'It's no cooler, is it? One thinks it will be cooler, with the rain. But it's just as hot.'

He put the bowl at her feet, and washed her feet and legs gently. Looking up, he said:

'Did you manage to get to the office?' She nodded, as though too tired to speak. 'No letter?'

Bates had agreed to let them use his office as an accommodation address. Madeleine said:

'Not from Carol. One from David, though.'

She opened her handbag and offered it to him. He gestured with his wet hands, and she held the letter while he read it. It was not very long, and did not say much. He realized things were hard, but they were bound to improve. They were still difficult in London, too. There was nothing he could do to help at the moment; there was a strict embargo on the export of such obvious currency substitutes as diamonds, and in any case they were unobtainable. In that respect all the resources of the Pale had been placed under guard in the silver vaults in Chancery Lane. She was to try to keep cheerful until things got better. He sent his regards to Andy.

'He doesn't say anything about coming out here,' Madeleine said.

'It sounds as though they're holding their own. Perhaps it will be we who go back there.'

In a tired voice, she said: 'The Royal Family have gone to Jamaica. It was on the News today.'

'For good?'

'For a prolonged State visit, they said.'

'That doesn't necessarily mean things are finally cracking up in London.'

'No.' She shook her head. 'And he wouldn't be allowed to say much in advance, would he? All the letters are censored.'

Andrew said: 'We should have heard from Carol by now.'

She nodded. 'Tomorrow, perhaps.'

'Bates didn't have any news of a job for me?'

'No. Not yet.' She put her hand down and rubbed his head. 'Don't fret, darling. There'll be a letter from Carol tomorrow.'

But the days went by, and there was nothing from Carol. After the second week they ceased hoping, because hope was a distraction from the grim concentration on living and enduring their conditions. Andrew managed to get a job working on building demolition, but lost it after a few days. Madeleine continued to work at the hospital, and from time to time contrived to get scraps of food from the kitchens. They spent as little as they dared, striving to build up a small store of cash; but it mounted pitifully slowly. In the third week, Andrew fell sick with some fever. Madeleine called in a doctor and got one of the mammy women to look after him while she was out at work. With these and medicines their money was gone by the time, four days later, he was able to get up.

He remained very weak for some time after this, and there could be no question of his being able to do any kind of manual labour. He hunted the streets, hoping that something would turn up, a miracle. He could remember, as a boy in his late teens, visiting London and looking for romance with the same hopeless persistence. His mind and body ached for release from this present helplessness.

On the Marina one day he turned towards the sea and thought he saw his sons: two white-skinned schoolboys, of roughly their age and build, stood looking out to sea. He started towards them involuntarily, but checked as he saw they were strangers. Then it occurred to him that even so they might be from the school at Ibadan, that they might know Robin and Jeremy. He crossed the road towards them, forcing a Rolls to swerve slightly. The white chauffeur glanced at him with contempt; the Nigerian businessmen in the back did not look up from their intent discussion.

The boys were also discussing something. He paused, catching the first words, and pretended to look out to sea.

'Ituno's jolly nice,' the smaller boy said. 'No swank about him at all. And he's a Chief's son.'

'So is Akki,' the other said. 'He's invited me to stay with him in the next hols. They have a terrifically big place up near Ife.' He gave a small embarrassed laugh. 'I made a bit of a bloomer about that. I thought they must be Yoruba, since it's Yoruba country. But they're Sobo.'

'It's a bit difficult, isn't it? Has he really asked you to stay there?'

'For a week. I wrote and told Dad straight away. They have a swimming pool a hundred feet long.'

It was not what was said but the tone of voice that brought things back to him; he remembered school, and the Fives Court, and overhearing two of the small handful of Jewish boys among his fellow pupils. There had been the same fencing unsureness, the glib pretence of acceptance into a society which, they knew at heart, would always deny them. He had been thirteen then, and had known enough to see through the appearance of confidence, but not enough to prevent him despising them.

Andrew looked down at his crumpled suit and worn dusty shoes. They did not appear to have noticed him yet. He turned and walked away.

Madeleine had had another letter from David, as brief and encouraging and uncommunicative as the first. Andrew was not sure whether she had written back or not; she made no mention of it. David, like Carol, seemed very far away – in the physical sense, obviously, but in other ways too. The closeness that had grown between Madeleine and himself was something which Andrew had never experienced before, nor imagined. He would have thought at one time that it would breed resentments, even disgust, but the opposite was true. Each day he looked forward more eagerly to the time when she came back from the hospital and they could be together. He wondered occasionally what would happen when David finally came out; since it seemed unlikely that Carol would sacrifice her present advantages for him. But this was a speculation without anxiety: he had won her now, and was confident he would keep her. Even in the wretchedness of their life, his bitter frustration with his inability to do anything about a situation which increasingly drove her to the limits of physical exhaustion, this was a transforming factor. He would have despaired without it.

The rains continued with only short intervals of respite; there was no let-up at all from the heat. The quarter in which they lived was a quagmire of mud, reeking with the stench of filth and decay, made worse by the dripping dampness. Andrew stayed in the hut much of the time scrubbing the walls and floorboards, trying to make something of the place. During the brief bursts of sunshine he went out into the streets, to get the air and loiter among the stalls, which opened like caves on to the running wet alleys of the streets.

One afternoon he got as far as the Idumagbo market. He had taken to coming out without shoes or socks, and with his trousers rolled up to his knees; it saved footwear and it was easier to wash his legs clean on returning than it would have been to clean the mud from the shoes. The local blacks, who followed the same practice for the most part, accepted this incuriously, and Andrew had noticed that other whites living in the native quarter were beginning to follow suit. He wandered round the market, looking at the bolts of blue and white cloth, the brightly coloured beads, the chalks and powders on the cosmetic stalls, with no self-consciousness. He was in front of the juju stall, staring at a neatly arranged pyramid of monkey skulls, when he was tapped on the shoulder, and turned round.

The man who had accosted him was a Nigerian, in immaculate white drill; he was about twenty-five, tall, heavy-boned, his skin gleaming with health and assurance.

'Excuse me, sir,' he said. 'May I have your attention a moment or two?'

He spoke good English with a sing-song cadence. Andrew felt himself pricked by flattery; he had been addressed as 'Sir', spoken to politely.

'Of course,' he said. 'As long as you like.'

'I represent Nigerian Television. We do a programme of topical interest. It's called "Every Day". You may have seen it some time.'

'No,' Andrew said. 'I haven't seen it.'

'We're bringing the cameras into this market today. We want scenes of interest, something to catch the attention of the viewers. In this case . . . a European – and English? – beside a juju stall – it has flavour, you understand?'

Andrew said: 'Yes, I understand.'

'An Englishman,' he repeated, 'and one who has – seen better days, shall we say? If you would care to co-operate, sir . . . merely allow yourself to be photographed – making a purchase, perhaps . . .'

Andrew shook his head. 'I can't afford that.'

'Well, naturally, we provide the money. And there's a small payment for appearing, a *dash* as it were. Usually ten shillings, but to a European . . . a pound, say?'

'Thank you,' Andrew said. 'I'll take it.'

'And allow us to ask you a few questions, perhaps? Nothing undignified, I assure you, sir.'

Andrew waited while the cameras were brought up. Another African came back with the first, and there was some discussion as to just what he ought to buy from the stall; there was a wide choice with carcasses of birds, dried mice and bats, ballooned gizzards and bladders, animals' intestines and limbs. Finally they settled on a small greenish object.

'As most suitable for an Englishman in your circumstances, you understand, sir. It is said to bring luck.'

Their faces had a peculiarly bland look which made him suspect that there might be more to it than this – that the purchase was one which might make him, despite the earlier reassurance, seem ridiculous. But they had paid over the pound, and five shillings for the purchase, and that was enough. He did his part for the cameras, noticing at one point that one camera had focused down to his bare feet, and waited patiently for the questioning that followed.

It was done adroitly; his past experience in the field enabled him to realize this. The apparent deference was maintained, but with a mocking edge; a wink over the shoulder to the viewing audience, as it were, inviting them to titter. As one who had organized and edited so many hundreds of similar interviews, Andrew felt a kind of ironic satisfaction at recognizing himself in the position of the victim. He co-operated with grave courtesy. At the point where he was asked what his earlier profession had been, and he told the interviewer, he had the additional satisfaction of seeing him thrown slightly out of gear. He recovered fast, and got in a few barbed remarks on the change of status, but Andrew felt that he had come as well out of the situation as could have been expected.

On the way back he bought a little meat, and prepared it for their evening meal. Madeleine, when she came in, sniffed the air and looked at him inquiringly.

'Meat?'

'To celebrate my new career on television.' He saw her eyes widen, and went on quickly before she could come to hope and so to the cruelty of disappointment: 'I was picked up by a roving camera in the market this afternoon. They gave me *dash* for co-operating. A pound.'

Madeleine smiled. 'I'm glad. But oughtn't we to have saved it?' She came over to him to be kissed. 'No, I suppose not. And you need building up still.'

'We both do.'

'I wonder if – Carol might see the programme.'

'I don't know. I tried not to look too pathetic.'

She pushed him towards a chair. 'You look pathetic now. I'll finish things off.'

'I bought a bar of chocolate as well,' he said, 'for a pudding.'

She laughed, but there was strain there. 'Madly extravagant! It doesn't matter, anyway. A short life and a rich one.'

It was two days later, an hour or so after Madeleine had gone out to work, that there was a knock at the door. Andrew was engaged in trying to repair the cane chair, patching a hole with raffia.

'It's not locked,' he called. 'Come in.'

He assumed it was one of the locals, though they usually made a direct assault on the door, only knocking when it was found to be bolted against them. But the door swung open, and he saw that it was a stranger, an African in a figured silk shirt and well-cut fawn slacks. As he came in, Andrew saw reversed calf tan shoes beneath the thick coating of mud. The man was stocky, about middle height, and wore thick black executive-type spectacles. His eyes peered into the hut, looking for Andrew.

'That's you, Andrew?' he said.

When he spoke, Andrew remembered him: the member of the visiting study group he had found looking helpless in the studios, and had taken to dinner at his Club. He remembered also the subsequent letter of thanks, from some address in Africa which at the time had meant nothing to him. He had thought about replying, but finally decided it was not worth it.

'Yes,' Andrew said. 'It's me. Come in, won't you? I can't offer you anything except a chair, I'm afraid. And I've got to admit that I can't remember your name. I'm bad with names.'

'Abonitu. You said you would call me Abo.' He smiled. 'I only found out afterwards it was the Australian slang word for aboriginal.'

'Now I remember. That was after several whiskies and a bottle of Burgundy.'

'Claret,' Abonitu said. 'A Latour.'

'You have a good memory,' Andrew said with admiration. 'Usually I drank Burgundy.'

'This one had been recommended. I remember the evening very well. Will you come out for a drink now?'

'I haven't been drinking much lately.'

'Please come. I want to talk to you. We can do it better with drinks beside us.'

Andrew said: 'Thanks. As long as it's not too good a place. My appearance isn't really up to a four-ale bar.'

Abonitu smiled. 'I shouldn't worry about that.'

Nothing much was said outside; they walked to the nearest main street and took a taxi to a bar on the Marina. It was new, with small porthole windows, discreet lighting, and thick wall-to-wall carpeting. In the lobby, a young Italian took off their shoes and eased them into blue and gold slippers provided by the house.

'This place still has Scotch,' Abonitu said. 'You will join me?'

Andrew nodded. 'With pleasure.'

The drinks were brought over to their alcove table. Abonitu raised his.

'To you, Andrew. To your good fortune.'

'Yes. And to yours.'

'Your case is the more urgent, I fancy.' He smiled. 'I saw your interview on the rushes.'

'Yes, I thought that might have something to do with your dropping in.' He sipped the Scotch, feeling it tingle, familiar and unfamiliar, against his tongue. 'For which I'm very grateful.'

The smile turned into a laugh. 'Friend, I could scarcely believe my eyes! To see Andrew Leedon buying a monkey's penis from a juju stall.'

'That was it, was it? They told me it was something one bought to bring one luck.'

'I suppose that is true, in one sense.' Abonitu's face relaxed into the somewhat anxious solemnity which was normal to it. 'You need not worry, Andrew. It will not be screened. I had you cut out altogether.'

Andrew shrugged. 'I wouldn't have minded. Do I have to give the pound back? I'm afraid it's mostly spent.'

'Andrew, it distresses me to find you like this. Believe me, this is so. When I saw your face on the monitor screen . . . I wished to find you, you understand, and yet the thought embarrassed me – to think that you might be embarrassed. Is this clear to you?'

'Roughly. You need not have worried, though. Embarrassment only afflicts those who are still managing to keep up appearances.'

'Such as myself? You are quite right. I think. That evening, when you gave me dinner – it was nothing to you, perhaps, but of great importance to me. To be accepted like that, with no sense of strain, to dine at a Club in Pall Mall . . . I had read about this kind of life, you understand. It was a wonderful thing, Andrew. I tried to say this when I wrote to you from Africa, but probably I put things badly.'

'I didn't reply. I'm sorry.'

'You were very busy, of course. This matter of appearances: it is true that in one sense I was pleased to see what had happened to you, glad to find you had been brought low. Is this honest enough?'

'Very honest.'

'And yet it is also true that I was embarrassed on your account — that I still am. I would like to help you. But you will not be offended?'

'Put the money on the table,' Andrew said. 'Then turn your head. I'll slip out quietly.'

Abonitu's expression was painful. 'It is not a joke. Would you like to work in television again, here at Lagos?'

'No whites need apply. I was told that in several quarters, but I went along to the studios all the same. They underlined it for me.'

'My uncle,' Abonitu said simply, 'is Chairman of the Television Board. He is the Oba Mekani Natela. That is how I have become a producer. I need an assistant, I can choose whomever I like.'

'Might it not make things difficult for you if you choose a white, though?'

'Nigerians have nothing against whites, as long as there are not too many of them, and as long as they keep to their place. You have perhaps heard something like that before?'

Andrew nodded. 'Something.'

'I am sorry. I should not have said that.'

'Better say them, Abo. They aren't going to worry me. Is this a firm offer you're making me?'

'Yes. A firm offer.'

'Then it's accepted.' He put his hand across the table, and they shook. 'I won't increase the embarrassment by going into details of my gratitude.'

Abonitu said hurriedly: 'Please don't. We will have another drink instead, to celebrate our future partnership.' He made a clicking sound and the waiter came for their order. 'Double Scotch again. That was not Haig, last time.'

'I'm sorry, sir. No more Haig.'

Abonitu shrugged. 'Serve what you have, then.' He turned to Andrew. 'In losing Britain, you have lost your home. I have lost a dream, a world which I could never enjoy but which I was glad to know existed. Who has lost more, do you think?'

'It may not be lost. The other side of the Fratellini curve . . .'

'No, that would be foolish optimism. I have seen the latest figures. Solar radiation has ceased to drop, but there is no sign at all of a recovery. It has found a new level. The ice age has returned.' He smiled wryly. 'The eternal snows will cover the White Tower and the Marble Arch.'

Andrew drank his whisky. 'How soon can I and my – my fiancée get out of that shack?'

'At once. You can stay in a hotel while you find a place to live.'

'She's been working as a ward-maid at the hospital. Can we . . . ?'

'We can pick her up from there as soon as we have finished our drinks. And then get what you need from the shack.'

There was a pause before Andrew said, 'If I'm not careful, I am going to embarrass you. I can't say . . .'

Abonitu drained his own glass. 'Shall we get a taxi right away, Andrew?'

4

They were in a hotel for a week, and then moved into a penthouse flat in a new luxury block overlooking the sea. It was strange how quickly one forgot the wretchedness and deprivations, and how easy it was to slip into the new way of life. For Andrew, of course, there were many associations; the old familiar jargon and techniques, to a considerable extent the old familiar jokes and viewpoints. There were two classes in this television world, he found: those with real ability, such as Abonitu, who kept things going, and the others whose function was simply to draw salaries and put in an appearance. But this in itself was a not unfamiliar division.

Madeleine and he found themselves quickly accepted by members of the former circle. The acceptance was perhaps a shade too quick, a little too emphatic, but there seemed no reason to doubt its genuineness. There were nuances that were wrong and there always would be, but in time these would be less important.

Meanwhile there was the pleasure of rediscovering comforts and small luxuries. The salary he was being paid was a very good one even by his old standards, and in this brash bustling society of Lagos, with its underside of poverty and ignorance, money received its full due. There were a number of new restaurants, with European chefs, where it was possible to eat as well as Andrew remembered eating in London; and although the threat of war with the Union continued to occupy newspaper headlines and television programme time, South African wines were still imported in quantity. Andrew had not drunk them before, and found himself liking them. The rainy season ended, and the cloudless skies returned; but there was air conditioning in their flat and the studios, and in most of the places they visited. Then there was bathing on the long white beaches, and golf before the sun got too high or in the late afternoon. All this apart, it was fascinating to be back on what was, basically, his old job, and he got on well with Abonitu who, although titulary his superior, deferred to him much of the time. It was a good life altogether.

Carol impinged on it at one point. He had a call from her at the studios, and arranged to meet her for a drink. They met in the bar to which Abonitu had taken him. When Andrew arrived, he found her sitting waiting for him, toying with a lace mesh glove. She smiled at him as he offered his hand to her.

'It's still strange, isn't it – us shaking hands?'

'In a way. What can I get you to drink, Carol?'

'Can you run to a Dubonnet? The real stuff? They have a few bottles here.'

'Of course. With gin?'

'No. I'm cutting down on the hard liquor. Andy, I'm so glad things are going right for you again. I can't tell you how pleased I am.'

'How did you find out that they were?'

'I saw your credit title, of course, darling. I don't watch the telly much here, but I had nothing to do that evening. The "Every Day" programme. Assistant Producer – Andrew Leedon. My God, that brought things back!'

'I suppose it did. You did know that things had been – going badly earlier?'

She was silent, moistening her lips. She said:

'Your letter? I didn't know at the time.' He said nothing, and waited for her to go on. 'When I saw your name on the screen – I was with my boss. I drew his attention to it. Then he told me there had been a letter, and something about what had been in it.'

'It was sent care of his office, but it was addressed to you. He opened it – and kept it back?'

'He's an odd person, Andy. Nice in some ways, not in others. He's inclined to be dictatorial. And jealous.'

'I met his wife,' Andrew said. 'A very nice woman. She has my sympathy.'

'Mine, too.' She put down the cigarette she had been smoking with a small angry gesture. 'Do you think I've enjoyed all this?'

'I'd assumed you had, but I haven't thought much about it.'

'I may have been promiscuous, but I never sold myself before. What alternative was there? I had the boys to think of.'

'You could have opened a shop; you suggested that for Madeleine and me. You did have some capital.'

'You can't imagine what it's like,' she said, 'to come out to a place like this on your own, as a woman. The first week I was in a hotel with the boys, watching my money dribble away, learning what it was like to be a white out here. With the men making the obvious crude advances. I was lonely and frightened. I didn't know anything. I did think about a dress shop. I went along to see it, but I got the feeling that the man who was showing it to me was a crook. I felt too scared to do anything, to make any decisions.'

Andrew said nothing, but he could understand what she was talking about. Men had always done things for her: nice safe men in a nice safe world. There had been two elder brothers, and her father had been devoted to her.

'We met by accident,' she went on, 'and he was very kind. He can be terribly kind. I was grateful to him. He got the boys into their school. Their fees are paid right through, by the way.'

'Generous,' Andrew commented, 'with a large hand.'

She looked at him; the flow of talk stopped and she was silent. Andrew did not help her out. When she reached into her handbag for another cigarette, he brought his own out, gave her one and lit it. She took the cigarette away quickly and bent close to the lighter flame, pursing her lips as though to blow it out. It was the beginning of an old, known gesture, and both knew it was deliberate. She drew her head back, and he extinguished the flame himself.

Carol said abruptly: 'You're still with Maddie?'

'Yes.'

'The last time we met – I wondered whether you might not be beginning to fall in love with her. Something like that.'

'Yes,' Andrew said. 'Something like that.'

'And when David comes out?'

'That's up to Madeleine. Haven't you got a stronger claim on him?'

'There are no claims, either way.'

'You still hear from him?'

'No. Adekema objected. I didn't write back.'

'I imagine David would understand all that. He's a pragmatist by nature. Isn't that one of the things that attracted you to him?'

She said in a low voice: 'Perhaps my standards have changed.' He looked at her, smiling slightly. 'My needs, then.'

'I don't think we change much,' Andrew said, 'at our age. Except through blinding lights on the road to Damascus. You haven't had one of those?'

'I think a lot about Dulwich,' she said. 'And dream about it. Do you know, in the last three years I never went inside the picture gallery. I was always meaning to.'

'The pictures were brought inside the Pale. But I don't know what became of them.'

'The Poussins that you liked and I couldn't bear. I wish I could see them again.'

'*Où sont les Poussins d'antan?* The winter has frozen over them, I'm afraid.'

Carol put her hand on his. 'Andy, look at me. Do you think I'm still attractive?'

He nodded. 'Very attractive.'

'You don't hate me – for what's happened, for everything?'

'No. I don't.'

'When David comes out, I think Maddie will go back to him. I'm sorry if it hurts you, but I think she will. If she does, do you think we could . . .'

'Turn over a new leaf,' he said, 'start from scratch again, make a go of it?'

'Don't make fun of me. I think I have changed, Andy. I've had my fill of some things – illicit sex, for instance.'

He said: 'It isn't certain that David will come out at all, is it? They seem to be keeping things under control over there.'

'I've heard differently.' Her mouth twisted. 'From authoritative sources. I don't think it will be long before it all breaks up. He'll come, all right. And when he does . . . ?'

'I've learned to take troubles as they find me.' Her face flinched slightly. 'I'll worry about that at the time.'

'We could see each other occasionally,' she suggested, 'for a drink.'

'I don't think it's worth it. Sir Adekema might object. In fact, I'm fairly sure he would.'

She said impatiently: 'I don't care about that.'

'You should, I think.' She looked at him, and he looked back steadily. 'I really think you should, Carol.'

Carol telephoned him again to ask if he would like to see the boys, during their school holiday. Andrew said he would, and looked forward to the meeting with a mixture of pleasure and apprehension. But the boys themselves kept the occasion on a level removed from intimacy or emotion. They were polite and pleasant, but in the formal way of well-brought up boys towards strange adults. They did not talk very much, and responded with deferential briefness to his questioning. He spoke to Madeleine about it later:

'In the end, I got the idea that they were a bit ashamed to be seen with me.'

'Probably we're all over-sensitive, out here.'

'I *don't* think so.'

'After all, they're white themselves. You don't represent any shameful secret.'

'But the alien strain, perhaps – the thing which can't be assimilated. They may try to avoid looking in mirrors, but it's more difficult not to look at one's father.'

'Or one's mother?'

'Carol's part of the assimilation. She has a coal-black boy-friend.'

'Do they understand that? I suppose so. But don't they resent it?'

'Children are like lovers – they don't make moral judgements. Or they rationalize them to their own needs. Robin looked quite embarrassed when I sent them your love.'

'You think you've lost them?'

'Yes.'

'How bad is it?'

'Not as bad as I once thought it would be. They're well and happy. When you lose people, I think a lot of the bitterness is due to guilt: one could have done this or that, and one didn't. I don't have that. And it can't be easy for them. Adolescence is bad enough, without their particular problems. In that respect, I can't do anything but make matters worse. Perhaps in a few years, when they've come to terms with things, we'll be able to get together again.'

She nodded. 'You may be right. All the same, I'm sorry – that you've lost them now.'

'Not finally.'

'Even temporarily. One's children. Even without having any, I can see that.'

He said: 'I may still have other children. It's not impossible, is it?'

She looked at him gravely for a moment, before she smiled. 'Not at all impossible. Aren't we going out to the Kutisis tonight?'

'So I believe.'

'You ought to change.'

'There's time enough. I feel like a drink. Can I get you one?'

'All right. Something small. Anything.'

She was sitting in the window seat when he brought the drink to her. The long picture window looked out over the dull purple flatness of the Atlantic; it was half an hour since the sun had flamed down beyond that distant edge. The few small clouds in the sky were of a metallic blackness, their outlines iron hard against the softer shades of night. Stars were already starting, here and there, in the moonless sky.

'Pretty,' Andrew said.

'Yes.'

He sat down facing her. 'Have you heard anything from David lately?'

'I had a letter last week.'

'Anything of interest?'

'Not really. Quite apart from the censorship, he's not a good letter writer. He's frank in speech and reticent on paper.'

'The natural antithesis.'

'Is it? I suppose. I knew a writer once who could only be frank in letters.' There was a pause, and she went on: 'I haven't been showing you David's letters lately – is that something you mind?'

'No. But I wondered about it.'

'It started when we were in the shack. There was something in one letter which I read as hinting that he might be coming out here quite soon. Things were so miserable then . . . you were still weak from that fever . . . I thought it best not to show it to you.'

'In case I realized how much you wanted him to come?'

'How uncertain I was. Afterwards, with the next letter, there was a kind of inhibition; it seemed wrong to show you that one without having shown you the other. You know how these things are. I was waiting for you to ask.'

'And I didn't ask. Till now.' She looked at him quickly, and he said: 'I'm not asking anything else, Madeleine. I'm leaving things to take care of themselves.'

'They will.' There was a touch of sadness in her voice. 'Things work out if you leave them.'

'Yes.' He contemplated her profile as she looked out across the darkening sea. For all she withheld, she offered more security than he had ever known in another person. He took her hand. 'I'll go and change. Mustn't be too late for the Kutisis.'

The maid, Anthea, took the telephone call from Wing-Commander Torbock while they were out for the evening; he was in Lagos on a turn-round and would like to see them if it was possible. He would call round at the flat the following morning.

That was Saturday. 'Day by Day' was a week-day programme and in consequence Andrew had his week-ends free. They had planned to motor up-country to one of the game reserves, and Andrew was a little put out at having to cancel this. At the same time there was something intriguing in having a stranger call on them.

It was just after eleven when Anthea let him in. She announced him in the clear accents that had once echoed through Kensington drawing rooms: 'Wing-Commander Torbock, Ma'am.' Madeleine had tried to bring her to a less formal address and demeanour, but without effect. She had been starving when Madeleine found her and employed her, and fear had bitten deeply.

Torbock was a large red-faced man, in his early forties, with a generous but straggly moustache. He looked as though the heat bothered him.

'Do come in,' Madeleine said. 'We had your message. I'm Madeleine Cartwell, and this is Andy Leedon.'

'Thank you,' Torbock said. He produced a handkerchief and wiped the sweat off his brow. 'Pleasantly cool in here. Damned hot outside.'

Andrew said: 'Is it too early for a cooling drink?'

'Not with me,' Torbock said with relief. 'Thank you. Anything on ice.'

'We usually drink South African brandy. They're doing a whisky as well now, but I should warn you it's aged with an atomic poker, or something. Not bad, though.'

'Anything you're having. You can't get a damn thing in the Pale.'

Madeleine said: 'You are from London, then. I wondered about that.'

There was something about him, Andrew thought, which seemed familiar but old-fashioned. The moustache? The easy expansive way in which he lowered his bulk into an armchair? Torbock smiled, and Andrew recognized what it was: the unconscious swagger of the Anglo-Saxon in foreign parts. It marked him out from the other whites in Lagos. Of course, although he might have seen some of the changes, they would not have affected him. His ties were still with England.

'Yes,' he said cheerfully, 'that's my parish. For the moment, anyway.'

'Do you know my husband?' Madeleine said.

'Yes. My name's Peter, by the way. I know Davey quite well. We used to lower the odd noggin together, while there was still any to be had. In fact, this is the object of the jolly old exercise – he asked me to bring a letter out to you. Dodging the censor.'

Torbock produced his wallet. From a mass of papers, receipted bills, documents and such, he produced an envelope and gave it to Madeleine.

'Thank you,' she said.

She looked at the envelope for a moment without opening it. Andrew, as a distraction, said to Torbock:

'What do you think of our view?'

Torbock levered himself up out of the chair again, and walked across to the window, Andrew following him.

'Pretty good,' he said. 'Especially if you like sea. I'm for the mountains myself. I lift up mine eyes to the hills, and all that. But that's a very nice stretch of ocean you have. Not an ice-floe in sight.'

Madeleine said: 'You'd better see this, Andy.'

Her voice was quiet and controlled, but he saw the tenseness in her face as she held the letter out to him. He took it and read it.

Dear Maddie,

Peter Torbock has kindly undertaken to get this through to you without benefit of censorship. I think this renders him liable to summary execution or something, so be discreet. You won't need to be for long, because the last balloon of the present emergency is due to go up quite soon. Anyway, I wanted to get a straightforward letter to you while there's chance.

The plain fact, Maddie, is that I've decided to opt out of the exodus. There's nothing heroic in this: I've just decided that I'd rather stay here. Things are going to be very difficult, but I don't think they will be impossible. I've learned a few things over the past months which I expect to stand me in good stead. And you know how lazy and difficult I am about new things. Long after I became a prefect, long after I left school, I used to have bad dreams about becoming a fag again. I still do.

It relieves my mind a lot to know that you have all made the grade out there, despite the initial setbacks. Andy is a very good type, and I couldn't want you to be in better hands. Give Carol my regards if you run across her: that all seems very long ago now.

I cheated you to some extent in saying I would be coming out myself eventually. I know you'll forgive this, as you've forgiven all my other cheating in the past. And it's all worked out for the best, hasn't it?

All the best to Andy. Love,
David

While he was still looking at it, Madeleine said to Torbock:
'You have some idea of what's in the letter?'

'Fairly roughly. I take it he's breaking the news that he's decided to stay on there.'

'He talks about the last balloon going up.'

Torbock nodded, and hissed out breath through clenched teeth. 'The airport's closing down shortly. The Government's moving out, to the West Indies. Other big bods are heading in different directions south.'

'And the rest,' Andrew asked, 'the ones left behind?'

'They'll have to manage as best they can.' Torbock added quickly: 'The bright ones like old David will be all right.'

'How soon?' Madeleine asked. Torbock looked at her. 'How soon does the airport close?'

'I'm going back there tomorrow,' Torbock said. 'It's a dicey situation. Even as a pilot, I'm expendable.'

She said in a dull voice: 'Of course. I can see you have to be careful.'

Torbock finished his drink, and Andrew poured him another. He watched with interest and with no demur as the liquor mounted in the glass.

'Very soon,' he said as he took the glass. 'I think I can say that I don't expect to be returning to this particular oasis of culture.'

'But you're not staying in England yourself?'

Torbock shook his head. 'No. But I've managed to swing myself on to the Cape Town run. That's where I aim to settle.'

'What makes you choose the Union?' Andrew asked.

'I'm white,' Torbock said. 'I've seen the way the whites are being kicked around in the rest of Africa. Even those who've managed to sneak into the higher echelons have to box clever.' He grinned. 'No offence meant. And I've no qualifications. The intake is strictly black as far as Nigerian Airways is concerned. And Ghana Airways, and all the other Airways. It may be tough in South Africa, but I've more chance of winding up as something better than a lavatory attendant.'

He was shrewder, Andrew reflected, than he looked. He said:

'There's pretty certain to be a war, you know. And the South African whites are pretty heavily outnumbered, even in their own territory.'

'I've thought of that one, too. Numbers aren't everything. And even if they were . . .' He shrugged. 'My wife died a few years back. No children. I've no dependants I'm bothered about. If there is going to be a war, I'd rather be fighting with my own side. And I'd rather be *fighting*, if you get me. Even at my age I stand a chance of getting behind a stick in South Africa. They'll want men.'

'Try and miss this block,' Andrew said.

'I'll aim on it,' Torbock said gravely. 'That's the one sure way I know of keeping any place safe.'

'Another drink?'

Torbock shook his head. 'Not now. I'm meeting someone for lunch. Nice to have met you folks.' He glanced at Madeleine. 'Any message to take back?'

'Can I deliver it later? You're not going back till tomorrow?'

'Crack of dawn. Seven a.m. take-off. Till then I'm staying at the Sheraton.'

'I'll let you have it there,' Madeleine said. 'Thank you for everything.'

'No trouble,' Torbock said. 'Glad to help.'

Andrew saw Torbock out of the flat. Torbock nodded in appreciation of the automatic lift.

'You live in style here,' he said. 'Don't get me wrong about the South Africa business. I think I'd settle for Lagos if I thought I could make it.'

'Good luck, anyway,' Andrew said. 'At any rate, if the worst happens you'll still be in a wine-growing country.'

'Don't go for it,' Torbock said. 'I'm a beer man. Remember Charrington's bitter? Sometimes I wake at night in a cold sweat, realizing I'll never drink it again.'

'It's a bad world to brood in. Good-bye, Peter.'

'Bye, Andy.'

When he returned, Madeleine was tidying up the room. The activity, he suspected, was a defence against intimacy; but something had to be said. He poured himself a drink while he thought about this. At last, he said:

'He will be all right, you know.'

She did not answer at once. She arranged flowers in a vase: large brilliant tropical blooms of which he still did not know the name. Over her shoulder, she said:

'There was nothing for him to come out for, was there? No one. Carol had gone her own ways. And he knew I was in good hands.'

He saw what she meant: if her letters to David had been less cool, if she had shown him she still wanted him, that might have brought him out here. He said:

'I don't think he made the decision on those grounds.'

'Then on what?'

'I don't know. What do we make our decisions on? Bits and pieces of motive. Pride, uncertainty, fear of running risks.'

'And there are no risks there? Can't you imagine what's going to happen when order breaks down?'

'A different kind of risk. He's a very proud man, isn't he?'

She stared at the flowers without touching them. 'Yes, a very proud man.'

'At least, you know,' Andrew said. 'And know it's his own choice. Certainty is the important thing. Once one knows something beyond doubt, one can accept it.'

She turned towards him and, after a moment, smiled.

'Yes, that's true. The worst is being unsure.'

'Are you writing back to him?'

'I think so. Yes. A little later, when I've had time to think.'

He patted the place beside him on the sofa, and she came and sat down. She dropped her head in the hollow of his shoulder. He put a hand against her neck.

'One thing I want to say.'

'Mm.'

'There's some satisfaction that he's not coming out. No, relief's a better word. I'm not going to pretend about that. But I wish he had come, despite everything. Do you believe that?'

She moved away from him, and he thought he had offended her. He looked down and saw that her eyes were fixed on his face, her expression serious but not angry.

She said: 'I don't think I've ever liked another person as much as I like you, Andy.'

'It's something,' he said. He smiled. 'In fact, it's quite a lot. Anyway, it will have to do.'

Her eyes searched his, but she said nothing. Then she put her face up for him to kiss her.

A small noise awoke Andrew in the night. He looked towards Madeleine's bed and saw that she was standing beside it, her body white in the moonlight that came through the net curtains. He said to her:

'What is it?'

She came to him. 'Nothing. I'm just restless.'

'Come in here.'

'I'm going to the kitchen to make myself a drink. Go to sleep.'

'I'll come with you.'

She pushed him down gently. 'No point in two people being awake.' Her lips brushed softly against his face. 'Be good, and go to sleep.'

'My mother used to say that,' he said.

'I know. You told me.'

He watched her, already almost asleep, as she went quietly out of the room. It was quite light when he awoke again. He saw that her bed was empty, and looked at his watch. It was half past seven, and he knew at once, with a clarity that was like a gout of pain, what had happened; and that it was too late.

She had left her note on the coffee table in the sitting room, pinned down under the ivory gorilla they had bought together in the Idumagbo market. She had neat regular handwriting, a hand that concealed everything and told nothing.

Darling –

I've looked in on you from time to time. You've been sleeping peacefully, and still are. It's a quarter past six, and as soon as I've written this I will be driving out to the airport. Even if you wake just as I'm leaving, and find this, I don't think you could be there in time. Please, please don't try. I shall leave the car at the airport, and you can pick it up when you like.

Don't think too hardly of Peter Torbock. He was very much against it, but he gave way in the end. I'm afraid I used pressure: threats and such. And he's not coming back here anyway. He's getting me on board at the last moment, as a hostess.

Will you understand this? I think and hope you will. I couldn't let him stay there on his own while there was a chance of getting back to him.

Dearest Andy, I do wish there was time to tell you how grateful I am to you for everything, how fond I am of you, how much I'm going to miss you. I wish I could have told you all this, instead of leaving a note and sneaking away. But I felt you would have found some way of stopping me – you would, wouldn't you? – for my own good.

But I hate doing it this way, just as I hated deceiving you when you woke in the night. I wanted to come to you then. I wanted it very much.

Please forgive me. The best of good fortune go with you – and my love always.

Madeleine

He read it through quickly, his eye darting down the page, at once searching and avoiding. Then he went out to the kitchen. The table was prepared for breakfast: fruit in the bowl, the coffee machine ready, bread in the toaster. But only one place set.

He stared at all this for some time before going back to the sitting room. Then he read her letter through again, slowly and carefully.

5

Outside the New Moon Cabaret Café, at two o'clock in the morning, the winking neon cast regular patterns of light and shade on the ranks of parked bicycles, and on the relatively few cars that stood between the night-club and the waterfront. Across the lagoon gleamed the still brighter lights of the Marina. For the most part the well-to-do preferred the places that had sprung up there, on the island, or the clubs well outside the city on the Ibadan road. In this quarter things were noisier, more vigorous, more frequently violent, the prostitution more blatant, the criminals more petty and more conspicuous. The opposition newspapers campaigned, on and off, for a clean-up, but this was generally recognized as a formal exercise in piety.

Andrew, who was half drunk, parked the car with exaggerated care, and waited for Abonitu to come round and let him out. The car was the Nigra Master, the smaller of the two models of the Nigerian-produced saloon, and of extremely flimsy construction. He had wrenched off the inside door handle on the driver's side some days previously and had not yet got round to replacing it. He could have wound down the window but it seemed simpler to leave things to Abonitu.

Inside the Fervid Four were beating out their usual brand of Dixieland. The combination was drums, two trumpets, and electrically amplified piano, and even without microphones the effect would have been savage in a room as small as this. The microphones, in fact, were working very efficiently. Andrew and Abonitu made for a table in the corner furthest from the music. The waiter, a scar-faced Dutchman, reached it as soon as they did.

'Brandies,' Andrew said. 'Two, and large.'

A couple of girls moved towards the table as the waiter left it;

the blonde headed for Abonitu, the Negress for Andrew. He knew her slightly. Her name was Suzie for the purposes of her present life, and she was from the North – a Hausa and a Moslem. She came of quite a good family, and had been cast off for immorality. She was shrewd and intelligent, and although she had no great physical appeal for him he usually enjoyed her company. At present he was not in the mood for it.

'You treating tonight, Andy boss?' she asked him.

He pushed a note across the table. 'Go and buy yourself one, Suzie. We're two tired men.'

'That's when you need the woman's touch.'

He shook his head. 'Tomorrow night, maybe.'

She grinned and left them, taking the blonde with her. The waiter brought their drinks over – service was prompt here – and Andrew rattled the ice in his glass.

'The Albert Hall, Abo,' he said, 'coupled with the Albert Memorial.'

Abonitu raised his glass solemnly. They had already toasted that night the Houses of Parliament, the Lyon's Corner House at Tottenham Court Road, Nelson's Column, the Chelsea Flower Show, the British Museum Reading Room, the King's Road, Admiralty Arch, the Samuel Whitbread, Peter Pan's statue, the Imperial War Museum, and Selfridges. The joke seemed less and less funny, but Andrew continued with it compulsively.

'Handel's Water Music turned to ice,' Andrew said. 'The Prince Consort's fingers frozen to his copy of the Exhibition Catalogue.'

Abonitu said: 'I remember going to a Promenade Concert.'

'They were *déclassé* in my circle.'

'I walked across Hyde Park in a daze afterwards. The music, the excitement . . .'

'The fellowship of the arts,' Andrew said. 'And no colour bar.'

Abonitu smiled. 'I worked that out, too. I do not deceive myself much, Andrew.'

'Then you should acquire the habit. Man, you'll never be happy without it.'

'Physician, heal thyself.'

'I'm winning,' Andrew said. 'One has one's setbacks, but I'm winning.'

'By drinking too much. You make it hard on your friends. Must I get cirrhosis to solve your emotional problems?'

'Do you know a better solution?'

Abonitu stared at him solemnly for a moment. 'I have found one,' he said. '*In vino solvandum est*. Is that good Latin?'

'It would fool me. Come up with your solution, and let us expose it to the night air.'

The noise of the jazz had been forcing them to speak quite loudly. Now as the number reached its crescendo and cut off there was comparative quiet. Abonitu's voice sounded very loud:

'Have you heard about . . .'

He stopped speaking and looked foolish. Andrew said:

'About what?'

In a much quieter voice, Abonitu went on: 'About the expedition?'

'No,' Andrew said. He drank more brandy. 'Not that I recall.'

'Tessili told me.' Tessili was Abonitu's uncle, Minister of Finance in the present Government. 'It's a hush-hush business, Andrew.'

'They always are.'

'No, this one really is. There could be trouble if it got out.' He smiled wryly. 'My entire family kicked out of their jobs at least. Their friends also.'

'A good point. Perhaps you'd better keep it to yourself.'

'No. I must explain to you the solution. We run the same risks, anyway, and for you the penalty would be heavier. You know that no governing authority exists in Europe north of the Mediterranean?'

'Yes. I know.'

'But the Council of African States has garrisons in two ports.'

'Genoa and St Nazaire. I see the point in Genoa.'

'St Nazaire is the most northerly port that is likely to remain relatively free of ice in winter. It offers the only year-round point of entry for northern Europe.'

His head was fuzzy with drink, and beginning to ache from that and the empested atmosphere. The piano had begun to play again, quite softly, without the amplification. There was a little clapping, and some shouts of encouragement. The Cheltenham Trio were coming on. They were the speciality of the house, three red-headed European girls who stripped each other in a long-drawn routine involving both fighting and fondling. Despite the name, only one of them was English. Only one was a genuine red-head; the other two were dyed.

'Why northern Europe,' Andrew said, 'why in God's name northern Europe? Who wants a point of entry to a cemetery?'

'There are enough reasons. The base is worth keeping. Eventually, when we have more resources, we may be able to do something there.'

'The War comes first. Don't forget the War.'

'One must take a longer view,' Abonitu said seriously. 'But, to come back to these ports: they are controlled by the Council, and they control Europe. It will be difficult for any individual country to make a claim outside the Council. The operation and the responsibility are joint, and will remain so.'

'Until you fall out.'

'Not you, we.' He smiled. 'Remember you are an African now, Andrew. I do not think we will fall out over Europe, even when the South African problem has been settled. It would not be worth it. Europe will stay under joint administration. But the British Isles – are they part of Europe?'

'We never did settle that question. I beg your pardon: they never did. It's a bit late now.'

'It is important,' Abonitu insisted. 'The ports represent a claim on continental Europe, but there is no foothold in Britain. There has been no sovereignty there since the Government left the country.'

'Pack-ice all round the coast – five miles of it in places.'

'Exactly. But, as I have said, one requires to take the long view. And it is being taken, in more than one quarter.'

'What does that mean?'

'Ghana is preparing an expedition to England next year. They hope to find a southern port ice-free in late April or May. It is believed that there will be a competitive expedition from Egypt. There are even rumours of an expedition from South Africa, though that seems unlikely.'

'But you can't hold a base there.'

'That remains to be seen. We know very little of the conditions. There are ways in which the difficulties may have lessened.'

'The natives, you mean, will have killed each other off? I suppose you're right. I take it what you are driving at is that Nigeria plans to join in the race to plant the flag. Let's hope the various expeditions don't get too tangled up.'

'The difference,' Abonitu said, 'is that the others are planning for the late spring. We are going now, in winter.'

'Across that pack-ice? Or by air? You couldn't risk those landing fields with ordinary planes. Helicopters?'

'There is an impermanence about air expeditions. There would be many difficulties. We have another possibility.'

The smallest of the red-heads, while one of the others gripped her hands behind her back, was using her teeth to pull articles of clothing off the third. The Africans near the front were making cries of excitement and encouragement that drowned the piano. Andrew's head was throbbing heavily now.

'Britain,' Abonitu said, 'had the world's only Hovercraft squadron.'

Andrew remembered the headlines; the squadron had been stationed in the south, outside the Pale, and their Commander had taken them out of the country in advance of the break-up. They had headed for Ghana, but there had been some trouble there and they had come on to Nigeria. The story of the trek had been blazoned for a short time, and then dropped.

'They would never make it,' Andrew said. 'God knows how they got here in the first place. You can't launch a five-thousand-mile expedition with twelve Hovercraft.'

'Eleven,' Abonitu said. 'One of them cannot be salvaged. But not five thousand miles. A few hundred only. They will be shipped to St Nazaire. After that there is only Brittany and the Channel.'

It began to make sense.

'St Nazaire is under joint control. Aren't the representatives of the other states going to object?'

'If they had warning, there might be objections. But by the time they can think of objections the expedition will be well out of the joint control area. They can wrangle then, but it will be too late to do anything.'

'Fuel? Food? I doubt if they could carry both.'

'Not so much fuel. Enough to reach Southampton. We have information of a fuel dump there which was never used: things collapsed too quickly in that part. They can carry enough food for two months. After that the idea will be to pick supplies up from a ship which will get as far north as there is open water.'

'It sounds risky.'

'Yes. Will you go, Andrew?'

'In what capacity?'

'An expedition needs documentation. I am quite a good camera-man. You will pass as one, with my help. And my uncle is the Minister of Finance. I think it can be arranged.'

Andrew was silent. He felt suddenly sober, and torn between excitement and despair: it was possible, it was fantastic, and it could lead to nothing. His eyes smarted. In the centre circle two of the girls were in mock-battle with the third, one sprawled on the floor clutching her feet, the other locking her arms and tearing at what was left of her clothes.

'We will make a documentary,' Abonitu said. 'Think of it. Black and white for the streets festooned with ice, weighted down with snow. And colour for the sunsets, the dying crimson glow over the frozen Thames. And a story, perhaps. You will find your lost love in the land of eternal winter.'

Andrew stared at him, blinking his eyes. 'Can you do it?'

Abonitu nodded his head. 'I can do it.'

'We'll drink to it, then.' He picked up his glass. 'Except that we seem to be out of drink.'

'We can fix that, too,' Abonitu said.

He flicked a finger, and the waiter came towards them at the trot.

The hangover with which Andrew woke the following morning was not the worst he could remember, but it was bad enough. He took four codeine tablets and made himself black coffee. He was drinking this when the telephone rang. It was Abonitu.

'The idea I suggested last night,' he said. 'What do you think of it now?'

'In the first place,' Andrew said, 'nothing planned by Nigerians is likely even to get off the ground. If it does, I can think of a dozen or more ways in which it's likely to crack up. The whole thing will be a fiasco. We would be risking our necks to no purpose at all. The city of your dreams is dead, Abo, and probably Madeleine is, too. If she isn't, I could never hope to find her in that wilderness.'

'Yes,' Abonitu said. 'I thought of all this, too.' He paused. 'Afterwards I saw my uncle, and fixed things. We leave for St Nazaire in two weeks. Is that O.K.?'

'Yes,' Andrew said wearily. 'That's O.K.'

PART THREE

The *Yoruba Diadem* docked late in the morning, and the eleven Hovercraft were off-loaded two hours after that. The savage whine of the turbines being tested split the cold quiet air of the port, and brought Council Control Officers hurrying to the quay. Andrew stood to one side watching while they argued among themselves and with General Mutalli, the leader of the expedition. There was dismay, and some anger, demonstrated in gesticulation and shouted protests: the shouting was not merely emotional for the noise of the engines was deafening. The Egyptian and Algerian Officers, it appeared, wanted the Hovercraft force impounded, pending a general Council decision. Mutalli outrode the storm with smiling courtesy. An hour later, the protests were still being made as the first Hovercraft slid forward, snow powdering into the air behind it, and made for the checkpoint. The barrier swung away as they approached it. Before four o'clock, Lagos time, the squadron was clear of the town and moving north across the frozen fields of Brittany.

Apart from Andrew, there were two other whites in the expedition force, two engineer-mechanics from the original Hovercraft squadron. Their names were Carlow and Prentice. Carlow was a thin young man with a continual sneer and a small greasy moustache. Prentice was shorter and heavier, a man about thirty who looked stupid and talked little. They kept to themselves, ignoring Andrew. On the voyage they had seemed to be drunk, most of the time, on Nigerian ersatz-gin. This relief would no longer be open to them, and Andrew wondered how they would take the deprivation. He neither liked nor trusted them.

There were just over a hundred Nigerians, the great majority of them picked officers and sergeants from the Nigerian Army. All were younger than Andrew; even Mutalli, a genial Ibo warrior, impressively tall and broad, was in his middle thirties. Discipline was easy and the general atmosphere cheerful and optimistic; there was no abating of this as the ship had steamed into colder waters. They laughed at each other as they paraded in Arctic kit, and went on laughing. When plans were talked over, although the final decision lay with Mutalli, all joined in with suggestions and criticisms.

Opinions had differed over the best route they should follow to England. There was a group, a majority Andrew thought, which was anxious to keep the sea crossing as short as possible, and argued for going overland to Calais before striking out across the Channel. The opposition was more concerned with the danger from the bands of starving Frenchmen who were known to be roaming the territory and who attacked, from time to time, the defences at St Nazaire. Their suggestion was for putting directly to sea and continuing on water, with suitable night camps on remote beaches, as long as possible – an extreme view wanted the approach to London itself to be made by way of the Thames estuary. Mutalli, when they had argued each other to a standstill, elected for a compromise. They would go almost due north, reaching the sea between St Brieuc and Dinard, and continue northwards to England. They would thus miss the worst of the local tribes, who were thought to have largely abandoned the Brittany peninsula, and would thereafter face no human hazards before reaching the Dorset coast. It seemed reasonable. It also represented, Andrew reflected, the most direct route to England. He had already realized that impatience lay not far below Mutalli's smiling surface. He hoped his judgement did not too much depend on it.

The weather was good – cold but very clear – and they made fair progress. After a little over an hour's journey, the leading Hovercraft, in which Mutalli himself was travelling, pulled away to a small piece of rising ground to their right, and the remainder followed. They halted in the prearranged close circle. Andrew and Abonitu were together in the last machine.

'We halt for the night,' Abonitu said. 'It is early.'

Andrew said, with some relief: 'Better than leaving it too late. The dusk's drawing in.'

'We have headlights.'

'Yes. I was afraid Mutalli would think of that.'

'Mutalli,' Abonitu said with quiet scorn, 'fears the dark. The Ibo are primitive. They circumcise their women, and are afraid to make love by daylight, or on newly ploughed land. And the night, apart from being the time for lying with their women, who are hideous as well as unresponsive, is for the Leopard men. He probably fears the juju of the dead Frenchmen.'

'You may be right,' Andrew said. 'But I'm in favour of an early halt myself. We're not in so great a hurry as all that, and I prefer caution in strange territory.'

Three guards were appointed for the night, on a three-shift basis of two hours on and four off. Andrew was missed off this roster, but both Carlow and Prentice were included – not, he noted, on the same shift. He overheard them talking to each other while the evening meal was being prepared, Prentice grousing and Carlow commenting, with a whining sarcasm, on what they claimed to be the unsoldierly qualities of the Nigerians.

The night passed without incident, and the day dawned clear and cloudless. There was some confusion and consequent delay in breaking camp and the sun was fairly high by the time they resumed the progress north. Not long after they started, they had their first glimpse of the natives – a group of seven or eight who scattered away as the Hovercraft came up. Andrew thought they were all men, but it was difficult to be sure since they were voluminously swathed in clothes. One of them, possibly bolder than the others, halted some three hundred yards away and stood watching as the squadron passed. A few miles further on they saw smoke rising from a chimney in a village to the west of their path. These things apart, the landscape was empty of human life. Occasionally animals moved against the snow – dogs, a fox, an unfamiliar large bird that rose ungainly and flapped heavily away – and towards the end of the morning a flock of gulls wheeled down from the north and hovered round them. They reached the sea half an hour after that.

Looking at the map with which he had been supplied – an old Michelin – Andrew concluded that they were probably some miles west of Cap Fréhel. The beach was as deserted as the land behind them. Ice stretched out in front of them, but some distance away there was the blue of open water. Nothing moved there. In the entire scene, the only living things were the men themselves and the circling gulls.

They brewed up their midday meal on the spot. Andrew expected that they would push on as soon as it was over, but there was further delay, consequent this time on the re-emergence of the anti-sea party among the Nigerians. At the very least, these wanted a halt to be made here, and the journey across the Channel begun the following morning, when they would have a full day ahead. Those who favoured pressing on pointed out that there was close on four hours of daylight remaining, and that, with the cruising speed of the Hovercraft something like fifty knots over clear water, they would have at least an hour in hand. It was objected that there might be a breakdown. The reply was made that the Hovercraft could float indefinitely and that a night on the open water was preferable in many ways to a night in open country such as this. But the weather might break. Unlikely, argued the opposition: the barometer remained high, the sky itself was almost without cloud.

It was Abonitu finally who crystallized matters. He said, after being silent throughout the wrangle:

'Time is going by. If we continue much longer talking, there will be no point in going on today.'

Mutalli nodded his large head. 'You are right. I think we will start at once.' He brushed aside the beginning of a further protest. 'We start. No more discussion.'

Carlow and Prentice were sitting near Andrew, and he saw them exchange looks.

'Proper bloody Karno's mob,' Prentice muttered.

'Hope you can flogging well swim, china,' Carlow said. 'You may have to.'

'Black bastards,' Prentice said unemotionally.

'Watch it.'

'They're too bloody busy gabbing to pay attention.'

'Watch it, all the same.'

Andrew caught the darting glance which Carlow gave him, and construed it: they had marked him down as possibly dangerous, presumably because of his friendship with Abonitu. He was surprised how little the realization affected him. Conscious as he was of his own whiteness of skin, he felt no sympathy with these two. They had probably, he reflected, picked that up, too.

The ice was thick for about a mile offshore; after that it cracked under the pressure of the downward jets and the Hovercraft, fanning out in line, left broad splintered channels in their wake. These merged into the open sea, clear and untroubled and of a bright sharp blueness. But there was haze where sea and skyline met, and it was not long before the coast of France was lost behind them. There was only the sky and the sea and the eleven vessels scattering rainbow-edged spray. The chatter of voices dropped. This was a different loneliness, a different immensity, from anything the Africans had encountered before.

Over the gently rippled contours of the sea, the Hovercraft made a better speed than they had done previously, and in this a relative weakness in the craft on which Andrew and Abonitu travelled became more evident. Gradually it slipped behind the other ten. They had fallen back, on leaving the ice, into column, and the distance separating the last Hovercraft from its next in line stretched out from fifty yards to a hundred and then to two hundred.

Andrew said: 'We ought not to lose touch.'

Abonitu nodded. 'They must see what is happening, and reduce speed.'

'Igmintu's craft is the only one that has a view of us. If they aren't looking out . . .'

'They will. It is quite light still.'

'No means of signalling between craft,' Andrew said. 'Another little flaw in the advance planning.'

The sea-mist seemed to rise quite suddenly out of the level blue ahead of them. At first it was no more than a change of colour in the water, a muddy greyness where the two blues met, but it broadened and took on height. Andrew thought that the craft in front would check, perhaps come to a halt for consideration of the altered conditions, but they went on. Their driver had swung off course to the west, slipping out of column in the hope of becoming more conspicuous, and they could see all the remaining ten. They saw them slip, one by one, into the wall of mist, and disappear.

Andrew said: 'We ought to back-track. If we get into that lot . . .'

Abonitu said urgently to the driver: 'Cut the engines! We will wait here in the open. They will come back for us.'

'We are a long way behind.'

'Never mind that. There is no sense in going in there.'

The man kept his hands on the control bar and made no attempt to slacken speed. Tendrils of mist swirled less than a hundred yards ahead of them.

'We must halt,' Abonitu said.

The man made no answer. Looking at his face, Andrew read fear: the fear of being left behind in this strange cold world of the north. He whispered to Abonitu:

'Get the controls away from him. It's the only hope.'

Abonitu hesitated. While he did so, the mist thickened, the tendrils, twisting and multiplying, sprang up behind and all round them, and the sky itself turned grey. Abonitu reached over and cut the engine, and the greyness seemed to be a silence, pressing in. They listened, and could hear the whine of the other craft, remote and fading.

Abonitu turned to him. 'And now?'

'I don't know. I don't know what Mutalli's thinking. He may be assuming the mist is patchy and that he can break through into clear water again.'

'I think so. He will be anxious not to delay, here on the sea. And probably he does not know we have dropped behind.'

The driver, his nerve somewhat recovered, said:

'You had no right to stop the engine. I am in charge of the engine.'

Abonitu shrugged. 'Go ahead, then.' He turned to Andrew. 'Surely, if we steer north by the compass . . .'

'There's probably nothing else we can do now.'

The engine started again, drowning the distant sound of the other craft. They plunged ahead, but with the mist all round there was little evidence of motion. Andrew, for the first time, felt tension beginning to mount in him. It was true that these waters no longer carried shipping, but there was always the chance of icebergs; a collision with one of those at something better than forty knots could only mean disaster. And there were reefs around here. Their course had been planned to take them clear of the Channel Isles but that did not necessarily mean they would be clear of the jagged rocks exposed at low water.

There was brightness, a softening and a glow, lost and caught and lost again. For a moment he saw the water clear for perhaps twenty yards ahead. The mist was patchy. Oddly enough, the brief moments of visibility were more frightening than the grey blankness had been. Andrew said to Abonitu:

'I don't like this.'

Before he could reply, the veil split again, the split this time widening and showing open water all round them. The mist stood off on either side; by some atmospheric freak they were in a channel between two banks of fog. The roar of engines dropped as the driver slackened off the throttle. It was an automatic act, indicating, Andrew guessed, his reluctance to plunge back into darkness from this oasis of light. The Hovercraft came round, too, as he swung on the control bar, moving slowly along the lane of visibility which ran in an easterly direction from their original course.

Abonitu said: 'If we go far off course it may be difficult to find the others again.'

There was floating ice ahead; nothing substantial, but it was the first they had seen since leaving the French coast. Cakes of it spun away from the Hovercraft's jets. Andrew stared out over it. He thought the channel was narrowing. After a few minutes, he was certain. On either side the mist rolled closer. This time it was the driver himself who stopped the engines. Silence immediate, and clear cut. Andrew listened but there was no sound at all except the slap of waves. The rest of the squadron was out of earshot.

The driver said nervously: 'I can't hear nothing. You hear anything?'

'I think we should press on to the north,' Abonitu said. 'If we do not find them before dark . . .'

There was silence while this sank in, followed by a burst of argumentative chatter. Andrew made an effort to master his annoyance at their volubility and their unconcealed nervousness. He saw Abonitu shrug his shoulders. Then he saw something else: further on the mist was lifting again. The view was still hazy, but there was a visibility of two or three hundred yards. He pointed this out to the others. The driver said with relief:

'O.K. We push on.'

'That's still west,' Abonitu warned. 'We're going off course.'

No attention was paid to this. The engines started up again and the Hovercraft began to move; not at full speed but at between ten and fifteen knots. The mist continued to thin out in that direction and, after a time, on the starboard bow also. About a quarter of an hour after re-starting the engines they came out into clear air.

The line of mist stretched north-east and south-west behind them. In front the sea was open to the horizon; and on the horizon there was a smudge of land.

'An island,' Abonitu said. 'One of the Channel Isles. But which one, Andrew?'

'Jersey or Guernsey, I should think. Too big for Alderney.'

The buzz of comment and suggestion broke out again. The general drift emerged quickly enough. After a couple of hours on the water and the encounter with the mist, there was a strong inclination to get back on land. Abonitu argued the importance of trying to regain contact with the rest of the force before nightfall, but without much conviction. Unless they went back into the mist, they would be bound to deviate further from their original course. In the end, he dropped his opposition. The Hovercraft slid on, at full throttle now, towards the distant island.

They met more floating ice a mile or two offshore, but the shore itself was relatively ice-free; the tides were fierce here and would keep the ice from accumulating. As they approached they saw what at first looked like icebergs, but proved to be granite reefs coated and festooned with ice. South of these, though, there was an easy approach to a shelving beach. They made their landfall there, halting the Hovercraft in the lee of a sea-wall. This, too, was of granite, but granite shaped into blocks and the blocks set together by human hands. There was no sign of life, and the wall, in one place had been breached by the sea.

The Africans, including the driver, climbed off the Hovercraft and scrambled up through the hole in the sea-wall.

Abonitu jumped down, his boots crunching ice and pebbles. 'Well, we are on English soil, Andrew.'

'Not English. British, perhaps. The Channel Isles had their own government.'

'What difference? Come on. We might as well follow the others.'

They emerged on to a road, plainly visible as such beneath its covering of snow. The snow lay even and unmarked. On the other side there was open land, a field perhaps, and, further off, houses. They gave no signs of habitation. The nearer ones had obviously been abandoned for some time. The landscape's desolation matched that of the Brittany coast they had left behind them. Andrew had a feeling of despair: it would all be like this, all a winter ruin. He had known there was no hope of finding her, but the knowledge was starker, barer now.

Abonitu touched his arm. 'That looks like a pillbox over there. You think they built defences against sea attack?'

Andrew shook his head. 'Not the islanders. The Germans. They occupied the islands during the last war, remember.'

There was general agreement on the desirability of brewing up coffee; the portable stove was brought up and snow was collected for melting. One of the Africans stood watch on top of the sea-wall. Andrew himself looked out to sea at intervals, but with no real expectation of seeing the rest of the squadron. One would hear them, anyway; the silencers had been abandoned for better working efficiency.

He was staring seawards when a cry was raised:

'Folks coming.'

He turned round. A group was advancing towards them along the road from the south. There was more than a score of men, mostly carrying rifles. A little in advance of the rest was a man on horseback. An attendant trudged alongside him through the snow: he seemed to have no weapon, but he was holding a short pole from which fluttered a rag of white.

'They look peaceful,' Abonitu said. 'But keep your weapons at the ready.'

The newcomers halted about ten yards from the Nigerian party. The horse, Andrew saw, was a cart-horse not a cavalry steed, but it made the impression that presumably was intended. Even on his feet the rider would have been a big man; on horseback he towered over the others, dominating the scene. He looked to be in his early forties; he had a heavy black curly beard, streaked with white. The fur coat he was wearing looked as though it might have been made up out of two women's coats. His voice was the only thing not in keeping – thin and reedy and cracking a little, though not, Andrew guessed, with nervousness.

He said: 'All right, Colonel. Do your stuff.'

The man with the white flag was older, in his late fifties or early sixties. He was badly clad, and looked cold. He said, in a tired voice but one that retained the clipped military accent of the British officer class:

'I present His Excellency, the Governor and Bailiff of Guernsey. Kindly state your purpose in making an unauthorized landing on these shores.'

Abonitu said: 'We are *part* of the Nigerian Expeditionary Force to Britain.' The word was lightly but unmistakably stressed. 'We are temporarily detached from the rest of our squadron and seeking shelter for a while. We intend no harm, and shall do no damage.'

The man on horseback ignored him; his eyes were on Andrew.

'You're white,' he said. 'What are you doing in this outfit?'

'The same as the rest,' Andrew said. 'I'm a member of the expedition.'

'Moving on soon?'

'In the morning, at the latest.'

'That thing you've got there. That's a Hovercraft, eh?'

From where they stood, the craft was out of sight behind the sea-wall. Probably they had been seen while still out to sea. That would account for the promptness with which this investigating force had appeared.

'Yes,' he said. 'It's a Hovercraft.' He thought it advisable to pick up Abonitu's cue. 'Part of a squadron.'

'And you got lost, eh? Engine trouble?'

'We ran into sea-mist.'

'Not used to the sea, I reckon.' He gave a piercing whistle through his teeth. 'You don't keep much of a watch, either.'

There were scrambling noises. Heads appeared above the sea-wall, figures in the gap which they had used to get up from the beach. A man with a sporting rifle jumped up easily beside the sentry on the wall, and stood grinning at him. Andrew understood what had happened. While the main party had been advancing along the road, under the flag of truce, another party had been sent silently along the beach. They were cut off from the Hovercraft. They would have to fight their way back to it, and they were outnumbered and surrounded.

He said, striving to lend his voice authority:

'This is a peaceful scientific expedition. We're not a military body.'

'But you've got guns, eh? Nice-looking automatics. Plenty of ammo, too, I reckon.'

He exchanged glances with Abonitu. The other Africans had been badly disconcerted by the emergence of the force behind them, but Abonitu looked unworried. It was he who said:

'We have weapons for defensive purposes only.'

The man on the horse said amiably: 'I was talking to the white man, Sambo.' To Andrew, he said: 'That smells like coffee you were brewing up when we came along. Haven't smelt that in months.'

'We're tightly rationed,' Andrew said. 'But we'll be glad to spare you a couple of tins.'

'That's very civil. Tell you what, you come and be my guest tonight. You'll do better than camping out in the snow.'

His eye on Abonitu, Andrew saw him nod his head slightly. The situation, from their point of view, was desperate enough; it was obviously better to try to talk their way than fight their way out of it. Another idea struck him. He said:

'Are your headquarters far from here,' – he paused slightly – 'your Excellency?'

'Other side of the island. Three miles, maybe.'

'Perhaps we could run you round there in the Hovercraft?'

The bearded face grinned down at him. 'That's a fine idea, providing you can take my men as well.'

He had thought that, once they were on the Hovercraft, there might be some opportunity of establishing a supremacy, but the Africans were too unready and the Governor's men too alert for the risk to be worth taking. Andrew took the controls himself, the usual driver raising no objection, and the Governor stood at his side watching intently. He had left the horse and a handful of his men on the road to make their way back overland: the remainder came with him, keeping a close look-out over the Africans, whom they outnumbered three to one.

They put out a hundred yards or so to sea and traversed the northern tip of the island. There were places where it would have been possible to take the craft on shore and cut across country, but Andrew ignored them. It was important, he felt, to give as little indication of the vessel's power as need be. With the same motive, he refrained from opening up the engines. They cruised at under ten knots, and as a result it was almost an hour before they came to the harbour of St Peter Port. The sun was almost down and mist, which already shrouded the smaller islands to the east, was coming up from the sea and rising among the terraced houses of the town.

The important thing was that there was a living town here. They could see movements in the streets – there was even smoke rising from a chimney somewhere – and faces looked down as the Hovercraft eased into the inner harbour. The tide was right out and the harbour bottom lay exposed, mud littered with cracked shelves of ice. Andrew brought the craft alongside the sloping granite ramp that led up to the town, and cut the engines.

'Come ashore,' the Governor said. 'We'll put a guard on for you. A good one.'

It was a difficult moment. Andrew said:

'I'd rather leave the men here.' He caught the Governor's wary eye, and said firmly: 'I'll bring my lieutenant, but I'd feel happier leaving the others on board.'

'O.K., Captain. Bring your lieutenant, and leave the others.' The acquiescence was immediate and showed, Andrew realized, that the Governor did not, at this stage, want violence if it could be avoided. 'We'll put a guard on as well,' he went on. 'She's the kind of job should be looked after, eh?'

Abonitu said to the others: 'Stay here. We'll be back in the morning.' He went to the stores and brought out two pound tins of coffee. 'Hope you'll accept these, your Excellency,' he said gravely.

'Take the coffee from Sambo, Colonel,' the Governor said. 'Coffee after dinner tonight. Take you back to old times, eh?' He laughed. 'You can come and have a sniff at my cup.'

They made their way to the Governor's residence, which proved to be a small second-class hotel in the town, still having the A.A. and R.A.C. recommendation signs swinging outside.

'I lived in Government House for a bit,' the Governor said. 'Too damn big and draughty for the winters we have now. You can't keep it warm. This place is different.' He led them into what seemed to have been a cocktail bar, nodding his head to the saluting sentry on the door. There was a fireplace, and a fire stacked up with sawn chunks of furniture. 'Take your things off and sit down, eh? Make yourselves at home. Drop of Scotch, Captain?'

'Very welcome,' Andrew said. 'Thanks.'

'Colonel! Scotch for me and the Captain. You can lick the cork.'

The Colonel brought drinks from behind the bar for the two men. There was no suggestion of offering one to Abonitu.

'Let's have a look at that bottle, eh?' said the Governor. The older man brought it to him and held it up in silence for inspection. 'Got to watch the level,' the Governor said. He grinned. 'Pinching my whisky's punishable by death, but you've got to watch it all the same. Here's to your very good health, Captain.'

'And yours, your Excellency.' Andrew sipped the whisky. It was a pungent malt, possibly Laphroaig. 'Do you have much of this left, sir?'

The big man winked. 'That would be telling. Enough for me and my special friends for a year or two. I can offer you a claret with your dinner tonight, as well. The Colonel used to be quite one for claret in the old days, eh, Colonel? He can pour it well. I let him have the bottle once she starts running dregs, but he still pours it well. How are things down in Africa, Captain?'

Andrew said: 'Not too bad.'

'You'll need to watch it down there. All those blacks. They'll bear watching, eh?' He downed his whisky in a gulp. 'Come on, Colonel. You can see an empty glass when it's under your nose, can't you?'

By the time dinner was ready, the Governor had downed six large Scotches – he had ordered Andrew's glass replenished twice – and was speaking more loudly and less precisely. At one point, he went out noisily to the lavatory, leaving Andrew and Abonitu alone with the Colonel. Andrew said to him:

'Your rank, Colonel – that's an official one, I take it.'

'Yes, sir.'

'But the Governor – he's not had military experience? Not as an officer, anyway?'

The Colonel hesitated. 'Not prior to the Fratellini Winter.'

'What did he do before that?'

The hesitation this time was even more protracted. He had been a commanding figure once, Andrew saw, but he was thin and stooped and wore spectacles from whose rims some of the tortoise-shell casing had stripped away. He said at last, his voice clipped:

'He was in my employ. A gardener and handyman.' He looked at Andrew bleakly. 'The connection has been a useful one to me, as you can see.'

Dinner was announced by a young woman in a maid's dress. Andrew had expected uniformed flunkies and this surprised him. The caress the Governor gave her as she came up to his chair explained things. He said to the Colonel:

'Take Sambo along to the kitchen and see he gets some grub, eh? Then you can come back and look after us.'

They ate in what had been the hotel dining room; the décor was typical and one wall still carried a framed list of instructions on times for meals. The maid served them with a rich-looking brown soup in which lumps of meat floated.

'Seal meat,' the Governor explained. 'We get quite a few around the islands these days. Not bad if you can get it cooked properly.' He drank with splashing vigour. 'Not bad, eh? There you are, Colonel. Sambo fixed up?'

'Yes, your Excellency.'

'You can start pouring that claret, then.'

The maid returned with small dishes of fish in a white sauce. The Governor waved his away.

'Give me some more soup.' He nodded at Andrew. 'You get tired of fish, eh? You want any more soup?'

'No, thanks. I'll have the fish.'

'Just as you like.' The Colonel carefully poured a few drops of claret into the wine glass by his plate, and he lifted it and sucked the wine in. 'Pour it out, Colonel.' To Andrew, he explained. 'I never used to like wine, but once you get used, it's not bad, eh? Have a go at yours, Captain.'

Andrew said: 'It's very good.'

'Eat your fish, then. Leave some room for the next course, though. It's a special one.'

It was meat, well roasted and cut into slices from, Andrew guessed, a shoulder. But it was not beef. He looked inquiringly at the Governor, who was watching him with drunken amusement.

'I can't place it,' Andrew said.

'Polar bear! We've had a few reported – they come down on the bergs – but this is the first we've killed. Not bad, eh? There's a lot of meat on him.'

'Very good,' Andrew said, 'but these surprise me more.'

He indicated the roast potatoes and greens which had also been put on his plate. The vegetables were fresh.

The Governor laughed in his thin voice, and looked at Andrew slyly.

'Not bad, are they? I never did like tinned stuff.'

'How do you manage it?'

'We'll come to that later. Colonel, my glass is empty again! Get weaving, eh?'

They retired for coffee and brandy to what the Governor called his study. It had probably been the hotel smoking room. Shelves had been fitted and filled with books, a good part of them gaudy paperbacks. A wood fire was burning here, too. They sat in armchairs before it, and the Governor stirred a large dollop of cream into his coffee. He said:

'All right, Colonel. You can trot along now, eh? I'll give you a ring if I want you.'

Andrew said, as the door closed: 'You seem very comfortable here, sir.'

'Never mind sirring. You can call me Emil. What's your name, Captain?'

'Andrew. Andy.'

'Pour yourself some brandy, Andy.' He laughed at the rhyme. 'You can pour me a tot, too. Hine Grande Champagne. I've got a few bottles of that laid away, too. You know, it's not a bad life here. We're organized. That's taken some planning, mind.'

'I'm sure it has.'

'This island's a triangle – seven by seven by ten miles. Not much ground, eh? And before the Fratellini Winter we had something like forty-five thousand packed on it. Not much of a proposition, eh?'

'How many now?'

'I can tell you to the last one. Five hundred and forty-five. And eighteen kids expected before summer – four of them mine.'

Andrew said: 'And the other forty-four thousand five hundred? That must have taken some organizing, too.'

'And without bloodshed. Well, very little. There was a bit of fighting at the start, while we were taking over. But none after that.'

He paused, and Andrew waited for him to go on. The Governor settled into his chair and stared at the fire with reflective satisfaction.

'We worked it out the island could run to about five hundred. That meant getting rid of the rest. Not easy, eh? Even if we'd wanted to kill 'em off, I doubt if we'd have been able to.'

'So?'

'We split 'em up in batches for a starter. The English settlers first, apart from the Colonel. Then the growers, the States deputies, the shopkeepers. Then all the parishes except St Sampson's and Vale – we were based in St Sampson's at the time. It worked very well.'

'What did you do with them once you'd got them in batches.'

The Governor laughed. 'We deported 'em! That's something you can do on an island. We didn't have enough boats to spare, but we got them building rafts on the west coast. We rigged sails on the rafts and put them out when there was a goodish wind from the north-east. They could reckon on making France with a bit of luck, eh?'

'With a bit of luck. You did this with all of them – the children, too?'

He said with slight and shrill belligerence: 'What would you have done? We gave them a chance, didn't we? We had kids, too. It was our kids or theirs.'

'Yes,' Andrew said. 'I see that. They didn't resist?'

'Give people something to hope for, and they'll go when they're pushed.' He spoke as though it was something he had learned by heart; Andrew could well believe that both the truism and the strategy had been worked out by someone else. 'And they went in batches, remember. People thought each batch was the last one, that we were going to let the others stay.'

'Even with numbers down to five hundred, it can't be easy to keep things going.'

'We don't do badly. In fact, it's easier than we thought it would be. There's more fish in these waters now – we only used to get cod here once in a way, but they run in shoals these days. And the seals. And there's whale, though we haven't brought one in yet. And then there's the glass.'

'Glass?'

'Guernsey's full of greenhouses – always has been, for the tomato trade. We get a short summer now, but we can use it. We can't do much heating, of course, but you can do a lot with cold glass. And where we could, we've double-glazed, cannibalizing from the less useful frames. We can grow potatoes, greens, fodder for the cattle. We even keep a few on tomatoes! We don't do much wheat – people can manage as well on potatoes.'

'It sounds like a well-run economy.'

'Not bad, eh, Andy? The others don't live too badly, and for me and my pals there are a few luxuries. And we've no worries. You're the first lot that's landed here armed since the crack-up, and we were ready for you, eh? It was a bit lucky I was over on the west coast when you were spotted, but we keep a force over there all the time.'

Andrew said: 'You took us by surprise.'

'It was easy.' He jerked a finger towards the brandy bottle, and

Andrew poured more into his glass. 'That'll do. That's a nice job you've got, that Hovercraft. I remember seeing them on the telly in the old days. Fuel?'

'Enough to get us to England. We know of a dump there which we think hasn't been touched. And they're sending a tanker up from Nigeria later on.'

'As it happens, we have a fair load of diesel here. They got stocks in when the first pinch came.'

'We have enough to get us to England,' Andrew repeated.

'There's nothing on the mainland.' The Governor spoke decisively. 'Nothing but a few gangs of yobbos. We've had one or two come over in small boats. There's no civilization left there.'

'What happened to them – the ones who came in small boats?'

The Governor smiled. 'We gave them three days' grace and sent them packing. You've got to be really useful to fit in with our scheme of things. Someone like you, Andy.'

'What makes me useful – the Hovercraft?'

Leaning forward, the Governor spat into the fire. 'You know the Channel Isles?' he asked.

'Not Guernsey. I spent a week on Jersey once.'

'There's the four islands worth talking about. Guernsey, Jersey, Alderney, and Sark. Sark's no good now – just a bloody frozen plateau. Same's true of Alderney. No glass worth mentioning. There's no glass on Jersey, either, but it's a warmer island. Guernsey slopes away from the sun, Jersey slopes towards it. I reckon you can still grow a little in the valleys – enough, anyway. And there's boats come out from Jersey, fishing, so they've got some kind of organization.'

'Haven't you asked them about it?'

The Governor laughed. 'We didn't like Jerseymen much to begin with. Less than the English, even, but at least they kept to their own island. Our ships steer clear of theirs, and they steer clear of ours. But there's going to be trouble one day. Twenty miles of water's no great distance. That's what we keep a guard on for – we're not worried about the Frenchies or the English, but the Jerseymen might try something. Unless we try something first.'

'And you think the Hovercraft would help?'

'I'll tell you,' the Governor said. 'When the look-out brought word at Cobo and I looked through the glasses and saw that craft of yours, it put the fear of God up me. It was almost as bad as seeing a battle fleet steaming up the Russell. It wasn't until you had beached and I saw that handful of black monkeys cavorting about that I began to get my breath back. There's a dozen ways we could use it against Jersey.'

'You think it would make you Governor of the two islands?'

'I think it would put my mind at rest.' He grinned at Andrew. 'I'd need a good Deputy on one of them, wouldn't I? How d'you fancy running your own island? A bit better than living with a treacherous lot of blacks, eh? And we could lay on the necessaries. Can't offer you virgins, but I can spare you one or two models nicely run in.'

Andrew tried to weigh up the man without paying too obvious attention to him. The one thing he was sure of was that it would be dangerous, perhaps fatal, to cross him. He said:

'It sounds very tempting. Can I sleep on it?'

'Sure you can, Andy! We'll have another chat in the morning.'

'My crew?'

'I've told you – I'm against bloodshed. We're out of raft wood, but we can spare them one of the old fishing smacks. There's some that aren't worth keeping. Perhaps they can sail it back to Africa.'

Andrew laughed. 'Yes. Perhaps they can.'

The Governor wrapped his hands together to make a huge conjoined fist.

'I like you, Andy,' he said. 'You're the kind of man I can talk to. I like to have somebody to talk to.'

'What about the Colonel?'

'I don't keep him to talk to. I keep him to pour my drinks.' He rose unsteadily to his feet and pressed a bell-push above the fireplace. 'And take my boots off when I come in from a heavy day.'

The Colonel knocked and came in. The Governor said:

'My bed ready, Colonel?'

'Yes, your Excellency.'

'Bed-warmer in position?'

'Yes, your Excellency.'

'You've not been touching her up, eh?' He laughed at his joke, and the Colonel gave an embarrassed smile. 'Got to watch him, you know, Andy. I owe it to the memsahib. How is the old cow today, Colonel?'

'She's a little better, your Excellency.'

'She doesn't earn her keep, you know. Still, we'll discuss that another time. Show the Captain to his room, Colonel. You feel like a bed-warmer, Andy? I can have one sent up for you.'

'Not tonight, thanks,' Andrew said. 'I'm a bit tired.'

'Nothing like it when you're tired! Still, suit yourself. See you at breakfast, eh?'

Andrew nodded. 'Good night, Emil.'

It was the right touch. With a satisfied grin, the Governor said: 'Nighty-night, Andy,' and walked clumsily out of the room.

The Colonel escorted Andrew up two flights of stairs in silence. When he opened the door of a bedroom, Andrew said:

'Abonitu – the man who was with me – where is he?'

'Floor above, sir. Room 302.'

'Thank you.' He glanced round the room. It was a typical hotel bedroom, with a Mediterranean scene in coloured tinfoil on one wall and a hunting scene print on another. The bed was double, with a chintzy bedspread. 'Very comfortable.'

The Colonel lingered. He said: 'Would you – might I come in for a couple of minutes?'

Andrew nodded. 'Yes, of course.'

He came in, carefully closing the door after him. 'May I ask a question?'

'I should think so.'

'The Governor assumed you were in charge of the Hovercraft, because you're the only white man. Is that true?'

'That I'm in charge? No. There's no one in charge officially. Abonitu carries most weight.'

The Colonel nodded. 'I thought so. I used to listen to the African stations on short-wave radio at one time. I got an idea of conditions out there. But, even if you're not in charge – I take it they might be willing to honour a bargain made by you on their behalf, if it was to their interest?'

'Go on.'

'He wants the Hovercraft.' There was no need to specify the he. 'He could have taken it by force, of course, but that might have left him without anyone who could operate it. He is not a very intelligent man, but he's wily.'

'Since you're being frank,' Andrew said, 'I don't mind telling you that I've been offered the job of Adjutant, with a view to eventually running Jersey as Deputy Governor.'

'Did you believe the promise?'

'No. Now tell me why I was right to disbelieve it.'

'The one talent he has is for using people. When he's got what he wants from them, he discards them. As an example, he manages to get better crops in the greenhouses by double-glazing a lot of them: it cuts the heat losses. That was the idea of a grower, a man called Grisson. He put him and his family on a raft, all the same.'

'You think he would discard me, once he'd got what he could about the Hovercraft out of me?'

'I know he would.'

Andrew laughed. 'I know practically nothing – nothing at all on servicing.'

'He thinks you do.'

'You said he's wily, but not intelligent. He told me about the deportation scheme. That was quite bright. Someone else's?'

The Colonel paused. 'Yes.'

'It has the flavour of a military mind. Yours?'

'Yes.'

'Over forty-four thousand put out to sea in rafts. Including women and children.'

'The alternative was bloody chaos and starvation for all. There are situations in which one can only choose between different forms of ruthlessness.'

'And you made your choice. No nightmares?'

'I have a military mind, as you've said. Strong in planning, weak in imagination. I didn't know what it would be like. I simply didn't know. Then it was too late. Yes, I have nightmares. I don't think he does.'

'No, I don't think he does. You say he discards people once they've served his turn. He didn't put you on a raft.'

'He hates me too much for that. In the old days . . . he's always had a good opinion of himself. I've told you, I used to employ him. He was a good worker when he put his mind to it, but he let himself be distracted too easily. And he was a boozer even then. I used to have to set him to rights. In the end I sacked him for drunkenness and incompetence. It was in the winter and there was no work going, except road relief work for the States. He came and begged me to keep him on, and I kept him. He won't forget that, you know, in twenty years. I need have no fears for my safety. Nor of my wife's. He has me while she lives.'

There was a silence. Andrew said:

'You spoke of a bargain.'

'If I got you out of here,' the Colonel said, 'and down to your Hovercraft – could you make a break for it? With a reasonable chance of success?'

'What precautions has he taken?'

'Four men on the Hovercraft itself, watching your blacks. A detachment above it, on the front. And he blocked the harbour mouth with three old boats at high tide.'

'The last item's a tricky one.'

'Tide would be out. They'd be grounded. The ebb will have pulled at least one of them over to expose her flank. You can take a ramp in those things?'

'Yes,' Andrew nodded. 'It might work.'

'If it doesn't, nothing else will. There's something else: they can do fifty or sixty knots flat out, can't they?'

'A little more. He doesn't know that?'

'No.' The Colonel smiled painfully. 'I used to follow the technical press. I spotted that you kept her speed down on the way round the island. If you let rip you'll shake those boys on board. After that, well, there's ten of you against the four of them.' He paused slightly. 'Or eleven.'

'Have we reached the bargain?'

'I get you off here – you take me and my wife with you. Fair enough?'

'I gather,' Andrew said, 'that your wife is a sick woman. What's the trouble?'

'Rheumatism. I could get her down there. It wouldn't be easy, but I could do it. Well?'

Andrew shook his head. 'No. I'm sorry. Even if it were just you, I couldn't promise anything. But this is an expedition and a sick woman would be an impossibility. You ought to be able to see that.'

'You won't get down there without me.'

'We'll have to try. I take it you're not going to denounce me to the Governor.'

'I could do.'

'No, I don't think you could.'

Their eyes met. The Colonel said wearily:

'No. I could plan slow death for all those thousands of people, many of them people I'd known, some of them my friends, but I couldn't denounce you to him. It's ridiculous, isn't it?'

Andrew said: 'It was a wild idea, anyway. She's better off here.'

'He humiliates her, too. If it was only myself, I wouldn't mind, but he humiliates her, and in front of his women.'

'But who suffers more from that? She? Or you, because it hurts your pride that you can't protect your wife from insult? Would you want to risk her life to make yourself feel better?'

The Colonel was silent for a moment. 'I would kill him – there have been opportunities. But the others would finish me off – he's popular enough with them – and then who would look after her? They would kill her, too, I think. There are no standards left.'

'I'm sorry,' Andrew said. 'There's nothing I can do, though, is there?' He offered his hand. 'Good luck.'

The Colonel said: 'Get into the bed, but don't undress. Don't go up to your Negro friend, either. I'll see to him. It might be dangerous to wander around just now. I'll come for you about three.'

Andrew looked at him. 'Why?'

The Colonel shook his head. 'Not decency. Not even a desire to help a fellow human being against the savages. I'm one of them now. Shall we say simple hatred?'

'Is it worth running this kind of risk for? You'll have to stay here.'

'It's worth it. Good-bye for now.'

On their own they would probably have got past the guard on the front door; there were several ways out of the hotel and the only danger after that was of being seen crossing the narrow street. They could have made it down to the front, too, through the maze of narrow alleys and flights of granite steps, coated with frozen snow. But they would have got no further. From the window of what had been a department store, the Colonel pointed things out to them. There were clouds in the night sky, but at this moment they did not obscure the moon, which was three-quarters full and high. Its light clearly showed the empty stretch of the front beneath them, the harbour drained by the tide, on the other side, and the patrolling figures between.

Andrew said: 'They're taking this seriously.'

'Yes,' the Colonel said. 'Your craft is about *there*.' He pointed. 'Under the harbour wall. The drain I'm taking you to has an outlet about thirty feet to the left of where she lies. And about ten feet above the harbour floor – try to drop as quietly as possible. I should wait for a cloud to cross the moon before jumping off. After that, you're on your own.'

'This drain,' Abonitu said, '– you are sure it is clear?'

'There was a grille at the far end, but it went in the storms last winter. It's clear.'

Andrew had some doubts about that when, with a final whispered 'Good luck', the Colonel dropped the heavy drain cover into place above their heads. The drain was a circular bore about three feet in diameter; crawling on hands and knees ice cracked beneath them and icicles broke off against their heads. They had the Colonel's parting gift, a Woolworth's pocket torch with a battery barely strong enough to give a faint flicker of light in front of them. Its value was only psychological; when the drain dipped suddenly to a thirty-degree incline, Andrew only knew it as he began to slide forward. He splayed his arms out against the sides and halted his descent. Behind him, Abonitu's voice called, low pitched but urgent:

'Andrew! You are all right?'

'A bit shaken. I should come down feet first if I were you.'

Their progress was slow after that. At one point a section of roof had collapsed, and the tunnel was practically blocked with rubble, which they had to shift laboriously and carefully, fearful of another fall. And there was a stretch where ice had formed to a depth of nearly two feet. They had to inch their way over it for something like thirty yards. The Colonel, Andrew decided, knew less about the drain than he had said he did, if he had been prepared to bring a woman crippled with rheumatism through this. It might not be clear all the way through. And if it wasn't . . .

There was a brighter glimmer than the torch's light ahead. He struggled on, and saw that it was moonlight. In a short time he was able to look out over the harbour floor. He could see the expanse of ice and frozen mud and, to his right, the Hovercraft. Away to the left was the opening to the outer harbour. Three grounded ships effectively blocked it. Their sides, frost-coated, were bright.

Andrew made room for Abonitu beside him. They spoke, whispering into each other's ears. They were uncertain how far sound might carry; above them, at one point, they heard the crunch of feet in the snow.

'I can see one man standing up,' Andrew said. 'One of theirs, I should think.'

Abonitu said: 'Yes. That is a rifle he carries.'

'Why didn't the others make the attempt to get clear? Not because they wouldn't leave us behind, surely.'

'No, not that. They are confused, frightened. What do you expect of Africans?'

He spoke with bitterness. Andrew said: 'Lucky for us, anyway. If we can keep close to the wall and not get spotted, we can get in by the rear exhaust. After that, we'll have to see how it goes.'

'We can do better, I think. I get in by the exhaust, draw his attention. He will perhaps think I am one of the others. If you climb the ramp, and drop down on board nearer the controls . . .'

'Yes, that is better. If you can, hit him as soon as she starts moving. Get his rifle and deal with the others. God, I hope the engines pick up!'

Abonitu looked out across the harbour. 'And then, we hit that at full speed. Will we clear it?'

'The one on the right offers the best chance. There'll be an air-pocket at the bottom, but with any luck we shan't lose our cushion. We will at the top, of course, but with the momentum we shall have we should skid over comfortably.' He shook his head. 'Not comfortably. But over.'

'Which way are the clouds moving?'

'Inshore. And slowly. That's a good one, above that small island. Ten minutes, I should think.'

It seemed to be longer than that before the cloud's edges trailed across the moon, and the scene darkened. Andrew went first, leaping for a dark patch of frozen mud. The noise of impact was loud in his ears, and he crouched down, looking towards the Hovercraft. But there was no sign of movement there. Some moments later he waved his hand, and Abonitu dropped beside him. They stayed motionless, not even whispering, and then began their slow hesitant advance towards the craft. They went separately, leap-frogging each other, and pausing after each stage. Once they heard voices above them, and stopped for several minutes, until long after they had died away into the night's silence.

The ramp beside which the Hovercraft lay was slippery with ice. Andrew moved up over the granite setts on his knees, trying to keep the steel studs of his boot from contact. Looking up, he saw that the moon would soon be clear of the cloud which hid it; already one could see its disk through the obscuring film. He glanced back and saw that Abonitu was poised for his boarding attempt. He himself was near enough to being in position. It would be better to leave the rest until Abonitu had attracted the guard's attention; continuing up the ramp before that might make him conspicuous. He waved his hand. Abonitu waved back and, in the same moment, heaved himself up towards the rim of the craft. He hung there briefly and disappeared inside. There was a faint clang of metal. After that, more evident noises, as of someone getting up, moving around. From the fore section, Andrew heard footsteps, the guard's voice asking something. He moved, as rapidly and noiselessly as was possible, up the ramp until he was above the level of the Hovercraft and he could look down into it.

There was a gap of perhaps four feet between ramp and craft; not a difficult jump, but unpleasant enough in these conditions and with a downward drop of five or six feet into the bargain. It would get no better by being looked at. He heard voices, Abonitu's and the guard's, and jumped quickly. As he landed, he stumbled, but recovered himself. He ran for the controls, heedless of the noise he made. The guard's voice shouted something, and there was an answering shout from one of the detachment on the front. A figure began to struggle out of blankets in his path; he kicked it viciously. There was a howl of pain; and he had reached the controls.

The engines coughed once and then came to life. He slipped her straight into reverse, praying that the steering controls had not been altered since he had brought her in the previous afternoon, and that she would retrace the arc of entry. Above the noise he heard the sound of a shot, and then another. The Hovercraft came clear of the ramp and wheeled out, beautifully, into the harbour. Andrew stopped her about fifty yards from the harbour wall, in preparation for putting her forward. In the moment of stillness, he saw a couple of figures, clearly Guernseymen, running towards him. One of them had a rifle, but seemed too confused to use it. He kicked the lever forward, and opened up to the full. As the craft moved, with violent, tearing power, they both fell. There were more shots now from the shore, and a shot nearer at hand, from the after section of the Hovercraft.

Andrew saw the beached ships ahead. The one he had decided to scale looked different from here, presenting an impossible angle, and his determination wavered. There was a gap between the other two ships, which might be wide enough . . . One of the two men was beginning to get up from the deck. Andrew made up his mind to go through with the original plan; at least the shock would be likely to throw them off balance again. He steered for the steel bulk in front. It widened alarmingly. As they swung into it, involuntarily, he threw an arm before his eyes.

The impact was staggering. Andrew was thrown against the control panel and felt the steering bar rip loose under his hand. The Hovercraft tilted sharply, and he thought it was turning turtle. But somehow she was riding over the ship, with a scream of engines and compressed air. There was a second shock, followed by startling freedom, and he realized she had cleared the obstacle and was, briefly, airborne on the other side. He was dazed, but sufficiently aware of what was happening to cut the engines. The third shock, even more bone-shaking than the others, came as the Hovercraft hit ground on the other side. She skidded, bounced, lifted, and slammed down again. This time she was still.

The silence rang in his ears. He had fallen, despite having braced himself, against the controls again, and his shoulder hurt abominably. But the only thing that mattered was whether the crash landing had damaged the jets. He went about the business of switching on slowly, with a kind of reluctance, afraid of learning the worst. But the engines picked up at once, and in a moment he felt the familiar shudder of vibration as the Hovercraft lifted on her cushion of air. He pressed the lever forward, and she moved.

There was clear moonlight, but he put the headlights on all the same. Spray swished high on either side as she reached the line of the advancing tide.

Abonitu came up to him as they moved out of the harbour mouth. He said:

'Very good, Andrew. But I would not like to do it twice.'

'Is the rest under control?'

'We've disarmed them. One of them is unconscious. He hit his head on the deck when we jumped. Do you want to be relieved now?'

'Yes.' He killed the engines again, and the craft settled down, rocking on a slight swell. The usual driver came up at Abonitu's beckoning, and Andrew moved out of the control seat. 'Are we going after the others tonight?'

'I am not sure.' Abonitu spoke, Andrew noticed, with automatic authority, in a way he had not done before. 'We need to stand far enough off these islands. The Governor is capable of sending his fleet out after us.'

'Does that thought worry you?'

'From now on, I take no unnecessary risks.' To the driver, he said: 'North at fifteen knots providing all is clear.' He looked out across the moonlit channel between Guernsey and Herm; reefs stood up, jagged and silvered, in the moonlight. 'Five knots till you clear this channel.' He put a hand on Andrew's shoulder. 'Let us see to our prisoners, Andrew.'

They were herded together in the after part, with five of the Africans pointing weapons at them. Abonitu said decisively:

'Ali and Kipuni, maintain your guard. The rest of you throw these men overboard.' One of the Guernseymen began to say something, but Abonitu cut across his words: 'I do this to save bullets. You are lucky. It is a short swim back to shore. Perhaps your Governor will give you a drink of his whisky when you get there.'

One of the men, a small swarthy man, said:

'You don't need to throw us. We'll jump.'

Abonitu said indifferently: 'Jump, then.'

The swarthy man pulled boots and outer clothes off, climbed

up the bulwark, balanced for a moment, and jumped. They saw his head break water and saw him strike out towards the shore. One by one, the others followed suit. The third man hesitated longer than the previous two, and one of the Africans reached up with his automatic and prodded him into leaping. Their heads bobbed away on the tide; one of them, treading water, turned to hurl some indistinguished curses. There was only the unconscious man left, slumped against the bulkhead, breathing noisily.

Abonitu prodded him with his foot.

'He will need help.'

Andrew said: 'Are you throwing him over like that?'

'Why not? He will have a longer swim if we leave him.' He grinned, his teeth white in the moonlight. 'Perhaps the water is cool enough to bring him round.'

He was lifted and manhandled over the side. His body slid into the water. Andrew watched, but he did not see him come up. To the others, Abonitu said:

'You can dismiss now. Ali and Kipuni, you stay on look-out. The rest can get some sleep.'

Andrew and Abonitu were left alone. Abonitu said:

'You handled things well, Andrew. Both in the breakout and back there, on the island. There was nothing I could do, of course. I had to leave things to you.'

Andrew was silent, waiting for Abonitu to go on. The praise had been more deliberate than patronizing, and he felt that something lay behind it. Abonitu made a small movement, and Andrew thought he might be going to repeat the gesture of putting a hand on his shoulder; but he did not.

Abonitu said: 'These others' – he jerked a thumb forward – 'they have little idea what happened. They were scared. They are pleased to have come out safely. I do not think they grasped the point.'

'What point?'

'To be frank, that matters hinged on you – on the fact that you were white and that the Governor assumed you were in charge of our party.'

Andrew nodded. 'I suppose not.'

'I think it will be better, Andrew, if they continue not grasping it. And also the others in the expedition, when we find them again.'

Andrew smiled. 'I see. Bad for morale?'

Abonitu's face was serious. 'Yes. And bad for you, too. There are resentments, and this was white man's territory.'

'Back there,' Andrew said, 'it still is. All right. What's the story?'

'Simply that we escaped during the night and got back to the Hovercraft.'

'That's very simple. I can remember that. Don't I get a medal for backing you up?'

In the half light, the bespectacled face peered solemnly at his. 'You are not resentful yourself, about this?'

'No. It just seems a little silly.'

'I assure you it isn't. I know my people better than you do.' Andrew started to say something, but held back before the words were uttered. Abonitu went on: 'You think they behaved badly back there? I do, too. Perhaps I can do something about that. You can do nothing. They will not accept anything from you: advice, censure, example – anything. Remember that.'

Andrew said: 'I'd be interested to know what you think you can do about their behaving badly. At present I don't rate our chances high in the next tight spot.'

'Something can be done, I believe.' His face had a tight withdrawn look. 'I cannot talk about it now.'

They cruised on at low speed through the night, encountering no mist, nor any other hazard. It was about six o'clock that the look-out reported flashes of light on the starboard bow. Swinging that way, it was soon possible to recognize the headlights of the rest of the squadron, spread out in a line that covered several miles. They approached, were called into line, and the squadron continued on its way. They saw the coast of England as dawn broke.

The squadron did not head for the shore then, but bore eastwards on a line parallel to it. The fuel dump for which they were heading was near Southampton and Andrew supposed that Mutalli had decided, the sea being calm and visibility good, to continue there before striking inland.

This was what happened. But the great estuary of the Solent, when they reached it, was choked with masses of ice, and they had to continue round the Isle of Wight. They saw no sign of life on shore. Towards Portsmouth it was possible to beach the Hovercraft: a shelf of ice stretched out to sea, but the high tide was washing over it, facilitating their passage.

Carlow and Prentice, Andrew knew, were in Mutalli's craft, with the purpose of guiding the squadron in to the fuel dump. There were several checks, and two or three false starts. But before midday they had reached the place: a low-lying windowless concrete block, its bleak outline softened by drifted snow. The squadron halted there.

The building was entered by a massive steel door. As they approached, it could be seen that this was swinging loose on rusted hinges – clearly at some time it had been dynamited to force an entry. There was a murmur of dismay as the significance of this penetrated: fuel, it was accepted, was the master key to the expedition's effectiveness. They hung back, staring at the gaping doorway.

It was Abonitu who pushed his way through and entered the door. He disappeared into the darkness of the interior, and they were silent, watching and waiting for his return. When he did, he was staggering under the weight of a metal drum.

'O.K.,' he said. 'Maybe they were looking for something else. Food, maybe. Anyway, the fuel is here, and untouched.'

There was a roar of relief and excitement. As Abonitu set the drum down in the snow, Mutalli rushed up and embraced him. Then he turned to the others.

'Everything's fine,' he shouted. 'Now we have dinner!'

2

They gathered, as usual, round the stoves, where the cooks were preparing the meal. Mutalli said to Abonitu:

'Now, you can tell us what happened to you.'

Abonitu said: 'First thing: the guard is not sufficient and not sufficiently alert.'

Three guards had been set, but they were paying more attention to what was going on at the stoves than to the outside world. Mutalli shrugged.

'We are safe enough here.'

'That was a mistake we made,' Abonitu said. 'They should be doubled, and they should be made to keep better watch.'

He spoke quietly, but with firm confidence. The bigger man looked at him for a moment, and nodded. He called to another African:

'Zaki! Double the guard, and keep them to it. Now, go on.'

Abonitu told it calmly and well, first stressing that the loss of contact with the main body had been due to the failure by the crews of the other Hovercraft to keep a rearward watch. He described the occurrences on Guernsey as he had told Andrew he would, simply saying that he and Andrew had been taken as hostages, that they had broken loose in the night and made their way back to their craft, and assuming, without actually putting it in words, his own as the lion's part in the undertaking. His account was listened to intently, punctuated by roars of approval which came, Andrew noticed, from the remainder of the crew of their Hovercraft as well as from the others. At the end there was a shout, a howl almost, of applause.

Mutalli said: 'Good job! Things work out lucky for us. Everything goes well.'

'Lucky that time,' Abonitu said. 'Next time, maybe not.'

'When you get lucky,' Mutalli said, 'you stay lucky. We're O.K.'

'Some things we have to do,' Abonitu said. He had raised his voice slightly, and the hum all round dropped to an attentive silence. 'Otherwise we won't stay lucky for long.'

Mutalli said, smiling but more watchful: 'What things?'

'We have to have better discipline,' Abonitu said. 'And delegated authority. One man on each craft who is responsible for it, and a man named as deputy to him in case he gets hurt or lost. We need to have decisions made firmly, and then kept – not chopping and changing all the time.'

There was a further noise of approval. For the moment, Abonitu had them, Andrew saw. Mutalli saw it, too.

'I'll think about it,' he said.

'It doesn't need thinking about,' Abonitu said. He stared at the bigger, more powerful figure of Mutalli. This was different from the usual independence displayed at meetings like this: it was a challenge, and the challenge was personal. Andrew saw Mutalli's hand drop to the knife they all carried at their belts. Abonitu turned away from him to look at the others. 'It has to be done,' he said, 'if we want to get back home when this is over.'

The agreement was quieter, more growling, but as positive as before. Mutalli looked around the assembled faces, and read his present isolation in them. He nodded in acceptance.

'O.K. Abonitu, you take charge of your Hovercraft from now on. I'll fix other captains soon. And you're responsible for discipline, O.K.? Set the watches, keep them to it, all that. Any trouble, I expect you to deal with it, not come running to me.'

Abonitu nodded: 'Just as you say.'

Mutalli grinned. 'Now,' he said, 'how's that dinner coming along? How is it, boys? You hungry for that stew?'

The situation had been well turned. He had made the minimum concession, and at the same time burdened Abonitu with the task in which he was most likely to incur unpopularity. And at the right time, Andrew guessed, he would strike at him. The usual undisciplined arguing did not affect Mutalli's supremacy; in a way, general and unfocused as it was, it confirmed it. But the emergence of an opposition centred on one man was quite a different thing. Andrew did not think that Mutalli would tolerate this for long.

The showdown, however, came sooner than he had expected. The squadron pushed on in the afternoon, north-east in the direction of London. They followed the Itchen valley to Winchester, where they saw the first signs of human life in England. Figures moved across the snow at the edge of the town. They fled to the cover of the buildings when Mutalli diverted the squadron towards them. The squadron continued on its way. A halt was made in later afternoon in the rolling empty country south of Basingstoke. When the Africans clustered, as usual, around Mutalli's craft, he called out:

'Abonitu! Set your guards, boy. Anything gets in this camp, you answer for it.'

'Are we pitching camp here?'

'How does it look to you?'

'A little early, I would say. We have quite a bit of daylight in front of us.'

Mutalli leaned his huge head slightly towards Abonitu.

'Shut up.' Abonitu was silent, watching him. 'You wanted discipline, boy, you'd better start taking it. I give the orders round here.'

Abonitu nodded. 'Yes.'

'Yes, sir,' Mutalli said. 'Remember that discipline.'

'Yes, sir,' Abonitu said.

His face was impassive, his eyes unwinking behind his spectacles. He stared at Mutalli and then turned away and made arrangements for the guard duty. The roster which he made up included Prentice.

Prentice said: 'I've done a guard already. Your pal, Leedon, hasn't done one yet.'

Abonitu said shortly: 'Leedon had a heavy night last night.'

'There are plenty of others,' Prentice said, 'who haven't stood a guard.'

Mutalli, within earshot, was watching the scene with amusement. Abonitu said:

'No arguments, Prentice. You'll go on guard, as arranged.'

Prentice looked at him in sullen anger. Carlow pulled his arm and led him away. They stood together, apart from the others, Carlow talking and Prentice listening. Abonitu continued to call out the names of those on guard.

Twelve guards had been set, on a three-watch rotation. In the morning only three guards were on duty; the fourth, an African of the Fulani tribe, was still in his sleeping bag when Abonitu went looking for him. He was not abashed by this. No one had called him for duty. His predecessor on watch, Abonitu found, should have been Prentice.

Neither Carlow nor Prentice was in the camp area. It seemed fairly clear what had happened. They had taken their automatics, and a good supply of ammunition and of food.

'The fools,' Abonitu said. 'How long do they think they will last on their own, out there?'

'They heard what you said about Guernsey,' Andrew reminded him. 'They probably think they can carve out a little kingdom on their own.'

'That was an island, protected by the sea. There is no comparison.'

Andrew shrugged. 'Or perhaps they think any kind of risk is preferable to going on with this.'

'This?'

'Life as a member of the lower orders. They're back in their own country now. Frozen up, but their own country.'

Abonitu's voice, when he spoke, had an impatient, almost truculent bitterness:

'One has to take life as it is. I thought you understood that, Andrew. It was a lesson your people taught us.'

'I understand it. I was suggesting that they might not have done. It's a thin line between hope and fantasy.'

They were standing by their own Hovercraft. Mutalli approached them, with a score or more of the men behind him. He said, in a heavy sarcastic voice:

'That was a fine guard you organized last night, boy. You really deserve credit for it. You don't mind taking the responsibility, I hope?'

'No,' Abonitu said, 'I don't mind that. We have to work out punishments, don't we? What I have in mind is no coffee for three days and extra guard duties.'

'Who for?'

'For the three who did duty on the last watch, and the three on the watch before.'

'Why so?'

'Negligence in not realizing there was a man missing. An elementary part of a sentry's duty is keeping in contact with his fellow sentries.'

'You got it worked out, boy, really worked out. You worked out how we're going to get those two bastards back?'

'We aren't.' He gestured towards wooded country to the south. 'Their tracks lead that way. They're shrewd enough to know that if they stayed out in the open we would run them down with the Hovercraft. But Hovercraft can't go through trees. We could go after them on foot, but they have at least two hours' start – maybe four. And I believe Carlow came from somewhere in these parts. It would be a wasted effort to look for them.'

'So we've lost our two mechanics? You take it easy.'

'No. But several of our men have picked up enough by now to handle minor troubles. And the big troubles were always likely to involve workshop repairs which Carlow and Prentice had no facilities for, anyway. We're not much worse off.'

Mutalli was plainly irritated, both by the reasonableness of Abonitu's arguments and by his calmness of tone. Almost shouting, he said:

'You can't trust white men. You ought to know that, boy! You ought to know you can't trust them.'

'I didn't choose those two for the expedition,' Abonitu said.

While the interchange had been going on, more of the Africans had been coming up to listen. They tended, Andrew saw, to collect around one or the other of the two men. Most were with Mutalli, but Abonitu's minority was a substantial one. And on the other side, there were signs that some were more impressed by the calmness than by the bluster. Mutalli seemed aware of this, too. There was a pause before he spoke, and when he did it was in a quieter, yet more venomous tone.

'Not those two. But you chose yourself a white man, didn't you, boy? Maybe you got to like white men, that time you went to England. You want to keep one with you – give you advice, tell you what to do, how to get discipline, how to set a guard on the camp? That the idea, boy?'

It had its effect. The swing of sympathy was perceptible. One or two of the others shouted angry phrases of agreement. Abonitu said:

'Leedon is a technician. He was chosen for that.'

'Like those other two bastards – both technicians. But you chose this one. You have any ideas on that situation?'

Abonitu said quietly: 'What ideas should I have?'

'I'll tell you mine,' Mutalli said. 'Maybe you'll pick it up from there. My idea, we've had enough of white men in this expedition. My idea, we make sure we don't have more treachery, when it hits us worse maybe. You're in charge of your craft, Abonitu. I leave it to you.'

'I'll speak for Leedon,' Abonitu said. 'You have nothing to worry about with him.'

There was a shout of derision at this. Andrew heard individual voices, raised in hostility. An African nearby shook a fist in his direction.

'You pick it up slow,' Mutalli said. 'All I'm asking you, you work out the best way of doing it. You think he's worth a bullet? The knife's just as quick, and more economical.'

He took his own knife from his belt, tossed it in the air, and caught it. The early morning sunshine danced on the blade.

Mutalli did not return it to his belt but hefted it in his large right hand.

Abonitu said, his voice still even: 'This is nonsense.'

Mutalli shook his head. 'You soft, boy? I thought you were the big hero, from what you said yesterday.'

'And barbarous.' Abonitu raised his voice slightly. 'What you would expect from an Ibo.'

There were other Ibo in the expedition, but they were greatly outnumbered by men from other tribes, notably the Yoruba. Andrew saw what Abonitu was trying to exploit. It was a dangerous gambit if it failed to work; and here it failed. There was a roar of anger from the Ibo clustered round Mutalli, silence from the rest.

Mutalli said, his voice steady but carrying an undertone of triumph:

'I'm giving you an order, Abonitu. You kill this white man. You kill him any way you choose, but you kill him. O.K.? That clear enough for you?'

Abonitu shook his head very slowly. He said:

'You're trying to make me look small. All right, I'm small. You're running this expedition. We all agree on that. You've made your point. Now let's get on with the work.'

Mutalli smiled. He offered the knife to Abonitu, hilt first.

'I've just given you a job. Maybe you didn't hear me?'

Abonitu shrugged, and began to turn away. Mutalli said, in a louder voice:

'I'm going to count up to ten. Before I finish, I want to see something happen.'

He counted the numbers out. Andrew felt fear crawl along his nerve ends. Abonitu's isolation was nothing to his; whether or not Abonitu succeeded in escaping from the trap, Andrew saw that Mutalli was determined on a victim. And the mob was with him.

Mutalli came to ten. Abonitu had said nothing, done nothing. He stared at the bigger man: his face was impassive, set in a brooding frown. Mutalli said:

'Disobeying orders? That's mutiny, boy.' He made a flicking motion with his head. 'O.K. Finish them off – both of them.'

As the other men began to surge forward, Abonitu spoke. His voice was sharp, and it stopped them.

'Wait.' His eyes fixed on Mutalli's. 'Are you telling them to murder me, Mutalli?'

'Not murder. Execute, not murder. You thinking about your uncle? I guess he'll still look after you, Abonitu. He'll give you a medal, boy. Does that make you feel good?'

'No,' Abonitu said, 'not that. I feel good because you have shown yourself for the coward you are. When you wanted the white man killed, you told me to do it. And now that you want me killed, you look to the others to do it for you. A brave man would do it himself – or try to. But you are not brave, Mutalli, are you? And, to make up for it, you are wise. Because if you came to me on your own, with a knife in your hand and no one helping, you think I might kill you.'

Mutalli did not answer. Instead, he tossed the knife from right hand to left, and back to right again. He held it by the hilt, the point upwards and pointing towards Abonitu. As he stepped forward, the others moved back, forming a rough circle in the snow. Two of them grabbed Andrew's arms, and pulled him roughly back with them. There was nothing he could do but acquiesce. Inside the circle, the two men closed on each other, both silent now. It was Mutalli who advanced more, but it was Abonitu who attacked first. When Mutalli was a couple of yards from him, he leapt forward, reaching with his free hand for the hand that held the knife, his own knife scything through the air towards his opponent's neck. The two men met and reeled together, grunting with the exertion, kicking frozen snow as they fought for footholds.

Abonitu gave way. He was borne backwards, and his arms pressed down by superior weight and strength. At last he managed, by a sudden twist, to disengage himself. As he did so, Mutalli's hand with the knife swept after him. His back was towards Andrew, but Andrew saw his spectacles spin through the air, a lens flashing sunlight. They landed in the snow between the two men, and Mutalli, moving quickly, stamped them with his right foot. Abonitu continued to back away, and Andrew saw also that blood was dripping from somewhere on his face. The small drops of red spread out on the snow. Around the two men, the other Africans murmured with excitement.

Abonitu backed as Mutalli advanced on a slow circuit of the ring. Once or twice Mutalli lunged forward quickly, but Abonitu evaded the attack. Mutalli began to talk to him, in a low mocking voice:

'Come on, boy. You not afraid, boy, are you? Let's see the big hero man fight. Come on, make it quick. You going to get cold, crawling around like that. Let's see that knife move, boy. Let's have some action now.'

Abonitu made a rush, as though goaded. Mutalli dodged, swaying with unexpected lightness and agility. His knife waved, and it was Abonitu's hand, this time, which dripped blood. The others roared. Mutalli said:

'I think I'll carve you up a little bit, boy. You got a lot of blood in you. Come right on in, and I'll tickle you some more.'

They continued to circle, Mutalli advancing, Abonitu retreating. The snow inside the circle was treading down under their feet.

'Come in,' Mutalli said. 'Come in again, boy. Come in, you brave hero man.'

He himself moved forward more quickly, and Abonitu backed off. It was beginning to turn into a chase. As Abonitu moved round the circle, hands pushed at him and prodded him. They could see the blood, and were beginning to shout for more. Andrew debated making an effort to tear himself free and run for it. Once Abonitu was dead, they would kill him. Nothing was more certain.

'If you don't come in,' Mutalli said, 'then I have to come and get you, don't I, boy? I think I'll get you right now.'

The circle grew a corner. They closed in on either side of Abonitu, forcing him to stand and give battle. He was at bay as Mutalli came towards him. Someone pushed him between the shoulders, knocking his head forward. At that, Abonitu leapt to his right, cannoning against the crowding Africans. Obviously he was trying to escape from Mutalli again, and as obviously he had no chance. The bigger man swayed to the left, swinging for him.

But Mutalli stumbled in mid-swing, his right foot slipping on a patch of frozen snow. He checked, and retained his footing, but he was off balance. In that instant, Abonitu flung his body forward. His head caught the other man high on the chest, his left fist simultaneously punching him in the stomach. Mutalli crashed back into the snow. As he hit the ground he twisted to one side, his hands reaching out to find a position from which he could regain his footing. One of them still held the knife. Abonitu brought his boot down on it and the knife fell free. He stared at his fallen opponent, at the hand flattened under his foot. With the other boot he kicked Mutalli savagely in the face, the head rolling back under the impact. Then he stooped, his own knife poised for the kill.

At the last minute, dazed as he was, Mutalli wrenched to one side and simultaneously swept his right arm round against the backs of Abonitu's legs. His knees crumpled and they were down together, rolling in the snow. But it was Mutalli's last effort. Abonitu sawed at him with the knife, wounding him in the arm, the body, the face, before he managed at last to drive the knife deep into the hollow of his chest. Mutalli coughed and lay still, a trickle of blood at the corner of his mouth.

Slowly Abonitu got to his feet. He looked round the ring of faces, assessing their reactions. Their expressions, Andrew saw, were blank for the most part. They had been shocked, as well they might be, by the outcome of the struggle, and were unsure how to take it. They were still capable of turning on Abonitu. It only required a spark from a small section – from the Ibos – to set off a conflagration of murderous hate and revenge.

As though aware of this, Abonitu stared most fixedly at the group of Ibo men, his eyes challenging theirs. He held them for a moment or two. Then, with deliberate and casual contempt, he kicked Mutalli's body.

'Take this away,' he said. He paused. There was a sighing exhalation of breath. 'Bury it,' Abonitu went on. 'We do not leave our dead for scavengers. The ground is too hard for digging. You will need to use the power drills.'

He turned on his heel, and walked away. The circle parted as he approached. When he had gone perhaps twenty yards, he stopped and looked back. He pointed to Andrew.

'Let that man go. And let the cooks get on with the breakfast. We break camp an hour from now.'

There was no attempt to challenge Abonitu's supremacy. When camp was broken, his Hovercraft moved off first, the others falling into line behind it. At the midday halt, the men scrambled from their craft and gathered round Abonitu's, as, in the past, they had done round Mutalli's. He had been busy, during the morning, with paper and pencil. Standing as far from him and as inconspicuously as possible, Andrew recognized that he had taken on stature, a conscious awareness of leadership.

He said: 'These are the names of the men who are to be in charge of each Hovercraft.' He read the names in a clear voice. 'They will be responsible to me. Each will appoint a deputy, to take charge in an emergency where he himself can't act, and report the name of the deputy to me this evening. I am appointing a deputy myself. That is Colonel Zigguri. If anything happens to me, he takes over. Is that understood?'

There was a murmur of assent. Zigguri, a Yoruba like Abonitu and the majority of the expedition, had held the highest military rank after Mutalli, and should have been named by him as deputy leader. He was a tall thin man with a pointed beard and a sober, watchful look. He nodded slightly towards Abonitu, a gesture of recognition and, Andrew felt, of loyalty. It was the best, the only possible choice. At the same time, Abonitu had taken care of the

Ibos. Two of them had been put in charge of Hovercraft; and those two, Andrew suspected, the ones who would have been most likely to cause trouble if left together.

'Some regulations,' Abonitu went on. 'At every halt one man will be detailed on each craft as look-out. No one will leave his craft until instructed by the captain in charge, and the captain will not give this instruction until signalled by me. Captains will be obeyed by crew members without argument or protest. Anyone feeling he has a complaint against his captain will report it to Colonel Zigguri. But first he will obey the order he has been given.'

He looked at them in mild but authoritative surveillance.

'That is all for now. Later I will talk to the captains.'

He dismissed them with a wave, and descended from the Hovercraft. They made way for him. He stopped, and looked back.

'Andrew, come with me.'

They walked together through the assembly and out, beyond the circle of Hovercraft, into the open country. They had halted in the lee of a hill, overlooking what was either a road or a frozen river. The white skeletons of trees guarded its flanks; from the way they hairpinned in the distance, outlining a narrow curve, it seemed more likely to be a river. It was difficult to believe that any Roads Committee in the Home Counties would have sanctioned or tolerated a bend like that. Some way beyond the curve, a long straight embankment more plainly marked the past existence of a railway line.

Abonitu settled his spectacles more firmly on his nose; the cut on his face had been high up by the right ear, and the adhesive plaster pressed against the spectacle arm.

He said: 'I shall have to be careful of these, Andrew. My only spare pair. It will not do to break them.'

Andrew said: 'Do you think it's a good idea – talking privately to me? I've been keeping out of your way.'

'Yes. That was thoughtful of you; but not necessary, I think. I have them now, and it would be a mistake to compromise in

193

anything. They will not turn against me because I talk to you privately. They would, if they thought I was afraid to do so.'

'You may be right. I had my fingers crossed for you this morning.' He looked at his companion. 'I didn't think you were going to make it, Abo.'

'Nor did I, at one time. But my family has always been lucky in battle. There is a story that one of my ancestors was lying on the ground, waiting to be speared, when the man who stood over him was struck by lightning.'

He smiled, as he said this. He was calm, unruffled, urbane. It was difficult to remember him kicking Mutalli on the face, gasping and groaning as he butchered the struggling man with his knife.

Andrew asked: 'What are you going to tell Lagos?'

Their link with Nigeria was through a powerful short-wave transmitter, previously kept on Mutalli's Hovercraft. Abonitu had had the set and the operator transferred to his own craft. A coded report was transmitted each evening.

'I shall tell them he has been accidentally killed, and that the expedition has elected me as his successor. That will meet their needs. They are proud of their democracy.'

'And when we get back?'

Abonitu shrugged. 'If we get back safely, it will not matter.'

Andrew said: 'What kind of a man are you?'

Abonitu turned to look at him. 'A black man. Some years ago, in your Parliament, one of your leaders said that all Africans are liars.' He smiled. 'But for Epimenides' paradox, I would say that also. Abonitu, an African, says that all Africans are liars. There is no paradox, really, of course. To be a liar is not to lie with every word one speaks. And we are murderers, too, and cheats and tyrants. Some of the time. It is just that you do not understand us, Andrew.'

'Why save me?'

'I did not save you. I saved myself.' He looked out over the white waste. 'Carlow and Prentice – I wonder where they are, if they are still alive.'

'Probably regretting it,' Andrew said. 'It must be lonely out there.'

'Then you will not follow them, Andrew?'

'Didn't you vouch for my reliability this morning? Wasn't that what the trouble was about?'

'Partly that. Will you follow them?'

'No. Why should I expose myself to the probability of freezing or starving to death, or being murdered by one of the surviving savages?'

'That is not an answer.'

'Then put it this way: I've made my choice. They hadn't, but I have. From that point, every action confirms the decision. Every day buries it deeper.'

Abonitu said briskly: 'Good. We reach London tomorrow. I shall need you for a guide.' He grinned. 'And you are the only one left to turn the cameras now; it would be undignified in a leader.'

'I should like to have had them turning this morning.'

'So should I. For my descendants – to go with the stroke of lightning.'

'London,' Andrew said, 'tomorrow ... What approach will you use? Up river?'

'It is the only sensible one, perhaps the only possible one. Andrew?'

'Yes.'

'How do you feel about returning to London like this?'

'I don't know.'

'Moved? Excited?'

'No. Numb, rather. A feeling of wanting to get it over and done with.'

'I am excited by the idea,' Abonitu said. 'And disgusted with myself, a little. When the princesses and queens of ancient Egypt died, they used to keep the bodies until putrefaction set in, before handing them over to the embalmers. That was because they found that otherwise the embalmers used them for their lust. London is a dead queen.'

'But not putrefying. Preserved in a deep freeze. There are no obstacles to your necrophilia, Abo. In any case, they had an easier and less unpleasant solution, surely – why not eunuchize the embalmers?'

'Because even eunuchs have some passions. Probably they hired the bodies out, to more complete men. For some sicknesses there are only unpleasant remedies. Do you not agree?'

'I agree entirely,' Andrew said.

Abonitu put his hand on Andrew's arm; it was a frank and open gesture, and although they were apart from the rest, they were in view of them. He said:

'I need you, Andrew. Not as a guide, nor for the cameras. I need you as a friend. If you leave me with my own people, I am lost. You will stay?'

'Yes,' Andrew said, 'I'll stay.'

The locks on the upper reaches of the Thames caused some delays; they had to be bypassed and at times this involved circuitous detours. Doing this near Teddington they found themselves crossing a battlefield, or a place of massacre. The snow was dotted with humps and larger mounds which here and there gaped to show frozen limbs thrust out in the agony of death. As the Hovercraft moved slowly on its way, Abonitu said to Andrew:

'You see that?'

A nearby mound showed signs of activity, of having been quarried almost. Bodies were freshly exposed. An arm had been hacked from one, a leg from another.

Andrew found he could look at it with no more than a tremor of nausea. He said:

'Yes. I expected that.'

'I, too. But to see it is something else. And there.'

He pointed. Andrew said: 'He was surprised. Something scared him – or her.'

A severed arm lay on the snow. It looked young, delicate. There was a gold-banded lady's watch on the wrist.

'He must have been very frightened,' Abonitu said, 'to abandon it. Can we head back for the river yet?'

'I think so. Heading north-east, through that gap in the trees.'

'Good,' Abonitu said. 'This place is unclean.'

They found human life again at Chiswick. At first there were odd figures on the banks of the frozen river, some retreating, as the Hovercraft approached, into the hinterland of buildings, others – bolder or more curious – staring and gesticulating. The noise of the engines blanketed any sound that might be coming from them, but one man was plainly appealing, in some terms, for help. As the Hovercraft continued up river, he began to run along the tow-path, trying to keep up with it. The crew watched him with interest and amusement, shouting encouragement and then, when he collapsed in defeat, jeering at him.

By Chiswick Bridge the activity was greater and more purposive. A mob that had gathered on the left bank spilled out on to the bridge itself. There were thirty or forty people, Andrew estimated; most of them male but with a few young and rough-looking females. The reaction was unmistakable here, too, but markedly different. They shook their fists and howled inaudible curses. Some stooped down and rummaged in the snow, looking for stones which they threw at the Hovercraft.

Abonitu said, smiling: 'The natives seem unfriendly.'

There was a whine in the air above them. Andrew said:

'One of them has a rifle.'

Ali, a Hausa and a Moslem who had been made captain of Abonitu's Hovercraft, said:

'We should go in, sir – give them a few bursts of fire.'

'To teach them a lesson, eh, Ali?' Abonitu said. 'They may go where they please, they may shin up the trees, but they won't get away from the guns. It is an old tradition. But here it would not work. They have too much cover and they can reach it too easily. We must press on, and take our chance on stray bullets. I do not think there will be many fired at us under such circumstances. They will be too precious to be wasted on folly of this kind.'

The river widened; Battersea Power Station lifted its quartet of chimneys, smokeless now, against the sky ahead of them. Abonitu said to their driver:

'Reduce speed. To five, and keep it there.' He looked at Andrew. 'A barrier? Alongside the river?' He raised his field glasses and stared through them. 'But it is not new.'

'We've reached the edge of the London Pale,' Andrew said. 'There were no fortifications there before I left, but I suppose they put them up afterwards. There had been attacks across the river. I suppose they got worse.'

'I see no signs of life.'

'No,' Andrew said. 'Nor do I.'

He felt the old misery invade him as he said it. How long, he wondered, could there be fresh recognitions of hopelessness?

They cruised along the broad reach of the Thames, flanked by empty silent cliffs of white. Behind them the western sky was lurid, with heavy banks of cloud lit by the declining sun. Andrew mounted the camera's tripod on its floating base, and panned from the frozen city into the sunset. It would be less effective, he reflected ironically, on television's black and white than on the colour film with which the camera was loaded, but effective enough to drive the unsubtle point home.

They passed the Tate Gallery. Under the usual anonymity of white, there were signs of the ravages of fire; broken windows showed glimpses of a gutted interior. The more important canvases had been removed before the crash – flown out to the southern countries for sale at knock-down prices to glean what foreign currency they could. There had been a boom, he remembered, in the Chantrey pictures, whose detail and magnificence had appealed to the African buyers: they had been brought up from the cellars and dusted over, and sold for figures which, while less than those they might have commanded in their Victorian and Edwardian heyday, compared very favourably with the revised values of Picasso and Braque and Matisse. But these had, at least, brought something: the abstracts had been impossible to sell. They had been put back on the walls, for the edification of the chilly survivors in the Pale. Presumably, after the final breakdown, someone had started a fire with some of them, and it had got out of control. He wondered about the sculptures. The small bronzes had been offered, but had not fetched anything that would justify their air freight. The larger pieces, of course, had been immovable. Presumably they still stood there, decked with ashes and snow drifted in through the broken windows: the Hepworths and the Epsteins and the Moores. Would they ever mean anything again? The Africans, even if the colonization project worked, had their own primitivism, a deeper, less artificial one, and too close for comfort.

Rounding the bend in the river, they saw the new skyline, the foreground dominated by the towers and traceries of the Houses of Parliament.

'Big Ben,' Abonitu said. 'There is irony for you, Andrew. Stands the church clock at ten to three – or nearly. Twenty to three, isn't it?'

'But of a winter night,' Andrew said, 'not a summer afternoon. It stopped in the February blizzards. The cold cracked a main driving shaft and they couldn't repair it.'

'And is there honey still for tea? This is worse than I expected, Andrew.' He turned towards the driver. 'Take her inshore, to the left bank. Just short of the bridge.'

'Here?' Andrew asked. 'Are you halting here?'

'Where else?'

'There are places that might be more easily defensible. The Tower, for instance.'

'The heart of England was here, when it stopped beating. What are you smiling at?'

'The poetic phrase. You have too much colour in your imagination.'

Abonitu shook his head. 'No. Not enough. This was London. To us, Rome was nothing by comparison, and Rome did not fall as this city fell.'

The expedition still suffered from the difficulty in communicating between Hovercraft in motion, but Abonitu had given orders before starting that the two rearmost vessels should take up a covering position whenever the remainder put in to shore. These now formed up in the lee of the Palace of Westminster and, again as prearranged, a landing party was disembarked and made for the steps. They moved quickly, purposefully, under their captains.

Andrew said: 'You've wreaked an astonishing change, astonishingly quickly. One wouldn't know them for the same men.'

'It has nothing to do with me,' Abonitu said. 'Or very little, at least. It is not what has been done to them, but what they believe they are. You have heard stories of the witch-doctors pointing a piece of bone at a man, telling him he will die – and he dies? I saw it once, when I was a small boy. The British told us we were simple ignorant niggers, and for generations we believed them. Then you brought our young men to England, and your liberals told them they were the white man's equal, and had human rights, and we believed them instead.'

'Was it as simple as that?' Abonitu shrugged, smiling. 'And now – with these?'

'Mutalli was a big man, but soft: afraid of making enemies, afraid of the possibility of rivals. Disorder and anarchy fed his vanity; order and discipline would have threatened it. So no deputy was appointed, no captains. As for the men, he wanted them to be a mob, and they were a mob.'

'All the same, the transformation is remarkably sudden.'

'All our transformations are.'

'But not lasting.'

'They may last. It depends.'

'In this case,' Andrew said, 'it depends on you, doesn't it?'

'In a sense, yes.' He turned his head, and his eyes, behind their spectacles, stared at Andrew. 'Or on you.'

'How?'

'Mutalli had another fear: of this country, of the ice and snow and desolation, and of all the things its name stands for. I know

200

what that fear is, and one's fellow Africans are no help against it. There is a temptation to turn back into the ignorant savage, frightened by ghosts and white devils.' He smiled. 'With you here, I do not think I will fall to that temptation; and the others will not if I don't.'

'If anything happened to you now, what would become of the expedition?'

'Who knows?'

He spoke with indifference and confidence. Above them, on the terrace, a head appeared over the parapet. Zigguri looked down, and waved.

'All clear up here,' he called.

Abonitu nodded. 'Right. We're coming up.'

3

As the winter evening deepened, various sightings were reported by the look-outs. A man was seen at the other side of Parliament Square, and another some distance off along the Embankment; then three figures were seen, in the direction of Charing Cross, making their way slowly across the river from south to north. It seemed certain that these, at least, must have seen the Hovercraft, drawn up in a flattened arc beneath the terrace, but they gave no sign. Looking through Abonitu's glasses, Andrew saw that one of them was limping. Two of them carried what looked like rough wooden clubs; the limping man had a bow fastened on his back and a form of quiver at his side containing arrows.

That night, Abonitu placed a strong guard, both on the building and the Hovercraft. Andrew had a watch himself, and in the small hours stood gazing eastwards over the moonlit roofs of the city. He had looked that way before, and at such a time of night, and the differences were not great. The streets had been quiet and empty then, the street lamps scarcely visible under the moon's overarching brightness. But great enough: nothing could hide the desolation and death. The soft lambent light, falling on the harshness of snow and ice, magnified rather than diminished them.

The morning came peacefully. That day Abonitu consolidated their position, erecting barricades where necessary, and sent two of the Hovercraft on patrol down river. They reported some signs of life among the wharves alongside the Pool of London, where three or four ships, one of them gutted by fire, were frozen into the ice, and the sight of smoke in various places, both north and south of the river. From time to time, during the day, figures were seen from the camp, but their movements had no apparent purpose. Inside the camp, the atmosphere was peaceful and relaxed.

But Abonitu did not relax the strict security arrangements, and mounted the same heavy guard at night. It passed without incident.

The first trouble came on the third day. In the afternoon, Abonitu sent a patrol out on foot, through the streets, with orders to proceed warily, along main thoroughfares, in the direction of Oxford Street. The patrol consisted of six men, under the leadership of one of the Ibos. They left soon after one o'clock; about an hour later there was a sound of shooting in the distance. It lasted for some minutes, and was succeeded by silence. Andrew, who was with Abonitu, said to him:

'Trouble. Are you going to send out reinforcements?'

Abonitu stared out towards the corner of Whitehall.

'No. No reinforcements.'

'Won't they expect you to?'

Abonitu looked at him. 'My own people, you mean? Yes, they will expect it. But others may expect it, too. Whatever happened is over. It may be they have met a small band of hooligans and put them to rout. If so, they will be back soon enough to tell us. But the outcome may not have been so happy; and in that case the other side may be waiting for us to send help so that they can ambush them.' He pointed. 'An ambush out there would be all too simple.'

The patrol was due back at four; by five, when there was no sign of them, they had to abandon hope. There was some uneasiness in the camp, and Abonitu called together all those not on guard and spoke to them. He spoke easily and confidently, but with grim warning. The purpose of the patrol had been to probe the dangers of their surroundings. They knew now that these dangers were great. For the time being, at any rate, there would be no further probes into the streets: the risks were known. This did not mean that they were in any danger in their stronghold; a few armed toughs could destroy a small patrol in the streets, but there was no comparison between such action and an attack against a position well fortified and strongly held. At the same time, what had happened obviously increased the need for vigilance. There might be more trouble; they must be prepared for it.

The attack came, in fact, during the night. The alarm was given when a figure was seen moving in the shadow of the Abbey, and a few minutes later there were shots, and a confused pattern of men advancing in an attack on the Yard. By the time Andrew got on the scene, things had settled down into sniping action on both sides, the attackers having taken what cover they could. Abonitu was directing events. He said to Zigguri:

'Go the rounds and make sure the guards in the other places are staying at their posts; they may attack somewhere else also. And tell Ali to form the rest into a reserve; we have enough to deal with these here.'

They watched, and saw one of the attackers hit. He did not cry out, but spun down against the snow. He lay still for a moment, and then crawled away to better cover.

Abonitu said: 'If we could have run a power line up here from the Hovercraft, and mounted one of the searchlights . . . we could finish them quickly.'

'I don't think it will take long, anyway,' Andrew said. 'They're not making much impression.'

'There is covering fire,' Abonitu said. 'Do you see from where?'

'No.'

'From the Abbey. They stationed men in there before they launched the attack. I am not happy about that. This is something more than a handful of savages.'

Savouring the irony, Andrew said: 'Yes. I suppose it is.'

'Well,' Abonitu said, 'we shall have to see how things go on. I think they have almost had enough for the present. There is another one running for cover.'

'Yes,' Andrew said. 'They've had enough.'

The atmosphere in the camp the next day was cheerful and confident; the failure of the night attack had dispelled the uneasiness following the loss of the patrol. A single Hovercraft covered the river – up as far as Staines, and down to the mouth of the estuary – reporting nothing beyond the same jeering stone-throwing mob at Chiswick, and the occasional sight of smaller parties and individuals. At the camp itself the day passed peacefully, as did the following night and day. The weather had stayed clear, but during that afternoon cloud thickened in the sky. Dusk set in earlier, and it was bitterly cold. Before night came, some snow was falling, and the wind was starting to get up. By midnight, it was blowing a blizzard, the snow sweeping in blinding gusts from the north-east.

The second attack was launched at the height of the storm. The main effort followed the lines of the previous attempt, but there was a secondary offensive from the direction of the gardens, and this for a time succeeded in obtaining a foothold. Andrew was not on the scene there, but it was clear from what was said afterwards that Abonitu had rallied the defenders to throw the attackers back. They left two men behind when they retreated, one dead and one badly injured, with a bullet through his chest. Three of the Africans had been injured, one seriously. Andrew found the dead and injured in what had once been the Lords' Robing Room; it was now a first-aid station.

Abonitu, as he came in, was quizzing the injured white man. He turned his head to Andrew, and shrugged.

'I can't get him to say anything. Would you like to try?'

He appeared to be in his early thirties, a thick-set man with an early jowl and full lips whose blueness showed how much blood he had lost; his face was very white. A dressing had been put on his wound, but blood still seeped through it.

Andrew said: 'Are you comfortable? Is there anything we can do for you? A drop of brandy?'

He stared, his face fixed in hostility.

'This is a peaceful expedition,' Andrew said. 'We don't want trouble. Can you tell us what's behind the attacks? Obviously someone is planning them – but for what purpose? Food? Arms? We have some, but I should have thought it was obvious we can defend them. It doesn't make sense.'

There was still no answer. 'Haven't you anything to say?' Andrew asked him.

He spoke then. 'Renegade bastard.' The words were spoken with difficulty. Pain crossed his face. He turned his head away, and lay without moving.

Abonitu said dispassionately: 'Leave him alone. He's dying.'

The man shuddered, but did not move or speak. Abonitu and Andrew walked away, out of the flickering illumination of the night-lights into the corridor's darkness, and Abonitu switched on his torch.

Andrew said: 'It was a closer thing tonight.'

'A lot closer. If they had managed to keep that toehold for long . . . I don't know how many more they have behind them.'

They passed a window; it was broken and the snow was blowing in, and drifting on the floor.

'If this kind of weather continues,' Abonitu said, 'it may not be easy to keep them out. Tonight one could not see five yards ahead.'

'I wouldn't say this is typical English winter weather. But more typical than the clear skies we've been having. The glass is more usually low than high.'

'Yes. I know that.' He paused. 'We had news from Lagos last night.' Andrew waited for him to go on. 'The supply ship is sailing north in a week.'

'That's a good deal earlier than planned.'

'We are gaining in importance. There were some, I knew, who did not believe we would get here, get to England even. And there was a political situation; if the expedition had ended in disaster, certain Ministers would have fallen. I suspect that the supply ship may have been ready for some time, but they would not commit it.'

'And they will now?'

'Vigorously. We are being reinforced to some effect. More equipment, more generating equipment, more troops. They want to make sure of a base here.'

'How long will it take the supply ship to reach us?'

'Twelve days, if things go well.'

'So, it's the next three weeks that are critical.'

'Yes.' He flashed his torch on an open door, and light reflected from fumed oak and heavy red plush. 'We are getting half a dozen Westland helicopters. And flame-throwers and napalm.'

'No atom bombs?'

Abonitu laughed. 'No. We have some, though – did you know that? They were sold to us before the crack-up.'

'For use against South Africa?'

'One supposes so. As a deterrent only, of course.'

His voice was sarcastic. Andrew said:

'Is there such a thing as loyalty?'

'As between nations, none: only self-interest. From an individual to his nation, yes, though prejudice describes it better, perhaps. I think it is only a true thing when it knows its object. Loyalty belongs to friendship, not to fancy.'

'And you can't have loyalty, I suppose, without the possibility of disloyalty.'

Abonitu shrugged. 'You can have no good thing, without the possibility of its opposite.' He looked towards a high eastern window in which the glass remained unbroken. 'Dawn breaking. They won't come back tonight.'

There were no further attacks on the buildings. Instead, the sniping began. There seemed to be two snipers, one in the Abbey and another stationed in a building at the bottom of Whitehall, though there may have been a number of men sharing the two rifles; there were shots from early morning until late at night. The snipers were not particularly accurate, but in the first two days one African was killed and two others injured.

The third casualty had occurred as dusk was drawing on; the blizzard had died away fairly quickly and this evening was clear, with the sun casting a jagged line of red along the western reaches of the river. Abonitu and Andrew stood on the terrace and had the report there: the man had been hit in the right arm, just below the shoulder. He was not seriously hurt.

'They're getting worried,' Andrew said.

Abonitu nodded. 'It is bad for their temperament; they never know when the next shot will come. They are becoming nervous – softening up. Another day or two of this, and then an attack again . . . things might go badly.'

'Yes,' Andrew said. 'They might. It's difficult to see what you can do about it, though. They'd probably like nothing better than to have you raid their positions.'

'I agree. I have been thinking about this.' He smiled. 'This is where I show I am a better leader than Mutalli was. He would never have been able to retreat.'

'From London?'

'No. Only from its streets. If we form a lager with the Hover-craft in mid-river we shall be out of range of anyone but a very good shot with a telescopic sight. And there is the psychological effect; our men will not feel hemmed in and overlooked as they do here.'

Andrew said: 'So you are prepared to abandon what was once the beating heart of empire.'

'Until the supply ship gets here. There is no point in risking things for a whim. In two weeks' time we will be invulnerable.'

Andrew made a gesture which comprehended the silent city all about them.

'How do you think they will react?'

'We shall have to see. Perhaps they will leave us alone out there.'

'I wonder.'

'We can be no worse off, anyway.'

'You're probably right about that.'

They moved out in the early morning, and set up the new camp in the centre of the ice, midway between Westminster Bridge and Charing Cross. The Hovercraft were stationed in a tight circle, linked by barricades brought over from the Palace of Westminster. On all sides there was a clear view across the level surface; the skyline of London, set back from them, was less intimidating in its remoteness. Andrew noticed a resurgence of cheerfulness and confidence among the Africans, a return to the carefree joking that had previously characterized them. They were good people to be with, he thought warmly. And they accepted him: he was sure of that now. They had come to venerate Abonitu, and they accepted Andrew as his friend and companion. The colour of his skin, despite the constant threat from all about them, no longer mattered.

There were two easy days with a peaceful night in between; then, as the grey dusk deepened into darkness, a new attack. Figures swarmed over the ice from the Embankment to an accompaniment of irregular gunfire. Abonitu waited until the vanguard of the attackers were some fifty yards from the Hovercraft before he ordered the searchlights on and gave the command for return fire. The attack withered and died on that instant; they fell and lay there, some silent, some moaning in pain, and the rest drew off. As soon as it was clear that the retreat was general and beyond reversal, Abonitu ordered his men to cease firing.

The searchlights remained on, throwing scarifying light on the scene. A man moved, got shakily to his feet, stared blinking into the glare. He was probably dazed; Andrew wondered if he expected to be shot down, or if he had lost awareness of where he was and what was happening. After a moment or two he turned and stumbled back towards the Embankment, clutching one arm with another. The scene remained bright and silent. A few minutes later, another man got up and made his way back. Others followed suit. Two men supported a third. Within quarter of an hour only two figures were left, crumpled and lifeless on the ice. At a sign from Abonitu, the lights went off.

'I don't think they will be back tonight,' Abonitu said with satisfaction.

Andrew said: 'No, I don't think they will.'

'Do you think it will mean anything – that we ceased firing, let them go back unharmed and take back their wounded?'

'What do you want it to mean?'

'That we are civilized men, not barbarians.'

'The important question is: what are they?'

'In the end, they must learn to tolerate our being here. We are doing them no harm.'

'Perhaps they think the traders and the missionaries will come later.'

'With gin and beads and bibles? It is absurd, Andrew. They know it is not like that.'

'We don't know what they think,' Andrew said wearily. 'And we can't find out.'

'Can't we?' Abonitu said. He took off his spectacles and rubbed them against the lining of his leather jacket. 'I wonder.'

There was quiet until the following night, when another attack came. This time, while the main and obvious thrust came from the Embankment, there was a secondary attack from the direction of the South Bank. It was more quietly and skilfully conducted than the northern attack, and a couple of the white men were within a few yards of the Hovercraft before they were spotted and exposed to the searchlights and to a withering fire from the defenders. As before, Abonitu called off the firing as soon as the attackers withdrew, but left the lights on in silent comment while the wounded were got away.

This time, though, the attack was renewed before dawn, and renewed with a difference. The lights illumined a contraption being pushed out from the Embankment: closer examination with the glasses made it possible to see that there was some kind of low-slung chassis mounted on small wheels and carrying, on the side facing the Hovercraft, a roughly made screen faced with metal.

'Ingenious,' Abonitu said. 'What do you think it is?'

'I think, one of those long trucks they used to use for transporting long castings. They have swivelling bogies at each end. I suppose they think they can get it up close enough to harass us.'

Abonitu smiled. 'They can get it up. There need be no trouble over that. Then we shall see.'

He waited until the truck had been pushed half way from the

210

bank. Then one of the Hovercraft was detached. It skirted the attackers in a wide arc and came up on them from the rear. They could hear the sound of shots above the roar of the craft's engines. Then, for a time, it cruised up and down on the far side of the truck, and the firing was further off – between the Hovercraft and the shore. It moved back into position in the lager a quarter of an hour after it had set off. The captain, a tall blue-eyed Fulani, made his report. There had been no defences on the other side of the truck; the men pushing it forward had been taken by surprise. After the first couple of fusillades, nothing had moved there.

'Good,' Abonitu said. 'That will do. Now try to get some sleep.'

Andrew watched the Fulani salute and walk away. He yawned. He said:

'I could do with some sleep, too, Abo. And you, I should think.'

'Yes,' Abonitu said. 'They are very persistent. But perhaps we have put them off for a while.'

Andrew crawled into his sleeping bag and fell asleep right away. He was awakened by the sound of firing and, looking up, saw that the sky was only a shade or two lighter than it had been when he lay down: he could not have been asleep for more than half an hour. Wearily he got to his feet. He felt sick and tired, and his head was beginning to ache.

The attack did not come to anything, but during its course another obstruction, a kind of armoured sledge, was pushed out on to the ice in the direction of the lager. There was no need to send a Hovercraft out to deal with those pushing it; it was abandoned less than twenty yards from the Embankment. The sky was rapidly paling now in the east, and the two abandoned fortifications stood out plainly against the level ice. Inside the lager, the cooks began to prepare breakfast, and Andrew decided there was little point in going back to his sleeping bag before eating. The wisdom of this was shown when another attack came, this time from the South Bank, no more than twenty minutes after the previous one. And this, also, left its abandoned strongpoint behind it, a few yards from the shore.

The pattern became plain during the morning; there was a succession of abortive attacks, and a succession of objects pushed out on to the ice which would serve as cover in future assaults. The attacks were pressed home only far enough to elicit responding fire from the defenders and to advance the mobile shields, The attackers had some casualties, but fewer than they had suffered before. The day wore on, the sun pale behind high barred clouds, and the nibbling attacks continued. In the afternoon Abonitu ordered his men to hold their fire, and sent one of the Hovercraft out to sweep close to the river banks, but it was impossible to get any rest inside the lager. Men dozed off for short periods but were continually being reawakened by the sound of firing, and towards evening an additional nuisance manifested itself: voices, using loud-hailers, began to shout abuse from the banks of the river.

The noise, and the erupting flurry of attacks, went on all night and all the next morning. There was no attempt to push the obstacles, of which there were now more than a score on the ice, far out; presumably because the attackers realized that to do so would be to invite being cut off by one of the Hovercraft. Their objective was plain: to keep the defenders on edge all day and night.

Eating his dish of sweetened and fortified maize mush, Abonitu said:

'We can't go on with this.'

Andrew said: 'No. They can handle this in relays; we can't.' He looked at Abonitu. 'Then what? Another move? Up river? Down?'

'Anywhere inside the city they would follow us.'

'Outside then.' Abonitu was silent. 'We can come back in after we have made contact with the supply ship.'

'Yes,' Abonitu said. 'I suppose that would be sensible. We move out now, and come back with our helicopters and flame-throwers and napalm. And this time we attack, hunting them down like rats through their narrow streets. That is not what I wanted, Andrew.'

'They give you no alternative, do they?'

Abonitu raised his heavy eyes towards the spires of Whitehall Court.

'What do they want?' he said. 'They are not savages – how can they be? A mind that one can respect is directing these harassments. If only one could make contact.'

'They don't appear to want contact.'

'But would they refuse it, if we went to them?'

'How?'

'An envoy, under a flag of truce.'

'Perhaps. Perhaps not. They have not offered anything like that to us.'

'They may think it is up to us to make the overtures. This is their country.'

'It would be simpler to pull out.'

'And return with napalm? This is London, Andrew. I want to warm my frozen queen, not roast her.'

'If you sent an envoy,' Andrew said. 'Zigguri? Do you think he could handle it?'

'No. Not Zigguri. Not any of the others, either.'

Andrew said slowly: 'Do you think I would be any good?'

'Only you would have a chance to persuade them, I think.'

'Persuade them?'

'That we mean no harm. That we want to help if we can. But I don't ask this, Andrew, unless you want to do it. I know there are risks.'

Andrew smiled. Fatigue lay on him with the distorting lightness of a fever.

'There always are risks,' he said. 'But I should think a white flag is still recognized in these parts.'

4

It was a lonely walk across the ice, carrying the short length of metal tubing with a white rag tied to one end. There was no sign of response until he was almost under the wall of the Embankment. Then a rope ladder was tossed over the side. A North Country voice called:

'Come on up, then.'

There were half a dozen waiting on the other side. They looked at him with a combination of curiosity and dislike.

'You're white,' the leader said. 'Any other whites out there?'

'No. No others.'

A small ginger-haired man said: 'Black bastards. I'd like to . . .'

The man with the Northern accent was about fifty, stocky, grizzled, clean shaven where the rest had straggly beards. He spoke across the other's words, cutting them to nothing.

'They sent you here? What do you want?'

'I've been sent to talk things over, with whoever's in charge.'

He stared at Andrew for a moment. 'All right, mister. We'll take you.'

The ginger-haired man was sent to report what was happening to someone who was presumably a local commander. The others walked with Andrew along the Embankment in the direction of Charing Cross; the ground was humped and uneven with ice and frozen snow. They cut diagonally across the road in the direction of Northumberland Avenue. The trees had a different kind of winter bareness from that which he remembered – probably the cold had killed them – and some had been cut down. Trafalgar Square came into view at the end of a long vista, and the small party stopped.

'Better be safe,' the stocky man said. 'Put a blindfold on him.'

They tied a piece of cloth smelling of machine oil round his face and afterwards he walked with a man on each side, holding him by the upper arm. He tried to judge the direction they were taking. They went diagonally across Trafalgar Square; after that he was less sure, but they were heading roughly towards Piccadilly Circus. Twice greetings were exchanged, and there were shouted inquiries about Andrew. The North Country man gave brief uninformative replies.

The man on Andrew's right side said: 'Steps here. Watch yourself.'

There was a fairly short flight, followed by a longer one. The softness of carpeting was underfoot. The North Country man said:

'Wait here. I'll go in and see.'

While he was away, Andrew said: 'Anyone like a cigarette? I've got a packet in my inside pocket.'

A voice said: 'Christ! How long since I had a fag?'

Andrew began to feel in his pocket. Another stronger voice said:

'Keep your hands where they are. We don't want anything from you.'

Discipline was good, Andrew noted; but that much he had gathered already. He said indifferently:

'Please yourselves.'

A door opened and footsteps returned. The North Country voice said: 'All right. Bring him along.'

They went through a door, down more steps, along a corridor. Andrew was led through another door, and halted inside.

'Take that rag off.'

Familiarity plucked at him, hovering on the verge of recollection. Behind his head, fingers tugged at the knots in the cloth. The cloth came free, and Andrew blinked. There were only two paraffin lamps in the room, but even this modest light dazzled him. One of the lamps hung from what had been a small electric chandelier in the centre of the room; the other rested on a desk facing him. A man was sitting behind it. Sound and sight clicked into recognition, as he spoke again:

'Andy! For God's sake, what brings you here?'

It was quite a small room, and windowless; it might have been the private office of a restaurant manager. There were useless strip lights round the wall, above an Attic-style frieze some three feet deep. The carpet was fitted, electric blue, and with a deep pile. David's desk was a quality job also; heavy mahogany with a red leather top. David sat in a matching swivel chair. The room had a paraffin heater as well as the two lamps, and he was in his shirt sleeves. He nodded to the men who had brought Andrew in.

'You can leave us alone.' The door closed behind them. 'Well, explain yourself, laddie.'

'I'm part of the expedition,' Andrew said. 'They sent me to talk things over – to see if we couldn't . . .'

'They're Nigerians, then?'

'Yes.'

'We thought Ghana – the squadron was supposed to have gone there.'

'There was some kind of trouble. They moved on.'

David nodded. 'But I don't understand what you are doing with them?'

'We're making a film record. I'm the camera-man. But things have been too hectic lately for camera work.'

'You volunteered?'

'When Madeleine came back . . . it was the only way to get here. Not that I expected to find her. But it seemed as sensible a thing to do as any other. It was Abonitu's idea.'

'Abonitu? The one who got you back into television?'

'Yes?' Andrew hesitated slightly. 'He's running the expedition now.'

'Is he?' David asked. 'Is he?'

'Madeleine – how is she?'

David studied him for a moment. He said at last:

'She's well.'

'Here, with you?'

'Not far off. Our dark friends – they sent you to talk to us. About what?'

'They want to know why they're being attacked – what they can do to stop it.'

David smiled. His smile had the same quality of easiness, smoothing out the lines of strain in his face.

'Nothing easier. They can clear out.'

Andrew said: 'Look, they mean no harm. It's only an examining force – no more. They're not planting flags or anything like that.'

'Not yet.'

'They want to help if they can.'

'That's the same canting phrase we took into Africa. You don't believe it, Andy. And we object to being colonized.'

'We? Who are we? A gang of street arabs, living in the ruins of a dead city.' He pointed to the lamps. 'How long will the supplies of paraffin last? I suppose you're living on tinned foods still. What happens when they're gone? Who's going to repair the buildings as they crumble round you?'

'You think we should welcome our dark-skinned liberators?'

His first shock and confusion at finding David, at realizing that Madeleine, perhaps, was in reach, had passed off. In their place he was conscious of old resentments – particularly resentment at his having been responsible for Madeleine's flight from Lagos. He knew this was unfair – that this, at least, David had done nothing to procure – but that only made his feeling more bitter. He said, with cold anger:

'I thought you prided yourself on the practicality of your approach to life.'

David nodded. 'I do, Andy.'

'And it's practical to let yourself slide into savagery – into cannibalism eventually – as long as you're waving a Union Jack?'

'Well, no, not quite that. But one has to take chances at times.'

'It depends on the odds and what you stand to gain.'

David looked at him, his face screwed up. 'Yes. I haven't given much thought to this lately. One has to concentrate on the job in hand. But I thought quite a bit about it before the final crack-up. As you know, I could have flown south. I could have landed in the warm sun, on my beam ends.'

'We would have helped you.'

'I know that. I've never been much good at taking help from people, but I suppose I would have got used to it. I might have even got used to being part of a despised minority, though that would have been trickier. But I'd had security all my life, and suddenly I realized I didn't want it. I wanted to survive, all right, but on my terms. And I thought there was a chance of doing that. Then, I was beginning to wield power, real power, for the first time. I didn't want to give that up.'

'Survive? As what – an urban Eskimo? And power over what?'

'It was obvious things were going to be hard for a few years. After that – well, it would depend on what we'd done with the time. It still does. We've managed to keep some kind of organization together.' He grinned. 'We're the biggest gang in these parts, and the strongest. We hold the old Pale, and a bit more besides.' The grin emerged again. 'My writ runs south to Brixton and north to St John's Wood. We're thinking of inviting the opposition to cricket at Lord's next summer.'

'And for Madeleine – is that sort of thing right for her?'

David said slowly: 'Madeleine came back of her own choice. I didn't ask for it, nor want it. I – I'm very fond of her, but personal relationships are a luxury these days. There's no time for them.'

'What is there time for, then? Playing gangsters in the rubble of a frozen broken-down empire?'

'Gangsters today. Government tomorrow.'

'And food? And fuel?'

'I don't know. At the moment, as you've guessed, we're largely living off stocks.' His expression was grim briefly. 'We fought to hold them. There was enough to share out, but we didn't share.

We condemned thousands to starvation, and killed them when they wouldn't starve quietly. And we kept the food: enough to last our lot through the winter.'

'The Fratellini Winter? You think the sun is going to start warming you again? I saw the latest figures in Lagos – radiation has stabilized, at the present level. England is out of the temperate zone for good.'

David nodded. 'We're in a cold climate. But we don't yet know how cold.'

'Cold enough to prevent you growing crops or keeping cattle. Cold enough to keep your harbours ice-locked eight or nine months of the year. You may get a few fish, or kill the odd seal, but you'll degenerate and die just the same. The Danes settled in Greenland in the twelfth century. It was warmer then. When the cold came back it killed them. I suppose each winter they thought the next summer would be better.'

'We get a few fish,' David agreed. 'From the Thames – would you imagine that? We cut holes in the ice and fish through them. I don't know what kind of fish they are, but they don't taste bad. But that's not what I'm talking about. Do you remember something you once told me: that precipitation is more important than temperature in producing ice caps? And I suppose one of the things that affects precipitation is global temperature. The weather's improving, Andy, even if it's still cold. Haven't you noticed it? That blizzard we had the other day was the first break in over a month, and that died out fast.'

'The country's still ice bound.'

'Though slightly less so. Even now, in winter, it melts a little each day. And as the days draw out . . .'

'Providing the weather stays good.'

'You know, I think it might. In the old days, the anticyclones that pounded eastwards across the Atlantic used to bring our rain. But they themselves were the results of all kind of factors, including temperatures. It's quite reasonable that cooling the planet might break the pattern. Perhaps Spain and North Africa are getting our storms these days. Any signs of bad weather on your way north?'

Andrew said reluctantly: 'Yes, there were storms.'

He grinned with a small boy's pleasure. 'There you are!'

'There have been seasons like that before, with the anticyclones running north or south of their usual track. It's a very little thing to build long term plans on.'

'Not plans – hopes, day dreams, if you like. The only long term plan at the moment is survival. We've got seed, though – corn and potatoes. As soon as the ground thaws enough, we'll start planting.'

'In London?'

'We'll send colonizing parties out.'

'You'll have to send them out a long way. Wouldn't a smaller city make a more useful centre?'

'We're staying in London for the same reason your dark friends came here. It's easier to hold it than it would be to re-take it. And holding London means holding England.'

Andrew said wearily: 'The words don't mean anything.'

'Don't they? Perhaps not to you, but I suspect they do to the darkies. If not – if this is just a fact-finding expedition – what are they fighting it out for? Why not move to quieter parts?'

There was no point, he felt, in concealing the truth. He said:

'I might as well tell you – there are reinforcements on the way. More men, more arms. They don't want to use them unless they have to. They want to work things out peacefully.'

David said slowly: 'Thanks for that. It's a help.' His eyes fixed in a stare. 'You could help us still more.'

'In what way?'

'Kill those lights for us. Can you do it?' He did not grasp the meaning at first, and showed his bewilderment. 'They run off batteries, don't they? You can cut the leads, or short them. Five minutes' darkness is all we need.'

Andrew gave himself time to think before he spoke. He settled in the end for practicality.

'What happens to me?'

'Lie low till it's over. It won't take long, I promise.'

'And then?'

'We'll look after you.'

'Will you? Can you look after yourselves? You've told me personal relationships are a luxury now. Even if I accepted that, I can't see what you would have to offer that would be tempting. And Abonitu is my friend. A friend I can trust, and who trusts me. You may not understand it, David, but you'll have to accept it.'

'Will I?' The smile on his face was one of confidence. 'Are you so sure we haven't anything to tempt you? Maddie?'

'Madeleine came back to you.' He felt a dryness in his throat. 'She made her decision. All I could do was accept it.'

'She came back because she felt guilty about me – she always did. You can't argue women out of these things. Maddie was made for sacrificing herself; she couldn't live with you out there while she knew I might be having a tough time here in England. But it was you she wanted, really.'

'No.' The ache in his mind was like the physical ache of resisting seduction. 'That's not true.'

David watched him. The confidence, the assurance, was still there, and with it, something else – wistfulness, almost. 'Anyway, you won't go back without seeing her. Will you?'

She was muffled up in a shapeless fur coat which she did not take off on entering the room. It was an impression without details; he did not really look at her until David left them. Then his eyes met hers, but he did not move towards her.

She said: 'I'm so glad, Andy. How can one say anything? I couldn't believe it at first. This sort of thing doesn't happen, does it?'

'You look well,' he said. 'Not starving, at any rate.'

She coloured slightly. 'We're rationed, of course, but there's enough to live on.'

He looked at her, thinking how incredible it was that she was alive, and that he had found her. There were so many things he wanted to say, but they were all banalities. It was Madeleine who spoke again.

'I hated leaving you, Andy. Believe that.'

'David's explained things,' he said. 'I was safe, well provided for, while he was in danger. You can't help having an over-developed maternal instinct, can you?'

She looked away for a moment. 'Andy . . .'

'Well,' he said, 'we're equal now, aren't we. David and I? He wants me to sabotage the expedition, and then stay on here. That will leave us both in the same boat. You can make up your mind without pity getting in the way. Isn't that the way it is?'

She nodded, not speaking.

'Some women would need time to make their minds up in situations like that – a few days or weeks, perhaps months – but that's not the case with you. Compassion may confuse you, but you know your mind. Don't you?'

'Andy,' she said. 'Darling Andy . . .'

'I remember when Abonitu first suggested getting on this expedition. We were sitting, nine tenths drunk, in a sleazy cabaret, and he looked at me out of those solemn bespectacled eyes and said: "You will find your lost love in the land of eternal winter." Fairy story stuff; he's very like a child in some ways. The next morning I could see what nonsense it was, but it seemed as simple to go as to stay.' He smiled. 'Nothing meant much after you'd gone.'

She looked at him, a brightness in her eyes that might be tears.

'But the fairy story came true,' he said. 'After a strange journey, I found you. As you say, the sort of thing that doesn't happen. And now it's happening. Distance and obstacles and dangers between us, followed by a conventional happy ending. I love you, and you love me.' He paused. 'It's true, isn't it? It is me you love. Not David.'

She nodded. 'Yes.'

'You don't need time to make your mind up? Those days or weeks – I was right in thinking nothing like that is necessary?'

'Yes, you were right.'

'I've imagined it often enough,' he said, 'but you can never imagine things the right way. Say it. Say it now.'

She said: 'It's you I love, Andy.'

He laughed. 'Then everything's all right, isn't it? Will David mind?'

'I don't think so.'

'Nor do I. He's never needed you the way I do, as a person. Has he? He's never needed anyone in that way. Isn't that right?'

She said, in a low voice: 'Yes, that's true.'

'I haven't kissed you yet.'

She came to him at once. Her body, muffled in fur, was real in his arms, her breath warmed his neck. He felt the shudder of her breathing, and saw how pale and thin the dreams had been, against this reality. This reality which mocked him.

'Say it again.'

'I love you. I do love you, Andy.'

He released her gently. He looked at her, and saw her lip trembling.

'What is it?' she asked. 'What's wrong?'

'Nothing. Nothing's wrong. You did it very well. David should be proud of you.'

'I don't understand.'

There was an impulse to be cruel. He had not imagined he could feel this, and it shocked him. Mastering it, he said, choosing his words, striving not to hurt her:

'It was a reasonable thing for David to try. He uses people, and somehow one doesn't resent it. And I understand that you would always do what he asked. But it wasn't necessary. I refused him, but you only had to ask me. You should have known that.'

She saw it now. She said: 'You think I was deceiving you – that when David came to fetch me to you he told me to pretend I loved you so that you would do as he wanted? And that I did this?'

He looked at her, not trusting himself to speak. She said, in a whisper:

'Have I ever lied to you, Andy?'

'Has he ever asked you to, before?'

Her eyes searched his. 'Why don't you trust me, Andy? Because I left you, and came back here? Did I lose you then? I regretted it afterwards. I regretted it bitterly.'

He said, with an effort: 'Acts have consequences, don't they? It's not the going back in itself, but what comes after. You were too quick, Madeleine, too glib. You aren't the kind of woman who can go from one man's bed to another's as easily as that. If you'd asked for time, I might have believed you.'

'It's true,' she said. 'I couldn't. But the supposition's wrong. I don't share David's bed.'

With bitter irony, he said: 'After you had left me there, you realized your mistake. So you refused David's attentions, and sat waiting like Penelope for your true love to come and find you. Is that what you're saying?'

'No. I never thought I'd see you again.'

'Then what? You let me make love to you at a time when you believed you still loved David, out of loneliness. What's different now?'

She did not answer at once. Instead, with a gesture part flaunting, part modest, she opened the fur coat she was wearing, and pulled it off in a quick movement. She faced him with the strange rich gravid lines of her body, under a blue jersey dress.

'This,' she said.

The realization dazed him. There was a pause before he asked: 'Is it . . . ?'

'Ours? Yours? Beyond the faintest shadow of a doubt. I had the first warning on the plane that brought me back here.' She smiled. 'I put it down to air-sickness. The next morning I had to look for a different explanation. I learned a lot of things then – about how I felt. But it was too late to do anything: the airport had closed and the Pale was breaking up. There was nothing I could do. Except survive. I wasn't sure I wanted to do that, but David kept me going. He's talked about the child a lot. He's sure it will be a boy. I think he's learned something about himself, too. He would like to have a son.'

'Things aren't going to be easy,' he said. 'No hospitals, medical equipment . . .'

'You're not to worry. Everything's going to be all right.'

The serenity of her confidence reassured him, but he still felt somehow cut off, uncomprehending. His mind went to David – David, in his little nascent empire, feeling at last the need for a son, for continuity. Involuntarily, he said:

'Poor David.'

She nodded. 'Poor David.'

It was this, the small conspiracy of love, that at last enabled him to make contact, to believe. He put his arms out, and she came to him, her body warm and loving and heavy against his own. In his ear, she said:

'You've asked a lot. Haven't you anything to say?'

'Only that I love you.' He tightened his hold. 'That I love you both.'

5

Abonitu had had a tent set up inside the circle of the Hovercraft. After greeting Andrew on his return he waited until they were alone there, sitting on either side of the small collapsible table, before asking how things had gone.

'Badly.'

'They won't come to terms?'

He poured brandy for both of them into small anodized aluminium cups, and pushed one across. Andrew said:

'The only terms are that you get out of London. They would prefer you to get out of the country, but they realize they can't enforce that.'

'They believe they can enforce the other?'

'Yes. They intend to try.'

'Why?'

'It's obvious enough, isn't it?'

'Has it occurred to them that if we were to pull out it would not prevent others coming?'

'They seem to regard the present evil as sufficient unto the day. They think they can begin getting the country back on its feet next summer.'

'That sounds optimistic.'

'Yes, it does.'

Abonitu nodded towards the cup that stood in front of Andrew.

'You aren't drinking, Andrew. I should have thought you would have welcomed a tot.'

'Thanks.'

He put the cup to his lips and drained it. The drink, warming him, made him realize how cold he was – bitterly cold, and scared.

'What's it like out there?' Abonitu asked.

'Frozen,' he said. 'Hopeless. But they still go on hoping.'

'Well organized? Disciplined?'

'As well as can be expected.'

Abonitu poured more drink into their cups, and lifted his own.

'So I must woo my queen with fire and the sword,' he said. 'There is no other way.'

'What do you propose to do?'

'What we agreed was sensible – move out until we can contact the supply ship. These are the crucial days; if they overcome us before reinforcements arrive, the whole thing is lost. Later . . . I've been thinking that perhaps the Tower would make a better base. A more ancient seat of sovereignty, and much more easily defensible. What do you think of the idea, Andrew?'

Andrew nodded. 'It sounds reasonable.'

'That lacks enthusiasm.'

'A good idea, then.'

'From the Tower we will be able to burn and bomb our way westwards. Along Cannon Street and Lombard Street and Cheapside. We will take St Paul's, Andrew. Do you think we could find a priest somewhere, to crown me in the Abbey when we get there? King Abonitu the First. How does that strike you?'

'As a joke? A little feeble.'

'Yes. Lagos would not like it. But the rest is serious, is it not?'

'Yes.'

There was a silence. Andrew heard someone go past the tent, whistling. In the soft glow from the small battery-operated lamp, he saw Abonitu's face watching his own. The light gleamed off black skin, white teeth between slightly parted lips, and accentuated the heavy negroid lines of feature.

Abonitu said quietly: 'What happened, Andrew?'

'Happened? I don't understand.'

'Out there. Something changed you.'

'Perhaps.' He stared at Abonitu. 'I found Madeleine.'

'Well?'

He framed the half truths carefully. In a neutral voice, he said:

'She's with David. She's going to have a baby.' He shrugged. 'That's all.'

After a pause, Abonitu said: 'Then your quest is ended, the hatred all done with.'

'Hatred?'

'Or love. Does it matter? The desire and hope of possession. That which brought us here, to this cold country.'

'Yes,' Andrew said. 'For me, done with. But not for you?'

'Not for me.' He drank the brandy. 'As for you, you have always depended too much on people, I think. Why are you smiling?'

'Because it's true, I suppose.'

'It is true. We all depend on others at times, of course. I have depended on you a great deal, Andrew.'

'Have depended? And don't now?' He gestured towards the outside of the tent. 'Have you got rid of your fear of their fear?'

'I think they are getting over it. Put fire in their hands and they will not be afraid. They will carry their sun with them even here.'

'The sun brings life,' he said, 'not death.'

The light caught Abonitu's spectacles as his head jerked upwards.

'I was waiting for you to say that,' he said. 'What am I to do with you, Andrew?'

The automatic rifle rested against the table on Abonitu's side. On the table were the two metal cups and the flask of brandy. It was almost empty. There was another flask, he knew, in the small chest by Abonitu's camp bed. He drained his cup with a slight shiver.

'Why should you do anything?' he asked.

'Because I cannot trust you now. There is the chance that you might betray us. And I can take no chances.'

He smiled. 'How does Abonitu the First deal with his first traitor? It's an interesting question.'

'I could send you back across the ice to them.'

'Unwise. I could be useful there.'

'That is true. Then?'

'There's a much simpler solution.' Abonitu watched him in silence. 'Send me back to Africa on the supply ship. You don't even need an excuse – there are others who can crank a camera. Young Numu. I'll go back and produce the first programme on the London Expedition. We have quite a lot in the can already.'

Abonitu nodded slowly. 'Yes. That is better.'

'And since I'm not to be trusted now, you'd better put a guard on me meanwhile.' He shivered. 'I'm still cold. Any more brandy?' Abonitu poured the remains of the flask into his cup. 'That's a thin measure.'

Abonitu smiled and got up from his chair. He went towards the chest. As his back turned, Andrew reached for the rifle. It made a grating noise, but Abonitu, opening the chest, did not hear it. When he turned again, the rifle was pointing at him.

Andrew said: 'No noise. I feel very nervous.'

'This is silly.' The black face showed nothing. 'What good can it do?'

'We'll see.' He rose to his feet. 'Do as I tell you. Walk past me and out of the tent. I'll be behind you. No cries, no warnings. Do you understand?'

'I understand that what you are doing is senseless.'

'I'll judge it. Now.'

He stood slightly to one side as Abonitu crossed his path. Moving quickly behind him, he had a sudden panic conviction that he would fail, that the blow would miscarry and give Abonitu a chance to grapple with him or, at least, to cry out. He changed his grip on the rifle, and swung it convulsively. As the butt came down on the side of Abonitu's head, he thought it was going to glance off ineffectually. But the shock jarred his hands and the heavy body in front of him crumpled and fell in silence.

He said: 'I'm sorry, Abo,' and began dragging the unconscious man out of the way. In the end it was easier to move the bed to cover him. He looked round the tent. It would pass any casual inspection.

It was quite dark outside. No one paid any attention as he

walked towards the nearest Hovercraft. A meal was cooking, and the smell of food was in the air. Someone was singing a song which he recognized as a Fulani lullaby. He climbed into the Hovercraft and looked out towards the city.

There was starlight in a clear sky, and the moon was rising; one could see the outline of the bridges to east and west and the unforgettable skyline. He looked at the luminous dial of his watch. A quarter of an hour; time enough, but with none to waste. He walked, unchallenged, unremarked, to the front of the craft. The guard glanced idly at him as he wrenched at the lead that fed the searchlights; presumably he thought some kind of maintenance work was in progress. The lead was hard to break: he tugged at it in vain for some little time before he managed to rip it free. He left it with the ends shorting against the metal casing, and moved to the next craft.

He had dealt with six before the first rattle of fire came across the ice. There were shouts of surprise and despair from the Africans as they tried to switch on the searchlights and found them useless. After that the confusion was extreme, but it did not last long. In ten minutes it was over.

6

The morning was bright, brighter by far than it had ever been in London in the old days. The sun's rays struck white flame from the frozen Thames, and dazzled from the surrounding buildings, still carrying snow from the last fall. Even the absurdly curved roof of the Festival Hall had a kind of dignity. The air was crisp, touched to sharpness by a breeze from the east.

David had Abonitu brought to him on one of the Hovercraft. He said:

'How are you this morning, General?'

'A headache.' Abonitu smiled faintly. 'We black men have thick skulls, as is well known.'

David grinned. 'I'm glad it's no worse.'

'May I ask what you propose doing with us?'

'I've been thinking about that. When Harold defeated the Norsemen at Stamford Bridge, he gave them twenty-four ships to enable the survivors to go back home and tell the tale. We can spare you one Hovercraft. You may be a little cramped, but you will be carrying neither arms nor supplies, which will simplify things.'

Abonitu said: 'I recall that story. And a few days later he lay dead near Hastings, and William had conquered England.'

'The English can learn from their mistakes, even when they're a thousand years old. If Harold had stayed in London while he gathered his strength, the story would have been different.'

'There will be other expeditions. How long will it take you to gather your strength?'

'Not too long, we hope. And perhaps we can discourage visitors in the short term. We are taking your cameras, too. We hope to get an interesting little film of the end of the Nigerian

Expedition – the disarmed survivors being packed off back to their supply ship. It will be effective, I think.'

Abonitu smiled. 'You have no television transmitters left, and if you had the programmes would not be received in Africa.'

'True. But now we have a Hovercraft squadron, I think it's time we started making civilized contacts again. I gather the Council of African States has a base at St Nazaire. If we take the film along, I imagine there will be some States who will want to use it, even if Nigeria doesn't.'

'Yes, that is true.' He was silent for a moment. 'This seems a pity. We could have helped you in many ways.'

David said: 'You still can. We're not too proud to accept aid, even aid with strings. Send us your traders, by all means – missionaries, too, if you like. The only thing we require is that you recognize our independence at the beginning, instead of after generations of struggle. It will be easier for you, too.'

'You are asking us, also, to learn from your mistakes?'

'Why not?' He laughed. 'Dominion status is the least we'll accept. Tell them that in Lagos.'

'They may not believe me.'

'If they're wise, they will.'

Abonitu nodded. 'Yes. I think you are right. Perhaps I will return – on a goodwill mission next time. Or as an Ambassador.'

'Ambassador would be better still. Bearing gifts from wealthy Africk's shores. Tobacco and coffee would go down best, I may say.'

'And brandy,' Andrew said.

'Yes,' Abonitu agreed. 'And brandy.' He turned to look at Andrew, their eyes meeting for the first time since the previous night. 'I was right not to trust you, wasn't I? But careless.'

Andrew said: 'I'm sorry. It wasn't easy, from any point of view.'

'You were careless, too,' Abonitu said. 'Or over-scrupulous. You allowed me to realize that your loyalty to me had ended. It was a fair warning. I do not think your friend here would have given such a warning.'

232

'No,' David said. 'I shouldn't.'

Abonitu's eyes were still on Andrew. His face carried an expression of regret. He said:

'I'm sorry you're not coming back with us.'

'Would you answer for my safety if I did?'

'We are a civilized people.' He smiled. 'It may be better, though, to wait for a time. And, after all, this is your home.'

'Yes,' Andrew said. He turned from Abonitu to look towards the city. 'This is my home.'

PENGUIN WORLDS

Classic science fiction introduced by brilliant contemporary novelists

Science fiction is a genre that gives us gripping plots and fantastical creations. It is also a genre that challenges us with fresh ideas about all kinds of things – politics, philosophy, technology – how the world works and what it means to be human. The Penguin Worlds project celebrates this incredible range, richness and invention, taking the very best from the twentieth century science fiction canon.

This series includes prescient environmental dystopia, a pioneering example of early cyberpunk, classic urban fantasy, chilling short fiction, and one of the most influential voices in feminist science fiction. Each one is a ground-breaking classic of its day; Penguin is proud to bring these classics to a whole new generation of readers.

Penguin Worlds is curated by Hari Kunzru and Naomi Alderman.

Hari Kunzru is the bestselling author of *The Impressionist* and *Transmission*. His new novel, *White Tears*, is published by Penguin in 2017.

Naomi Alderman is the acclaimed author *Disobedience*, *The Lessons* and *The Liars' Gospel*. Her latest novel, *The Power*, is published by Penguin in 2016.